THE
DOUBLE SNARE

A Simon and Schuster
Novel of Suspense by

ROSEMARY HARRIS

SIMON AND SCHUSTER · NEW YORK

Library of Congress Cataloging in Publication Data

Harris, Rosemary
    The double snare.

    (A Simon and Schuster novel of suspense)
    I. Title.
PZ4.H3158Do3   [PR6058.A6915]   823'.9'14   75–656
ISBN 0–671–22036–5

1

"There was this garden, with cypresses."

"Yes?"

"They were dark against the sky. I was walking up toward them."

"Yes?"

"The sky—it was light, with that sort of light, you know, that comes before a storm, or after it. Watery. Or it could have been evening light."

"Yes?"

"The slope—it was uphill." I laugh uncertainly, pointlessly. "And I began to run." I wish he would look at me. My hands are drenched with sweat. The handkerchief I squeeze between my shaking fingers is damp with it.

"You began to run? Why?" This at least is an improvement on that eternal "Yes?"

"I don't know."

He sighs gently and stares out of the window. He's probably thinking of his girl, the dark-haired Neapolitan I see him with on Wednesdays. I am being a bore—a blank, blank bore: a question mark. At the thought of my blankness I sweat again.

"I—I was frightened."

This time his gaze does swivel round to me, accusingly. "A moment ago, signorina, you said you didn't know why you were running."

I search the blankness, hopelessly. "What I meant was, I didn't know why I was frightened into running."

He says nothing but makes a note on his sheet of paper. It's covered in notes and things which look like noughts and crosses. Is he playing ticktacktoe? The noughts would be suitable. The sweat is now running down my spine—my spine is stuck to my nightdress, and my nightdress to my hospital dressing gown, and I'm stuck to my chair. The heat is intense. The cold inside me is like the cold in a refrigerator.

I try again. "When I was running uphill the grasses round me were all dark—so it must have been twilight, I think. There were heavy stones in the grass. There was a—a thing like a vault. Large, and oblong. I saw it against the sky, on my left. Whatever I was running from must have been coming up the hill. There was a house."

"Ah . . ." He scribbles. "Where was this house?"

I drop my handkerchief on the floor and bend to pick it up so that I have time to still my quaking. If he doesn't say "Yes?" again at once, I may place the house. I clutch frantically at the handkerchief and, metaphorically, at the sliding screen of memory.

"Yes?"

Now he has lost me my house. It's gone back into the darkness. Was it even connected with the garden, the cypresses, the—graves? I feel that it was, but whether it was to the right, the left, behind me, or even what I was running to, I can't tell. With his eternal "Yes?" he's broken the connection. My house is switched off and drifts back into its separate darkness.

"I feel sick . . . I feel terribly sick, and my head aches. I want to go back to bed." To my blank bed in my blank room with its blank walls. "Please, that's all I can remember." Hysteria starts rising in me. "Please—"

For an Italian he's a remarkably silent man. Even in my panic I wonder if he says more to his girl, or if they never talk. He sighs and presses a bell, and a nurse comes hurriedly to collect me. I'm passed from one to the other, an unsatisfactory Olympic torch whose flame has gone out. As I stumble doorward he says encouragingly, "Well—we have got something, at least." Then he spoils it by sighing again. But I smile over my shoulder at him, desperately. If only I were his girl! She undoubtedly knows where she comes from, where she's going to, who she is.

But we have got something. We have two whole cypresses.

The nurse puts me back to bed and covers me up like a dog covering something undesirable in the garden. Not for the first time I wonder why so many people connected with healing have this tinge of brutality. Is it because they must be so healthy for a demanding profession that they've never felt pain or weakness? "Not for the first time"—so I've thought this before. Have I been in a hospital before? I put my face in my hands, and the sickness rises in me.

"Please. Can I have a basin?" But I'm sick on the bed before she returns. Now she has every reason to dig me out as though I were undesirable. Luckily the mattress is rubber and the undersheet too. The mess is sorted out and I'm put back to bed like a nice clean bone, and the basin's left propped on my stomach. I lie back and shut my eyes and hear her dump some rustling papers on my bed and go away. I lie thinking of nothing, for there's little enough to think of except those cypresses.

After a time I do begin to concentrate on them. They're compulsive—and the vault, and the hill: the only bits of my past that I've remembered in all these five long weeks. I think of them in Italian, and then in English. My mind makes the switch with no trouble at all: I'm faultlessly fluent in both languages. They've tried me against a professor of English, and against Italian students. I'm not only correct, I know the current slang. There's nothing to tell which country I was born in, but they believe I'm Italian. Perhaps those two cypresses will lead to my Italian home. Is this an encouraging thought, when the fear I felt made me run uphill? And if I'm Italian, why has no one claimed me yet? My diaphragm heaves, and I press on it with my left hand. The right is still heavily bandaged. It was badly injured in the accident.

I lie looking at it, thinking of its treachery. An able

right hand—ah, that would be a treasure at this moment. A hand which could automatically trace a signature might be surprised into truth. An accustomed flow of movement, the body thinking, whorls of ink making the mark: an identity. I've tried with my left hand, but if I'm bilingual I am not ambidextrous; and my left hand is a fool, a clown. It writes like a drunk two-year-old. It's as though fate, having made a trap, had tested it thoughtfully in all directions to show the prisoner there's no escape.

Blank walls in a blank room; I'm frightened to leave my cubicle, for outside everything is new. A baby couldn't be more surprised by everything than I am. No wonder nature allows such a slow growth of consciousness, or the baby would hang onto the womb howling, afraid to come out. Just as I'm afraid to come out and face a new city, a new country, an extraordinary, unknown world, filled with people who know it and each other.

Footsteps at the end of the corridor. Tense, I shut my eyes. My mother, my father, two sisters, or an unlooked-for brother? Someone from a consul, searching for missing persons? My surgeon, my analyst? (For they've taken great care of me here, they've never had such a problem before.)

It's none of them. Only Chiara. She hums the monotonous tune that she's always humming whenever Sister sends her round with soft drinks or coffee. I keep my eyes shut but can feel her presence hovering in the doorway. Gloating. Chiara's peering has done almost more to undermine me in the last weeks than anything else. Her gluttony for other people's sensations is intense, and she lives off my disaster like a parasite.

"Still remembered nothing, signorina?"

"Nothing," I say, suppressing my cypresses. But I haven't suppressed Chiara. Clumping footsteps and an overwhelming smell of garlic tell me that. I open my eyes angrily to find her looking down at me.

"What do the doctors say to that, I wonder?"

I feel a retch coming but manage to hold it back.

"To think of poor papa and poor mama waiting desperately somewhere, always waiting. Not a poor husband, perhaps—" At this point she always glances at my ringless left hand as though to make sure that none has suddenly materialized on it. She's like an insatiable child who wants the same tale over and over again and is only happy when no word is altered.

"A thankful lover, maybe." I put my cold hands—cold on this hot day—beneath the sheet.

"Signorina, you're always heartless."

"Mindless and memoryless too. Go away, Chiara, it's too hot to gossip. And I may be sick."

That was bound to remove her. She's over by the door in a flash, for she wouldn't care to hold the disaster's head. But she has an instinct for triumph. "That other lady has gone out today."

"What other lady?"

"The one who came in and out for treatment, then had a minor operation. Read about you in the papers. I let her have a quick peep at you when you were asleep. She said it was heartrending, and you so young."

Visiting the animals is free on weekdays.

"Next time someone wants to see me, charge them."

She gives a quick little nod and slips away, forgetting to offer me lemonade or coffee.

Charge them . . . I think drowsily. From what I know of Chiara, she probably did.

2

Morning. The doctors' round is over. The briefness of their visit shows how tired they are of me. The subject of my cypresses has been raised, but the specialist merely frowned as though he thought I was making them up as a pointer to resurrection. The day nurse is sick of me too. She says I may dress for a while and go into the garden, and says it as though decreeing punishment. There's only one nurse I like—the short girl with the sweet expression and bubbly laugh; but she, unfortunately, is away.

At least I'm offered help as I stumble about my cubicle, making do with that clumsy left hand. It's hard to arrange my hair, which has grown while I was in the hospital and hangs almost to my waist. When we're ready I ask for the accident photographs again. But the nurse refuses. The doctor thinks I'm too morbidly interested in them, and trying to force my memory too often will never release it. He would sooner I got my mind onto other things, for some unexpected association may do the trick when deliberate efforts fail. She hands me Italian and English papers, leads me out into the garden, and arranges me in a deck chair in the hottest corner. One or two patients from the surgical wards are limping about on crutches. Near me Signora Pacetti, whose husband was in a motorbike crash, placidly winds wool onto her hands while waiting for him to emerge from the physiotherapy room. We exchange smiles and nods. I open the papers, hoping for a miracle.

Half an hour later I lay them aside. I'm sweating from tension and the usual disappointment. My memory is as dormant as though it lay fathoms beneath a turgid ocean. It's left unstirred by—in the Ialian news—scooter accidents, denouncements of communism

and adultery, landslides in Sicily, the ex-queen of Greece, the Pope blessing the faithful. (Am I one of the faithful? A visiting priest seemed ready to claim me zealously for his particular brand of heaven.) And the English news has no better effect. Why should my buried memory care about immigrant problems, inflation, or an interviewed countess speaking about a fabulous family miniature which someone has pinched? Poor Countess—incredible though it may seem, the painting wasn't insured. I study its photograph and wonder why people always fail to insure what they're going to lose. I doubt if I insured my memory. Still, Countess, be thankful it's only an Elizabethan miniature which is missing. It might have been some bit of you, and how would you like that, I wonder? Better to mislay a Nicholas Hilliard, any day.

"You're better, signorina? I'm so pleased." Signora Pacetti has a pleasant voice.

"Yes, I suppose I'm better. At least I'm promoted from that sort of chaise longue plus dressing gown."

We laugh together politely.

"Is your husband better?"

"I believe so, but what a time they keep him in physiotherapy! Look, I've wound all this wool, and now I'm starting a second skein." She draws it out of a capacious bag and waves it at me. I'm glad to have her here. She's companionable, sympathetic, not ghoulish like Chiara. Even as I'm thinking this she gives me a sideways glance and says in motherly tones, "I hope you'll never be such a foolish girl as to take lifts from unknown young men again!" Then she turns pink and starts hurriedly winding up her wool.

I hasten to reassure her, and we both sit in silence. My thoughts go back to the accident photographs, but this would annoy the doctor, so I wrench them away with an almost physical effort. They linger instead on the police findings. It seems strange that the boy I was with is now fully documented, while I'm not. The car went off the road and plunged deep into the valley before the fall was broken. I, the passenger, was flung clear, but the driver was inextricably wedged in his seat, among the flames. A horrible thought! The engine number wasn't destroyed, so the police were able to trace the car, which had been stolen that morning from a village square forty kilometers away. It belonged to a well-known businessman, and when accounts appeared in the local paper the young thief's family had reluctantly gone to the police. His Christian name was Dino, but he belonged to a wild gang that had nicknamed him Il Nero. They admitted to having seen him drive the car away. No, they were sure there'd been no girl with him then, and Il Nero had no girl with auburn hair, so far as they knew. (Further inquiries proved them correct.) But he had a persuasive tongue, and with such a smart car had boasted he was bound to pick up something special. He had a habit of "borrowing" cars, picking up girls, and returning both—the worse for wear—a day or so later. This last bit of information entranced the journalists, and since she's a good Italian wife and mother, it's very sweet of Signora Pacetti to speak to me. Perhaps she's firmly decided I'm English after all.

"The picture didn't look like you, signorina," she ventures at last.

I stare at her, confused. My mind has been following its own obsessive thoughts. How strange—there must have been a time when I was free of them!

"What picture?"

"The one in—the one they took of you and put in all the papers. They should take another, now you're so much better. You mightn't be the same girl."

"The doctors might be interested—but they'd never manage to interest the papers now. I'm stale news."

"All the same, they should try," she persists. "For one

thing you look, oh—so much younger." She's dying to know something and too polite to ask.

"They say I'm under twenty-one."

"So young? I wouldn't have thought it—" She looks at me doubtfully, is conscious of rudeness, blushes again. "Of course, you've been ill. . . ."

How tactful of her to separate my mind from my body—perhaps my remaining blankness doesn't seem illness to her?

"They're quite certain. I suppose they tell from my teeth, like a horse."

We both laugh, dutifully. She's plainly relieved to see her husband limp toward us across the grass.

"Signorina!" He smiles. "You're better?" He looks slightly surprised to see me there, which is explained when he continues, "I thought, that is, I heard they were transferring you to—"

Signora Pacetti rises very quickly, stuffing the skein of wool, all tangled, back into her bag. Her voice has a higher note than usual. "But of course she's better, Edmondo—she is up and dressed!" She pats me hurriedly on the arm, takes hold of his, smiles at me, grimaces at him, and burbling frenziedly about how her cooking will be spoiled, leads him away.

Now my sweating isn't caused by sun or weakness.

"I heard they were transferring you to—" And her confusion. There are two other hospitals they could send me to: the big general one in the town and the local asylum. Why should mention of a general hospital cause anyone confusion?

This brilliant sunshine is intolerable; and the strolling, sitting, ordinary people, who know exactly what they are, become a nightmare reminder of my uncertainty. Like an animal, I want to creep into the dark and hide. I'm shaking all over as convulsively as someone in a fit. I must hide it. No one must see. My mind's blank, but my body must be well. The doctors must see that I'm fit enough to go out, take a job. (What job?) I shut my eyes, as if that might hide me. Don't let anyone pass, don't let anyone pass— The shaking grows more violent, as though I'm handling an electric drill. Just let the other patients and the nurses keep away until it goes— But I can feel the shadow as it falls across my eyelids, cutting off the sun's ferocity.

"Signorina Maria? Signorina Maria!"

(The staff gave me a name so that I shouldn't feel too anonymous; but here in Italy could you come closer to anonymity than Maria?)

Ave Maria, gratia plena . . .

There is more confusion. Somebody calls out. A man's heavy footsteps approach quickly. I grip my knees, trying to steady my hands. But both hands and knees are jerking like a puppet's on a string. As I open my eyes a white sleeve comes down between me and the light. The nurse's calm, cold hands grip my right arm, turning it underside upmost, and the needle pricks home into the vein as the sky draws two faces toward it and then falls on me.

Chiara appears with two large tablets before I have my supper.

"Back on these," she says, shaking her head happily. "And two more tonight, the sister says."

"She never said it to *you*." I push her hand crossly away. "I don't want them, anyway. They make me feel woozy and worse than— They don't suit me. If the nurse is too busy to come herself, they can't be all that important."

"The nurse said *I* was to give them. So hurry up. Had a bad day, haven't you? We all thought you were getting more normal."

Something boils within me: fierce anger, as ruthless as Chiara's pretended pity.

"No one will ever think that of you, Chiara. And if

14

you want a boyfriend, instead of that sloppy little girl I see you mooning about with now and then, you'd better start washing your hair—every other day wouldn't be too much." Firmly I close my eyes, congratulating myself that even on such a day I'm able to quell the little beast; the sound of her slippers goes pad, pad, pad, away from me, toward the door. . . .

It's true that the tablets make me woozy. When my supper comes, I eat it in a haze—remote, remote even when the doctor slips in to see me. He takes my pulse, asks one or two questions, looks at my chart. There's another doctor with him. Young, white-coated, with eyes like eggs which have been boiled too long. We aren't introduced, and my own doctor avoids my eyes. Outside the door they have a long, low discussion. Even through the pill haze I can reason enough to suspect the newcomer of being an advance guard from—

It's a suitable note on which to end the day, and my mind winces away from definition. I drift into sleep thinking of cypresses and inquisitive birds which look like Chiara and lay hard-boiled eggs.

3

The sun is streaming into my room when I wake. The pills have really done their work. I'm calm with the calmness of a log. It would need an elephant to move me off the strand where I've stuck on my river-of-life journey. All the other little logs are floating tidily down the river toward their proper destinations. I lie supine, waiting to be moved.

As on every morning, I do the deliberate mind-delving which may dredge up something—another cypress, perhaps? But when nothing happens I don't cry. I lie placidly saying to myself, "Who are you, where do you come from, where were you born?" Click, click, click—the cogwheels turn over, not connecting. I've thought of Ravenna, but it might just as well be Timbuktu.

"*Buon giorno,* signorina, you're better today, yes?" Here she is. My friend, the small sweet nurse with the bubbly laugh and kind eyes. She arranges my pillows as though I were a child.

"Giustina, how good to see you! I thought you weren't back for another week?"

She grimaces. "We're short of staff—so, holiday cuts. But I've a fortnight later, and then we'll go to the sea, Mario and I. But you didn't answer my question, signorina? And no grapefruit?"

"No grapefruit, thanks. I don't know if I'm better, but I'm probably going away."

She looks at me severely. "What sort of talk is this, now! They've put you back on the pills, I see. They never suited you."

I smile at her as she fusses round me. But I'm silent. I won't upset Giustina by telling her they're sending me to the asylum. However, later in the morning, when she comes to tell me that my own doctor is bringing another one to talk with me, I see that she knows. She looks at me surreptitiously, and is obviously upset. Dear kind Giustina, who really cares about her patients.

Dr. Carlo—is it his Christian or his surname?—isn't quite so bad as I first thought, and attempts to put me at my ease. Although he tries almost too hard to bridge the gap between the normal and abnormal—he might be used to it by this time!—he is, within his limits, sympathetic and encouraging. He's well aware of my instinctive horror at the transfer, and tries to make it easier for me by saying that I'm only going to the wing where they deal with outpatients and neurotics.

"You'll probably soon be an out-patient yourself, signorina. But now you need more intensive treatment than you're getting."

"I've lost my memory," I say desperately, "I'm not mad."

"You could manage in the outside world then?"

I am silent.

"You see, you're not ready to go out yet—out of the hospital, that is. And there's nothing they can do for you here that they haven't tried already. There is, too, a desperate need for hospital beds—physically sick and surgical cases."

"Can *you* do anything for me?" I mutter, my hands plucking at the sheets. He's looking at them, and I will them to stay still.

"Naturally we hope so," he replies easily, "or we shouldn't be taking you. We'll send for you this afternoon—" He talks on, and while he's doing so I'm aware of a flurry in the doorway. It's Giustina, who murmurs something in my own doctor's ear. He gives me a quick, amazed glance and hurries from the room with her. Dr. Carlo eventually gives me a last encouraging smile and goes too, repeating his promise of sending transport as though it were the biggest treat I could expect. It probably is. I stare at the ceiling and wish heartily that the car which trapped Il Nero had trapped me too.

And then something happens—

My own doctor comes back into the room. He's smiling broadly. He says, "Signorina *Giulia?*"

And waits for a response.

I sit there staring at him.

He plumps down on the end of my bed unceremoniously. If he weren't such an imperturbable man I would say he's bubbling with excitement. "The name 'Giulia' means nothing to you? It does not have the same impact as, say"—he almost giggles—"those cypresses?"

"Should it have? No, it hasn't— Has somebody—is someone—" I falter. I should have been delighted, but instead I am filled with fear. My limbs turn to boneless jelly. I have never really understood before how awful it would feel to be confronted with someone who knows me intimately whom I may not recognize. Even, perhaps, a husband.

"There's a lady in my office. She has come to learn of your presence here. From the photographs she cannot be quite sure, but it's almost certain that you're her niece by marriage. Her name is Signora Carmina Carminotti."

There is the same complete blankness.

"That, too, means nothing?"

"Nothing at all."

He sighs. He's a nice man and he's terribly disappointed. Plainly he'd hoped I would rear myself up in bed crying, "Aunt Carmina! Of course, and the villa, etc." But all that comes to my overburdened memory are the words: ". . . with this key Shakespeare unlocked his heart . . . The thing became a trumpet; whence he blew soul-animating strains—alas, too few!"

"You've thought of something, signorina?"

I repeat my unlucky find, and he looks positively disgruntled. One cannot say my mind is out to help him. These aren't the sort of words one would have expected from the Italian niece of a person so obviously Italian as a Carmina Carminotti. I'm filled with panic. Do I really want to meet this woman? Still, perhaps she can push the log off its sandbank into the river—and less alarmingly than Dr. Carlo. Yes, I'm trapped between the devil and the deep blue sea. My pulses thud.

He sees something of this conflict in my face. He gets up and holds my wrist. After a moment or so of silence he says: "I think you can see her. Don't worry. I'll come with her. And until all this is settled I shall ring Dr. Carlo and tell him to delay." He pats me on the shoulder and goes out of the room. Within five minutes he's back, holding the door open and announcing, "Signora Carminotti."

A woman walks into the room, stands still, and takes stock of me. For perhaps ten seconds we take stock of one another. With the sure instinct I've developed, I know exactly what she'll say before she does so.

"But, Giulia! My dear, dearest child—"

Her voice is deep and harsh and must have been extremely sexy. Now it has the slightly masculine tones that such voices sometimes develop in middle age. She's an elegant woman, black hair smoothly pulled back into two large curls behind her ears. Her figure has thickened, but must once have been willowy in the model's fashion. She's only of medium height, but her obvious vitality makes her seem taller, yes—almost to fill the room. She has been beautiful, and perhaps it's the gradual loss of beauty that has made her mouth, above that originally perfect though now slightly heavy jawline, turn downward self-pityingly at the corners.

"What a thing to happen! My poor, poor little Giulia —" She advances toward the bed, and I watch her come with apprehension. For there's another thing about that voice which my developed sixth sense understands. Although there are notes of excitement and pleasure in it—and alarm?—there's not one hint of fondness.

I cannot for the life of me think what to say. "Hello, Aunt Carmina" to a complete stranger? Eventually I manage to stutter, "Are—are you really—my—my aunt?"

"Oh, but my dearest Giulia!" She has reached my bed and is patting my hands with firm, hard little pats as though I were a dog. She bends to kiss me, and I get a waft of subtle, expensive scent. "You know," she says, turning to the doctor as though I've embarrassed her— which I probably have, "I never thought it would be so—difficult not to be known! And by someone I nursed on my own knee as a baby. Those large, beautiful blue eyes—"

"My eyes are brown."

"All babies' eyes are blue at birth, and yours were particularly blue. Like periwinkles."

The doctor fiddles with his stethoscope. *He* doesn't know what to say either.

The signora, my aunt, turns back to me. "Now you see what happens when you're such a naughty little girl, eh?" The arch reproof is quite out of keeping with her appearance. "Your uncle and I, we're well accustomed to your not writing. That's the young of today, no? But Enrico—when we reached the next port he was really worried by no letters. So he goes ashore and wires to these people you had vaguely said you might stay on with in Switzerland—but no answer." She sits on my bed and motions imperiously to the doctor that he's to station himself in the only chair. "Then the good Frauleins are on holiday, of course, so no use to wire your school. I assure you that I have to calm Enrico—he would have us fly back home and see the police!" She snaps open her crocodile bag, looks absentmindedly in its mirror, and snaps it shut again. "But I say, this is how the young are, no? And yet," she sighs heavily, "in this case he was right, poor boy. I feel most responsible. Yes,

I've failed in my trust." Although she ostensibly blames herself, she sounds more as though she's accusing me.

"It's not so like the *upper-class* Italian young," says the doctor thoughtfully.

"It's not her fault—or mine—that *she* wasn't brought up as a young woman should be!" she flashes back at him. "A convent would have been much more suitable— I always said so—but her parents left all these ridiculous wishes, which we scrupulously—"

I'm in a daze. My parents, then, are dead? The tremor starts up in my hands and I bury them hastily beneath the bedclothes. My doctor looks at me.

"Signora, I think we'll now leave the signorina to think over the fact that she is found. She doesn't know who all these people are whom you speak of, but it will right itself in time. This, in her present nervous condition, is a strain for her. So we continue our conversation in my office. I'll send the nurse with a sedative for you, Signorina Giulia. Is there anything you wish to ask your aunt before she goes? I think it would be inadvisable for you to leave today."

"Please—how old am I?"

"Nineteen. You've just left finishing school."

"And—and Enrico?" Who is Enrico, that he's so frantic when he doesn't hear from me?

"Your first cousin. My son." She rises and looks thoughtfully at me, as though thinking of something more. Then she shakes her head as if refusing further comment, and all she adds, a little drily, is, "We shall be anxious to learn, my Giulia, what you were doing in the car with that poor young man who died!" Doesn't she believe that I *cannot* know?

She leans over and kisses me again with dry lips. As she straightens up she notices the limp rag of blue dress lying on the chair back, my only day garment. It was what I was wearing on the day of the accident, and it failed to provide any clues, for it was old and obviously homemade. Its shabbiness is in strong contrast to her own elegance.

"Is *that* what you're wearing? It looks as though it needs a good cleaning." She sounds intensely disapproving. "If they can lend you something here I'll take it with me and have it dealt with. Nerina shall send us from the other house those clothes you were wearing there last summer. They may still fit you."

Obviously she's happier with the subject of clothes than with me. She shakes out the shabby garment and tucks it beneath her arm, and somehow I feel she's shaken some strain out of herself as well. She gives a relaxed little wave, says, "We leave you with much, much to think about, eh, my Giulia? I'll come and see you again tomorrow, and take you home, if the good doctor allows it." And follows him from the room.

I hear his murmur of "Just in time . . . possibility of transfer to . . . ," and then, from farther down the corridor, a little shriek as my aunt presumably learns of Dr. Carlo.

Her going has sucked the tension from the room as though by vacuum cleaner, and I feel as if the oxygen has gone as well. I lie there scarcely breathing, not much happier to be found than lost. The only object in the room that really seems part of my own identity is the large, expensive leather bag that was found open beside me after the accident. Like everything else, it provided no helpful clues, only the unnecessary proof that I'm feminine—lipstick, comb, face powder; all of them were international brands. Everything else must have spilled out and burned. Now that bag seems like my only friend. Exhausted, and even before Giustina can bring my sedative, I fall asleep.

Only to dream about those cypresses. This time I'm standing between them, looking down the small steep hill up which I had run, seeing the tomb oblong and grim ahead to my left. What I'm looking for is my home—the home from which I ran? Surely from where I stand it should be clearly visible.

All at once I'm conscious of vulnerability. A target on the skyline—that's what I could be for anyone looking up the hill from either north or south. Sideways the trees protect me, one on either hand.

The mood of fear passes; why should anyone want to harm me? It's so peaceful on the hilltop in broad daylight. And yet here's a funny thing: the valley ahead of me is dark. Try as I will, I cannot see the house nor its inhabitants. All are hidden from me. I turn to face the other valley and find it's daylight there. Below me is a river in full flood. Small craft and logs drift down it, easily riding the current in the center stream. It looks so peaceful, so ordinary, and yet the sense of menace is as strong from this side as it was from the direction of the house.

The dream breaks as another gets imposed on it. I'm driving a van, faster and faster and faster. Someone—some thing—is chasing me. Terror grows. The road winds, a drop upon one side. Faster. The van sways. There are dark trees on my right. Only the trees are safe. I put my hand out of the driver's window to touch one. It turns into my cypress. Touching its foliage I wake. . . .

I am found. I am Giulia. Ahead of me lies my first meeting with people I've known all my life. The black leather bag on the hospital table is more familiar to me. If it could speak! I reach out and drag it into bed with me, fondling it. What good workmanship; it's better made than the dress that Aunt Carmina whipped away so scathingly last night. Soft leather and a fashionable shape. I was immensely pleased when he gave it to me—it wasn't even my birthday, just a sudden surprise. I lift out the contents to examine them fruitlessly once more. Why did this lipstick, this comb, have to be so

23

carefully anonymous? And why doesn't even the knowledge that I'm a Carminotti (or at least a Carminotti niece) bring back something?

My heart pounds suddenly. *He—* Yes, I had thought "he gave it to me—it wasn't even my birthday." One small piece, an infinitesimal one when you think of the average memory's scope, has detached itself from hidden depths and floated to the surface, like a bubble long trapped beneath weeds in a pond and suddenly released. I fondle the bag again, as though it's a primitive god that might be coaxed into speech by kind attentions. He gave it to me, he—Robert, *Robert!* Or Roberto? Anyway, not Enrico.

I stroke the bag again while I look inward, oblivious of sunlight. A long, long way away—like looking down the wrong end of a telescope—I see a pattern which forms into a face. A man's face. Dark hair, blue eyes— bright blue eyes like periwinkles (no, that was Carmina talking), a narrow-lipped mouth which has a sensual, attractive shape. Perhaps I never considered the toughness enough. . . . How strongly both the weak and the tough can inflict pain. . . . Yet the first feeling the bag gave me was one of happiness. I lean my forehead on it, trying to remember. But there's no further response. Whatever's holding down the bubbles is too strong, and too wary, to be moved by my own efforts.

4 | It's a wonderful evening—hot as Hades, but beautiful all the same. The shutters have been flung wide open to let in air which moves with the gentleness of a moth's wing against flesh tired by the day's ferocious heat. Benedetta moves silently round the table, a little old humble woman, very bent, whose eyes, when she straightens up, are far from humble and hold something stony and ageless in their gaze. She was sent from the convent many years ago to clean and cook. Service to the convent and service to the Family, this has been all her life. When she comes to offer me more *frutti di mare* it's as though some ancient spirit from the past stands beside my chair.

I shake my head.

"Giulia, you must eat—" Enrico bends forward solicitously. There's a crease at his waistline when he bends, but in a few years' time that won't be possible. His face is mournful, amiable, too fat already. If his mother really had his interests at heart she wouldn't constantly press food on him. There's something nice about him, something attractive, something comic, and something else.

"If she won't eat, she won't," says Carmina tartly. ("For heaven's sake, child, stop calling me aunt—you never did before, and it makes me feel about a hundred." That was what she said yesterday. I was relieved.)

"But, *Madre mia,* food is so important." A look of ridiculous anguish crosses his features at the thought of someone refusing food.

"Too important—to you," says his father drily. Uncle Vicenzo is as dried up as his voice. I wouldn't dare call him "Vicenzo," it would be asking for a snub. His small

25

eyes, bloodshot above pouches, run over me like insects. I can almost feel them.

"She doesn't want too much food." He speaks across me to Carmina. "Doesn't want to spoil her figure. You all thicken up too fast. Pity." He wipes his mouth on his napkin with a fastidious shudder after one glance at his wife's immaculately held-in waist.

Perhaps it's small wonder that she immediately presses more food solicitously on her son.

Uncle Vicenzo now addresses me: "Don't you think he's too fat?"

Impossible old man. I wonder if we've had many rows *à quatre* between the candle flames. Enrico looks sulky but firmly helps himself to another slice of *quiche*. I sip my wine. Carmina gives me a look as though summing up my silence.

"It doesn't make men attractive to young women, does it, my dear?" goes on the old demon. "Not unless they've plenty of money as well as plenty of suet." His laugh sounds like a hiccup. His son reddens. "I'd plenty of money at one time, but I was never fat, eh, was I, my beloved Carminetta?"

"If you'd had a few wits it would have been better than money or a figure," replies the beloved venomously.

The old man laughs quite heartily. "Well, we cannot say that our remarkable friend Cosmo has no wits, eh? And he's fat too, but attractive to women. So they say. Though no money—yet. How did you like our witty fat friend, our good doctor, Giulia?" Again those little eyes travel over me as though walking up and down my pink dress.

I hadn't liked him. He was full of solicitous warnings about what care must be taken of me, and solicitous inquiries about my memory, almost as though he was warning me against letting it return too fast. It had been on the tip of my tongue to tell him about the leather bag and "Roberto," but at the last minute I'd kept silence, as I had to my own doctor at the hospital, who had somehow depressed me about those cypresses. This had put me off telling anyone small discoveries. Superstitious perhaps, but I found such negative reactions so disheartening that I feared they might even cause the gates of my memory to close for good. I certainly wouldn't want to confide in Carmina's beloved "Cosmo," who was overbearingly paternal with his hand-patting and soft voice, and radiated sexual self-confidence. I had seen her looking at him, and wondered fleetingly if she had helped contribute to it. Now, as Uncle Vicenzo dwells sardonically on Cosmo's fatness and his charms, I suspect myself of being right. What a household—although perhaps no worse than many others. At least I feel some sympathy with the plump, faintly endearing and obviously admiring Enrico. Yet somewhere within he must surely secrete the genetic pattern of his parents. Unless they adopted him?

Benedetta brings fruit and cheese, and places them in the ring of candlelight. I start to peel a pear.

"She doesn't like Cosmo," interprets Uncle Vicenzo.

"I didn't say so, Uncle." Is the wicked old man determined to put Carmina against me? What else can we start to wrangle about, I wonder?

"That looks like a delicious *burino*."

Enrico at once cuts a huge slice with the best bit of butter for me. I applaud his unselfishness but accept a smaller slice. If they didn't adopt him, I'm wondering if Carmina had an unselfish lover.

"And he dandled you on his knee," says Uncle reproachfully, giving a cackle of dry mirth. "Am I correct, Carmina?"

"Who?" I say, startled.

"Why, our fat witty friend, of course. That's a very pretty pink dress you have on, my dear."

"Nerina sent it up from the other house," says Carmina automatically.

"How peculiarly well it fits you. One would really

expect you to have grown since last summer. Or has one stopped growing at nineteen?"

Following this conversation makes me tired. I've been here a day and a half and still feel no more at home than when my feet crossed the threshold. But I've come to the right place, whatever it's like; there's no doubt of that. The first thing I saw when I went out into the gardens was the hill rising steeply up before me, and there at the top my two cypresses, and the stones and vault between me and them. It's a comfort to know that when my memory does work it does so accurately.

Benedetta brings coffee, but Carmina waves her away. "Take it out on the terrace, it's too hot in here. Not that it will be cooler outside," she says to me, "but we can pretend it is. This heat exhausts me."

"You're lucky, my dear," says Uncle Vicenzo, feeling for his rubber-tipped cane, which has slipped beneath the table, "that you don't drive into town every day to sit in an office."

"That office of yours is air-conditioned, which is more than can be said for this villa."

"Still, it was very hot today," complains Enrico feelingly. "I wish you wouldn't insist on our always going in together, Papa. I'd far sooner have my own car and come away when I choose."

I'm a little surprised. Enrico must be twenty-three or -four. Surely he has his own car?

"That," says his father, rising and grasping the stick firmly in an amazingly strong old hand, "is what I'm afraid of—you'll never make a lawyer if a little thing like heat can put you off. Courage, Enrico"—he taps his son on the shoulder as he passes him—"you shall have your own car soon enough, and a good one it shall be." He touches my arm and waves me ahead of him toward the garden.

The air, though just as hot as Carmina has foretold, is beautiful with the scent of night-opening flowers. The dark shadows seem quite solid, as they do in heat, and from the direction of the lily pond comes the croak of little frogs. We arrange ourselves in comfortable chairs on the flagged terrace, and Carmina efficiently and Enrico languidly dispense coffee. Then my cousin seats himself at my side. It's not unpleasant to be admired by Enrico, but it's obvious that his mother has somehow emasculated him, which makes his attention less flattering than masculine admiration usually is. Idly I wonder if other men have been fairly attentive to me, and if Roberto was one of them.

"Giulia"—Enrico hitches his chair a little closer—"you don't remember anything more at all?"

"I don't think you should go on and on asking her if she remembers things," says Carmina in a warning voice. This should be solicitous but doesn't sound so.

"I don't mind," I say perversely. "There's such a lot I ought to know. Tell me about Switzerland. If I was at finishing school there, perhaps we should go to visit it."

"The doctors think you should take life simply for a bit. No rushing around anywhere. And no going out alone either. We don't want you suddenly going off into a daze and getting lost. A fugue, Cosmo calls it. Such a strange word."

"Is that likely to happen?"

Carmina shrugs. "We mustn't take chances. I hope you're going to be tractable, Giulia. You've been a headstrong piece ever since you were born, I believe. And look what it's brought you to now."

A more sensitive person wouldn't have said that, but 1 respond meekly enough, since I can hardly gainsay her knowledge; she and Vicenzo have been my guardians since my parents were killed in an air crash ten years ago. I was first schooled in England—my mother was English—and then in Switzerland. From what I've seen of Carmina so far I must have been an unwelcome charge, a girl growing up into rival womanhood. Small wonder that she was so often traveling when my holidays were due! Apparently I liked spending them in Switzerland—or so I'm told. And sometimes at the "other house," with their accommodating housekeeper Nerina. Of course motherbound Enrico traveled with his mother, and without father, who was too busy in a substantial law practice to accompany them.

I find myself wondering how well I got on alone with Uncle Vicenzo; perhaps the as-yet unknown Nerina acted as a buffer. Last year they bought themselves this villa in a countryside convenient to his office and said to be cooler than their own house tucked some thirty kilometers away. It's a luxurious villa. Vicenzo must be doing very well to afford it. This is the first year we've actually occupied it, although last year there must have been plenty of coming and going to see how the decorations were getting on. All things considered, it's clever of my memory to have picked on this place for its only flash of recovery—other than "Roberto." Perhaps, as Carmina undoubtedly is, I'm impressed by luxury. Tentatively I'm testing out what sort of a person I may be. I cannot get over a feeling that the older Carminottis regard me with a certain scorn.

Beside me Enrico shifts and clears his throat. His hands clasp and unclasp themselves between his knees.

Ever since I came home there's been a sense of something left unsaid. Perhaps Carmina gave me one clue when she spoke, in the hospital, of Enrico's fussing about me. Was he on the verge of a proposal? Then it's certainly best to ward it off. Pick of the family though he is, I can hardly imagine marrying him. Besides, there's the enigmatic Roberto! For all I know—and I'm quite sure Carmina doesn't trust me—I may have got myself engaged already. Up there in Switzerland? Yet I don't feel Carmina's anxious either to stop or start her son proposing; it's a different sense I get. If she wants to ward it off, as I do, it's because she feels he's going to put

his foot in it somehow. I don't know why I'm sure of this, but I am.

"When you've drunk your coffee, will you walk round the gardens with me?" he asks.

"I'm feeling rather lazy still."

"My dear Enrico, a little more of this hustle in the office and you may do well after all. I shall not despair."

"We might all take a small stroll," says Carmina very finally, "and then Giulia should go to bed."

"But, *Mamma mia*—"

"Talk to her when she's less tired tomorrow morning. Your father can send the car back for you from the office." This has definitely clinched the matter, whatever it may be. As I stroll between her and Enrico down the sweet-smelling walk, Uncle Vicenzo tapping his stick behind us, I can see my two friendly cypresses, spears of darkness against a deep blue sky.

5

Benedetta brings my breakfast tray a little earlier than I expect her and informs me that when I'm up the signorino will be waiting for me in the drawing room. I savor my roll and butter but am a little apprehensive. There are enough undercurrents in this family already without my adding to them by upsetting Carmina. I don't want to stay on here in an atmosphere of hostility. And where else can I go till outsiders see me as normal? I've not asked myself before what I'm living on. My uncle and aunt? Surely not. They don't look charitable. Perhaps my parents left me some money. But at least Enrico's shy admiration doesn't seem like the blatant maneuvers of a fortune hunter. And he's a lawyer; perhaps he's simply expecting to talk about finance.

It's a beautiful day anyway, and warms me right through to the bones. There's a flutter of sparrows on my windowsill, and a bright brown eye peers in—an instinct for crumbs. I dispose of my last crust, which disappears under a soft rush of feathers, and then go downstairs.

Enrico greets me awkwardly. For so large a man his fluttering is ridiculously sparrowlike. He talks too much, then not at all, seats me in a chair, fiddles with papers at a desk, and looks quite desperate.

"I suppose the family friend is coming up today?" I make conversation.

"Cosmo? No, I don't think so—yes, I suppose he is. It—it must be very odd without a memory."

"Odd is the word. But otherwise I feel almost normal—which may surprise your Dr. C. He wants to have another look at my hand. I'd no idea how dependent one could be on two hands till I tried to dress using only one. It's coping with hair that's hardest."

"Yes—uh—it looks charming though."

"Like a bird's nest. Or so Carmina says."

"Ask her hairdresser to set it for you, then. Or no, I—" He looks more confused.

"She seems to think I'm made of glass—shouldn't meet anyone or go out." I've been surprised by her solicitude. She looks more the type to tell someone to pull herself together.

His silence is oppressive. At last I say bluntly, "What's the idea of this interview, Enrico? Business or pleasure?"

His dark complexion can't redden much, but what it can do, it does. Large and clumsy, he lopes across to the desk and extracts a bundle held together by a rubber band.

"It's—about some letters of yours. These."

"Letters of mine?" (Not "Roberto's," I hope!)

"I really think you'd understand better, Giulia, if you read them yourself. They start at this end—" He's more assured now, the lawyer overcomes the shy man. "Here. Will you take them?" He places them in my lap, and I stare at them fascinated. The first one commences, *"Mio caro* Enrico—" in a schoolgirlish hand.

"They begin when you're almost sixteen—" He swallows, and puts his hands together as though they might comfort one another.

"They're all to you?"

"Yes, yes." He sounds impatient now, eager to get it over, whatever it may be. "Here, I forgot how awkward that hand is." He slips the band off the letters for me. There are about twelve of them; evidently I'm not a good correspondent at the best of times, as Carmina has already trenchantly asserted when I was in the hospital. The first three are written in that schoolgirlish hand. The others are typewritten, and signed with the same unformed and flourishing signature. It appears that Vicenzo, good businessman that he is, gave me a typewriter and insisted I should use it to augment the finishing school's more exotic accomplishments. No one could say I showed much secretarial aptitude. There are clusters of wrong words roughly scratched out, but the letters at least become longer and more readable. The tone of the earlier ones is of cousinly affection but almost entirely self-concerned. Then comes one which, with all this buildup from Enrico, doesn't surprise me.

". . . no, I'd no idea that my parents and yours always thought it a good idea if you and I should get married one day. It's new to me, and truly, Enrico, I feel far too young to decide anything like that. Why—I've hardly met anyone, and you can't want to marry me, can you, when we've always fought by the end of the holidays? I can't see that our parents had the usual Italian reasons, either. It's not as though we've land adjoining each other's, or something like that. Don't want to sound unkind, but have I a colossal dowry that no one's ever told me of? It's not unpleasant to ask, is it, because we're like that as a nation, aren't we? I mean, my Italian side tells me that we are. Anyway, it's nice of you to be so pro the idea—I don't feel pro or against. I simply feel it's unreal, unbelievable. Please tell Carmina and Uncle Vicenzo that I couldn't think of anything like marriage till I've left school. In our country it's a life sentence, after all."

I put the letter carefully aside, to pick up the next. The self I cannot remember was out to avoid the subject, for this one deals firmly with other things, skiing, German lessons, and envy for the smartness of a girl from Brazil. But the next letter returns to it on a slight note of distress.

". . . tell Carmina and Uncle V. to lay off, can't you? I've had letters from both, and I don't know which made me feel more like leaving for Siberia. Carmina's plainly insulted that I'm not swooning already with love and excitement, and Uncle V.'s was worse, he takes it all completely for granted as arranged. It's not. I won't come home at all for the holidays if this sort of thing goes on, and they can threaten to stop my allowance till they're blue in the face, I don't care."

And the next—

". . . glad everyone's mollified and quietened down. Good thing I haven't anything like Carmina's explosive temperament, isn't it—must be my cooler English side coming out, I suppose. Just promise not to keep on at me when I come home, eh, Enrico? We'll see how everything goes. I've not said I'm against it, just don't want to be pushed; it makes me dig in my feet, like a mule."

There must have been a break for the holidays then, because when the letters started again they were different in tone, more grown-up, more affectionate. I glance sideways once at Enrico's hands. He's almost cuddling them to him for comfort or moral support.

". . . yes, it was a good time, and you were very nice to me, Enrico. But don't think this has decided anything yet. I really can't begin making promises now, even though I may feel more pro the idea than before. We've been reading Shakespeare with Miss Howard—new English mistress—'Men are April when they woo, December when they wed.' Ever heard that before? One sees plenty of it when looking round—and as for the other girls' parents! But there's one thing I'll say for you: even when you're fighting you don't show Carmina's flashes of sheer brilliant bad temper—sorry!—nor the sarcasm that makes Uncle V. so shriveling somehow. Write again soon, then I'll write back."

Reading this I feel a bit indignant, and sure that they pressured Giulia—me—in a way unfair at her—my—age. Yet it seems that after this letter the idea had taken root and grown of its own accord, with its own life, as though inertia had taken hold of me and allowed the Carminottis to rule the matter as they pleased. I don't really care for this quick submission after so spirited a start.

It's not at all what I feel myself—or hope myself—to be like. Of course, in these matters we Italian girls, for all our volatile temperaments, have centuries of passive acceptance of male dominance in our blood, whatever our matriarchs may achieve inside the home. And yet, looking at Enrico's kind, fleshy face, I find it hard to believe that anything Italian in myself had ever knuckled under quite so fast without a good deal of parental bullying. But what about the mule reaction in the earlier letter? This puzzle makes me frown.

The last letter, especially, holds the core of all Enrico's present troubles—and now mine.

". . . I agreed that when I got home we'd be formally engaged. But it's no good fussing about being dragged off with Carmina on another lazy cruise just now, Enrico. *I* want these last few weeks with friends. The person who has a right to complain must be Uncle V., surely he's tired of managing alone when she drags you off. I suppose he's hoping I won't follow the example! Well, I'll admit that I've not been too happy about your mother and our marriage. Reading between the lines, I've a good idea that it's she and not you who chose the ring. Why did you send it to me, anyway? I'd call it the perfect bribe if I didn't know you better! I love wearing it (away from school), but nothing's settled, see? If I hand it back you'll be able to sell it easily. Your mother certainly has perfect taste. But any woman would sooner have a lover's bad taste than his mother's good one. Don't expect me to write a lot, because life's bound to be hectic here."

I lay the letter aside. Easy to see, as Enrico obviously did, that I was having second thoughts. Easy to understand why I had wanted those last wild few weeks— days—which ended in the accident. Roberto. What, in heaven's name, had he to do with them? And straight into my mind come words that the excellent Miss Howard must have taught me: "Who is Silvia? What is she that all our swains commend her?" They aren't very suitable for a man. . . .

"Now you can surely understand—" bursts out Enrico, as though the strain of waiting for me to speak has been too much for him.

Yes, I can—and feel sorry for him. Almost sorry, too, for Carmina and Uncle Vicenzo, whose expert parental plans had received so sudden and unexpected a spoke in the wheel. But sorrier still for myself—it's an awkward enough situation. To me it seems one best dealt with by a clean break. Without my memory of the chains carefully forged by my aunt and uncle I know very well that I don't wish to marry Enrico, pleasant though he probably is. I say so, not attempting to hide the harshness of the truth. What's the use?

The distress this causes him is very apparent. He turns quite pale with emotion. "Oh no, but dearest Giulia—" He argues, pleads, and walks about the room.

I harden my heart, though it's tough on him if it took him so long to bring me round to the idea in the first place.

"Listen, Enrico, I met you for the first time the day before yesterday—"

He winces, turns to me hurriedly with denial on his lips. I hold up my bandaged hand. "Yes, can't you see that's how it feels? I know the hospital staff better than I know you! We *have* to leave the whole thing. I won't marry someone I hardly know. Surely you've sense enough to see it? You want to start afresh, but I say we have to wait till I get my memory back."

I stand up as though to emphasize my words. "Perhaps I will remember—soon."

The idea doesn't seem to give him much pleasure. A look of suppressed anger settles on his face, lending it a likeness to his mother's.

"Giulia, you must try and see it from my point of view. You're impossible! After all these months and months of waiting for you to make up your mind I go and buy the ring, and then you—then this has to happen."

"It's hardly my fault," I say tartly. "You don't imagine it's fun for me, do you? They were just going to put me in an asylum when Aunt—when Carmina wandered in. And speaking of Carmina, she never told me how the family suddenly came to hear I was in that place?"

"Oh, what does it matter? Some woman who was in there talked about a girl—" He shrugs it off impatiently, then turns on me with an accusing stare of his dark eyes. "And you say it's not your fault, but it's just the sort of thing she would have done—"

"She—who?" I ask, bewildered. "Carmina?"

"*La madre* never behaved like that in all her life! But no, Giulia *mia*"—he comes toward me and grips me by the arms—"you're not getting out of everything so easily as this, first turning me on, then turning me off, allowing yourself to be picked up by a sordid little gangster on the run! We don't know a thing after you left Switzerland, anything may have happened, do you hear? And then you've the effrontery to stand there and look at me like that and say you won't marry me! You should be glad to marry anyone."

He glares at me and lets me go. I'm blazingly angry. Yet there's something unreal about Enrico's rage, almost as though he's deliberately worked himself into it, or is really filled by another, totally different emotion. I turn my back on him, feeling slightly sick, and start to shake, just as the door flies open, and there stands Carmina. Are we in for a scene with the loving mother? Luckily she spares me this. Enrico, who might have expected sympathy if she's been eavesdropping, gets no more than an indecipherable glance. While I, shaking increasingly, am ushered out into the hall, where Cosmo's bulk and deprecating medical smile await me in a conspiratorial manner which sets him in league with my betraying body against myself. It's not surprising that within half an hour I'm so sedated I can barely speak. But one half-formed thought goes round and round in my mind like a bird shut in a room. Didn't—didn't Enrico, when he first saw his mother standing there, look slightly scared?

6

A day in bed, and everything seems better. Surely there's nothing to be worried by after all, and the impression I got—that Enrico was frightened by his mother—was one of those crazy exaggerations that my groping mind is prone to now. Carmina has really been sweet to me, and even pats my hand with those hard little pats which are more like an assault on quailing skin.

"This stupid son of mine!" She shakes her head. "I warned him not to try and rush you, Giulia. Perhaps it was a mistake to tell you anything so soon, but your uncle thought we shouldn't keep from you just where you stand—or stood." She smiles charmingly. "Everything must now take its time." Perhaps her beloved Cosmo warned against hurried renewals. I smile back guardedly. There's something I want to know; before, I've been too embarrassed to ask.

"Carmina, am I—that is, have I money of my own?"

"But surely!" she says readily. "Were you afraid you're living on charity?" She doesn't wait for a reply. "If your mind's running on business matters you had best speak with your uncle. He thought you weren't up to it yet."

Why was I thought up to that scene with Enrico, then?

My uncle does talk to me. It's all very civilized, over a glass of dry vermouth while Carmina and Enrico sit outside on the terrace where the evening flowers are already starting to scent the air.

"You want to know your—er—financial position, my dear."

"Yes, please, Uncle."

"Very natural. Love, sickness, beauty—all pass; but a

good solid interest in the price of stocks and shares we might describe as an eternal verity." He looks at me from wicked little eyes. "I'm happy to tell you, Giulia, that you are all right. Yes, *quite* all right. It's one reason I—we should like you to marry with our son."

That's honest anyway. And more or less what I suspected.

"You don't look surprised, my dear, and in fact no one but a fool would be. There are other reasons, of course, why we would like it. You have a strong character, sometimes regrettably strong." Snuffle. "Enrico has not; he will be very much what his wife makes of him. You were—are, no doubt, healthy. You're exceptionally pretty. I don't think we need worry too much about the children.

So the old rogue has summed me up as a potential good brood mare. "Except that we happen to be first cousins," I say tartly. "Yes, it's more or less as I thought, Uncle Vicenzo. I didn't think you and Carmina would have pressed us to marry if I'd been poor."

"You're quite sensible, my dear. Anyway, you're far from being a pauper; nor are you what we might call a great heiress. You're comfortably in between. My brother and his wife left you all they had. As your guardian and trustee I've endeavored to fulfill my duties. After careful discussion with your other trustee, Basilio Giambollino—now, alas, dead—I sold your property in the South and in England to invest the sums acquired, with your other monies. But this is all very tedious. When you're quite recovered Enrico shall bring you to my office and we'll go into it in detail and explain it to you. Suffice it to say in the meantime that you're not here on charity." He smiles his close lawyer's smile and levers himself upward with his stick. "Shall we join the others in the garden? Doubtless Enrico wishes to take you for a little stroll and explain that he didn't wish to press you too hard or upset you yesterday."

I take a deep breath. "Uncle, there's one thing I must make absolutely clear. Whatever relationship I had with Enrico ended with that motor crash. We're getting to know each other now for the first time. Without promises."

"Of course, of course. But it's most annoying to have one's plans upset when everything's going well. Why did anyone invent the motor car?" His smile is urbane as he ushers me out onto the terrace. "It will be your decision, Giulia, and you may trust us to agree with that."

One tiny unwelcome thought flickers like a running spider through my mind: Why should he feel I might not trust them? In such casual sentences people often betray themselves.

"Have you taken your pills?" asks Carmina sharply as I settle by her in a chair.

"I'm feeling better and don't really want them."

But she overrules me in her usual arrogant manner and Enrico's sent to fetch them. They aren't the same as those doled out in the hospital but are some favored medicine of Cosmo's. They still have the unpleasant side effect of plunging me back into that silly mindless haze which makes me feel like a disembodied robot.

"Six a day," says Carmina as, weakly protesting, I swallow two with water. "And you're to obey Cosmo, Giulia, and not treat us to fireworks. He doesn't think you were sedated long enough in that hospital. Dr. Carlo says he would put you on deep sedation for at least three weeks."

I give a slight start. Dr. Carlo . . . The asylum doctor? How can she know what he says, what possible cause—?

"Don't look so thunderstruck, my dear! Our friend has known Dr. Carlo for years. We shall have his expert advice on treating you if you don't shortly improve. So you see, dearest Giulia *mia,* you're being excellently well looked after." As she leans backward and closes her eyes her face looks like an ancient Roman mask, with harsh lines round the corners of the mouth, and a dominant nose.

The sedative is just starting to fog the corners of my mind. All the same I wonder, fear cutting into the haze, if she's just uttered some sort of threat. I lie back in my chair and stare across the coming dusk at those two cypresses.

We're still sitting there, and I'm beginning to wonder if we—and those cypresses—are turning into stone, when Benedetta comes shuffling out onto the terrace, her ungainly movements disturbing the flower-scented air so that a waft of it comes to me strongly and for a moment rouses me from apathy.

"The signora is wanted on the telephone."

Carmina sighs and goes. The two men start chatting in low tones.

"Well, *cara mia?*" asks old Vicenzo when she returns.

She's silent, biting her lip. I get the impression she would like to call him a fool, but for once feels constrained by my presence. "People have started ringing up—that's all," she says shortly.

"Ah? May one inquire who?"

"Beatrice"—more shortly still.

"One wonders how she heard. I suppose the hospital staff will talk in spite of that doctor's promises. Doubtless we shall have the press on us very soon. Giulia will not see them, of course. The strain would be very great. My dear"—he turns to me—"we shall regretfully confine you to the garden for the moment."

I'm not regretful. Probably no one who hasn't suffered from my type of disaster can tell the fear that former—or indeed any—contacts induce in me.

Carmina frowns very heavily and twists her fingers together in an uncharacteristic way.

"After all, the contessa's not our *neighbor* here, Carmina," Uncle Vicenzo soothes. "She's very fond of Giulia, but she is old and would hardly drive all the way from our old neighborhood to—"

"She talks of coming. She's all agog. Heaven knows what she has heard!"

"Giulia's not nearly strong enough for these emotional encounters."

How thoughtful is my uncle for my welfare! Yet for the second time I recall that I was thought strong enough for that discussion with Enrico. Thinking of Enrico, who all the time sits watching me hopefully, I think suddenly of something else.

"Didn't you give me a ring? So where is it?"

"What?"

Now they're all three looking at me.

"The engagement ring," I persist, gazing at my hands. "Perhaps they stole it in the hospital!" Irrepressible mirth rises at the thought of those solemn specialists pulling a ring from my finger while I lay unconscious. "Or perhaps someone else was first on the scene of the crime."

"The—crime?"

"The accident, of course—I was merely joking." I glance from face to face. All three stare at me like owls startled in daylight. "Still, perhaps some thief did find me first. . . . Obviously I must have had it with me. You did say you—no, it was in that letter, wasn't it?" I turn to Enrico.

"But—but dearest Giulia, of course." He swallows and looks nervously at his mother.

"Yes—and we never thought of it till now," she says, gravely nodding her head. "How very—wise of Giulia. There may have been a thief, as she says. How distasteful." Indeed, the downward lines at the corners of her mouth look as though she finds something acutely distasteful. "Yet you are vague, Giulia—you know I'm always complaining of your vagueness."

"Then perhaps I left it behind me in Switzerland when I stayed with friends. The police would scarcely have stolen it!"

"Or perhaps," puts in Enrico with a grimness that seems foreign to his nature, "you lost it when you went to some cheap *trattoria*—with your pickup."

I feel myself flush beneath the accusation in their eyes. And yet behind it I feel there's almost something else entirely, some sort of watchful amusement.

"Such a beautiful ring too," sighs Carmina. "I chose the design for you myself. Modern, but a Renaissance copy. And that superb emerald! Enrico himself went to the gemmologist to find one that would be worthy of its setting."

I'm suddenly touched that they should have thought so much of my return that a considerable material disadvantage had been, till now, completely overlooked. Considering that they're people who value material things very highly, it *is* touching, to say the least. My heart warms to them in a way it never has before.

"I'm very, very sorry if I was careless," I say sincerely. The apology sounds ridiculously inadequate in these circumstances.

"I'll get you another," declares Enrico, which makes me regret my words.

"There's no hurry." I avoid looking at his angry flush. Since their insurers will probably pay up, it is even odder that they haven't thought about the ring before. Trying to smooth things over, I venture, "Could you draw the design for me? It would be interesting, and might help me remember things." With so much tension in the air, my sedative has lost all its effect.

"With pleasure." He sounds less sulky, and goes to fetch paper and pencil. The design, when drawn, is truly beautiful. Black pearls support a great square-cut emerald in the center, and other, smaller emeralds are set in the sides of a heavy gold mounting. Although it sounds vulgar, it's exquisite, and could have graced the hand of a Bronzino sitter.

"Lovely," I say inadequately.

"Yes, a very lovely piece of work." Uncle Vicenzo squints across at the design. "And one wonders where it has got to now, eh? Eh?" He levers himself upward with his stick. "It's almost the dinner hour—if you've all finished your vermouth we might save our good Benedetta the need to fetch us. As for this young woman, it's my opinion that she should have her meal in bed. Rest, that is what you need to remember, my dear Giulia. Rest, rest, rest . . ."

And rest I do. It seems to have become the refrain on everyone's lips, even old Benedetta's. Total inertia engulfs me, perhaps because of Cosmo's drugs. Usually I'm urged to swallow these after meals and before Carmina's ever-watchful eye. But even when I manage to slip the pills into my handkerchief my inertia remains. Perhaps I've deteriorated since concussion, but sometimes I suspect uneasily that I'm getting more sedatives, in my food—although I try to thrust this thought from me, as being purely paranoid. However, one thing's quite certain: I'm being daily exposed to Enrico rather as one exposes a girl to German measles in the hope that she'll catch it early on. He seems to do less and less work at the office, and spends more and more time at home, saying he works better at his documents away from Uncle Vicenzo, who seems so irritable just now. Enrico's presence has little effect on me, except to annoy. Far from my getting the measles, one lengthy bout of them already seems to have left me immune.

But Carmina's badly infected by the passion virus, as becomes clearer when Cosmo makes endless unnecessary visits to the Villa, ostensibly to see me. I often hear them talking afterwards in the drawing room beneath my bedroom, and then long expressive silences. I keep thinking how strange it is, the people who attract each other. And how bored I am by Enrico's stressed devotion and the heavy, silent pressures of Carmina and Uncle Vicenzo, all obviously aimed at getting me engaged again as fast as possible.

Engaged quickly—but not quickly well. This idea suddenly pops into my sluggish brain with the surprise effect of a bursting balloon. I sit up with an energy that's amazingly unlike what I've been feeling. I've been so lulled into rest, and Enrico, and more rest and more Enrico, that I've simply not seen the numbing effect this has had on my former strong desire to get better. I've ceased to *want* to remember things! But it won't do; of that I'm sure. If I'm to escape these schemes I'll need a mind of my own. There must be some way to improve it, although I don't think there's much use asking the doctor. I'll eat less; I'll take still less of that drug, even if it means sticking my finger down my throat after meals. Somehow I'll keep notes and write down every thought that crosses my mind which could be of service. This idea makes me feel so tired that I fall back on my bed and stare up at the ceiling.

Outside it's very, very hot. Perhaps the heat's partly responsible for my languor. One thing is clear anyway: it's no use asking someone to buy me exercise books and pens. They would simply look at my still-bandaged hand pityingly and tell me not to worry about things like that just yet. But they won't stop me from laboriously tracing out my thoughts—and laborious it will be, with my incompetent, clumsy left hand, which writes like a three-year-old's in great sprawling letters, tilting backward. Resolutely I determine to steal sheets of Carmina's good stock paper from her desk in the drawing room downstairs.

7

Which I do. Tracing the letters with an unaccustomed left hand, how my admiration grows for the persistence of small children! I meant to record my thoughts, but what I most obsessively record are the small things other people say and do which, taken one by one, are innocent enough, but together add up to a disturbing whole. First there's the day when I last pinched Carmina's paper from her desk. Afterward I strolled alone through the gardens, down a path not explored before, between high whispering grasses and scented wild flowers. My sandaled feet moved over the path almost soundlessly. If I looked to my right and upward I could see the cypresses, my friendly sentinels, on the top of their steep hill. Behind, and to my left, the house was silent and shuttered in the sun. I reached a small gate and leaned on it, looking across a flight of rough stone steps into a dusty road. Two men were coming down it, scythes over their shoulders. They were chatting together, their countrified accent sometimes too thick for me to understand. As they drew level with the steps they looked up and saw me. The younger grinned. The older shielded his eyes from the sun and stood looking at me.

"*Buon giorno,* signorina! A lovely day."

"Lovely," I agreed.

"And more beautiful now," said the younger, with a look of exaggerated lechery, followed by a laugh. He was very young. I laughed back.

"Is it?"

"But assuredly!"

They both leaned on their scythes; a little conversation was more desirable than work. "You're a visitor here, perhaps, signorina?" began the older man.

"Oh no, we're all—" I broke off. There was a sound of footsteps scurrying along the path behind me. I looked over my shoulder and saw Carmina coming, her poppy-red dress almost too violent a color in the sun. It dazzled. I screwed up my eyes, and the dress turned to a scarlet blur, while her face stood out white with temper.

"Giulia!" She sounded breathless as though, before she reached the path, she had been running. *"What* are you doing down here?"

"Doing?" I turned from her and looked at the two men, who were now leisurely shouldering their scythes. "Why, nothing. Exploring. Having a friendly chat."

She reached my side and glanced over the gate. The men were now walking up the road, not quite so slowly as they had approached.

"Farm laborers . . ." I would have expected her to sound scornful. But there was something different in her voice. She had taken hold of my arm; now her grip slackened. All the same she shook me slightly, as though I were a small child who had run away.

"You mustn't go straying about like this! I was quite alarmed when Benedetta came to say you'd gone toward the road."

"Alarmed? I was in the gardens. I'm only leaning on a garden gate!"

"You might have gone out of it. You might have gone down into the road and got killed. You might have wandered off and—" She turned me round to face the house and began walking me back toward it.

"And gone into the village, I suppose, where you could easily have found me. Carmina, aren't you being a little too dramatic?"

"Dramatic? After what has already happened? After you've already taken a lift from someone you didn't know—who is dead?"

"We don't know I didn't know him! I may have lost my memory, but I'm not mad, Carmina."

"Of course you're not mad, dear," she said soothingly in a way which cast some doubt. "But it doesn't appear to me that you understand your state at all. You've forgotten everything once. You could forget again."

"But you know all about it this time. You and the police together could easily find me if I went wandering."

"We—your uncle and I—don't want this sort of scandal in the family."

"To lose one's memory is hardly scandalous."

"That depends on the circumstances," she retorted. "Luckily, and because of the time lag between the story in the papers and our finding you, or indeed searching for you, nothing—we hope—has been publicly said which connects you, a Carminotti, with anything that could affect your family in the eyes of other people. And we must hope that your uncle still has some influence with the press."

I dragged my arm free. "Dino Il Nero may have been scandalous, but why need we assume I am? Won't people sometime have to know I've lost my memory?"

"We hope not. It will be better for us all if it's never known. The things people could say!"

"But that old contessa who rang up—"

"Heard about your accident, yes. That you were unconscious, certainly; not that you had—"

"I see. So that's why I'm being kept so close, as if I were a disobedient child!" I felt my face flush in the heat and with deep-seated anger.

"It's because you're not well," she responded coldly. "See, you're already upsetting yourself again." Her thick, determined fingers felt for my pulse. I knew it bumped under her touch. "Go into the house, have something cool to drink, and then lie down."

"But I am *not* a child!"

"Then don't behave like one. Disobedience, when you're so sick, is very silly." She gave me a firm push between the shoulder blades, propelling me toward the house. All the revolt went out of me just then. I obeyed sulkily, like the child that she had called me.

Cosmo came that afternoon, a fact which I recorded, too, on my sheets of paper; he wasn't due till the next day. He had a talk with Carmina before he came upstairs to me. When he had examined me, he sighed.

"We're not progressing very fast, are we?"

I didn't reply.

He shook his head. "I've been having a little talk downstairs. With your aunt."

"I know."

There must have been something in my tone, for his eyes moved sideways as though trying to escape a dart.

"I was sorry to hear about this—fractiousness. It's a sign of some irritability somewhere."

"In my aunt, I think."

He raised his eyebrows. "You're unkind, Giulia. Your aunt's thoroughly concerned for your welfare. She and I have been wondering if you were allowed out of the hospital too soon." He smiled, showing his healthy red gums. "Unless you can bring yourself to be more equable, my dear, more docile, we may feel we should reconsider it."

He patted my hand, much as one soothes an animal in its cage. It struck me that the people I most dislike here are determined patters. This thought, bubbling up spontaneously, made me realize that I truly do dislike Carmina, something I'd been firmly keeping from myself.

By this time I'd grown edgy, or probably I wouldn't have seen the next incident in a sinister light at all.

We were eating our midday meal. I, bored but less torpid than usual (I had successfully evaded at least three tablets), was watching a dragonfly hover like a small helicopter above the flowers on the terrace. The telephone rang in the hall. Carmina rose to answer it. I often wondered why she didn't always leave this to Benedetta. Carmina's feet in their high-heeled shoes tap-tapped quickly across the polished boards. Idly watching the dragonfly, I listened to her answers—the door was open behind me. I heard her draw in her breath sharply. Her voice altered in some subtle way, hard to analyze.

"But no, indeed—she's not here. You have your dates wrong, I believe. . . . What? . . . I can only tell you that we simply don't know. Please don't ring again—as soon as we do know when she's coming, we will telephone—she will, I mean. . . . But it's ridiculous! I promise you— . . . Of course she'll be very sorry to hear you were misled. Certainly I'll tell her, and then she'll get in touch with you herself. . . . Goodbye."

Tap-tap came her approaching step. There was brisk anger in it, I thought, as I switched my glance from the dragonfly. Her face showed nothing unusual but a heightened color. Uncle Vicenzo watched her in silence. For some inexplicable reason, both he and Enrico covertly studied me. Carmina sat down and helped herself to more salad from the huge round bowl. I could hear the angry tap-tap of her shoe's toe beneath the table, as though violent, irritable restlessness had taken hold of her.

"I wish people wouldn't worry us at mealtimes."

"Ah?" said my uncle intently. It was as though he waited for a cue.

"Yes—they have no consideration. Do I ring anyone at such a time? I have more consideration, much more."

"You are always so thoughtful, *Mamma mia.*"

"And yet," said Carmina turning to me, "each time our dear neighbor Giovannina goes away and lets her villa we have a flood of these silly calls from *her* friends, saying they thought she was there, and when will she be coming back? We're not a telephone exchange, and next time Giovannina goes away I shall beg her to make it clear to everyone."

"But, *Mamma mia,* it's the first time that—"

"Doubtless it's the first of many," she snapped. "Give your cousin some more *spinacio,* Enrico. She still eats too little."

While I obediently swallowed spoonfuls of vegetables that Enrico heaped upon my plate I was dwelling on the discrepancy in Carmina's glib account. If this Giovannina's villa was let, but her friends thought her still in residence, then they would surely ring there? And whoever took the call would say when she was coming back. Carmina had clearly lied. The caller wished to speak with someone else. My cheeks burned and I kept my eyes downcast. What caller?

Roberto . . . I was certain now that Carmina knew all about Roberto; she was keeping us apart. Since they strongly wished me to marry Enrico, it would explain so much. For instance, why they seemed more eager to get me re-engaged than to recover. I longed to face her with it: "Was that for me—was it *Roberto?*" Yet instinct held me back. This could be all imagination. Their stares of amazement could be genuine, the next step possibly a quick return to the hospital, with "suspected paranoia" attached to me as a new label.

I tried to appear intent on my food. "How well Benedetta does this delicious spinach." I heard the tiny sigh that escaped Carmina as she relaxed again.

After the meal I wandered out into the gardens, having escaped Enrico by drawing his attention to documents waiting for him on a side table. I strolled farther up the terrace than usual, wondering in desperation what to do if my memory showed no sign of coming back. There must be some treatment that would help? It seemed unlikely now that Carmina would encourage it, and though I might boldly ask if Dr. Carlo could help me, I shrank from this course, which carried with it the threat of an asylum. I could only cling to gradually fading hopes that something, anything, would happen to bring my deadness back to life.

". . . but we've tried it," said Carmina's voice close by.

I started.

"She hasn't had very long as yet. We should not allow ourselves to be stampeded."

Of course! The voices sounded close enough to startle me, but the explanation was simple: they were in the small room leading from my uncle's study, at the corner of the house, the shutters wide open. I stood very still. Eavesdroppers may hear no good of themselves, but someone without a memory may hear of her past. No scruple restrained me. I kneeled by the flowers and began pressing earth firmly round their roots. If I were discovered . . . A passion for gardening! What else was I fit for?

Unfortunately Carmina must have moved away. Her words became indistinct; try as I would, it was hard to catch more than a few.

". . . dangerous enough—"

"Try and keep calm, my dear!"

". . . waiting . . . could bring it back . . . what then?"

"Then we should have to make a different plan, should we not? But things have a habit of working themselves out, which an impatient woman like yourself will never admit to—"

Straining my ears, I distinctly heard her sound of annoyance. She must have turned toward the window again, for her next words came clearly: "*Time* works things out, as a rule. Vicenzo, we have no time."

"Entirely a matter of opinion, my dear. But I'll think it over. Perhaps we should apply more pressure— If sudden action's called for, it can be taken. And there's always Dr. Carlo—though I should be loath to involve him too far, as you may imagine. Now, shall we go into the garden? Pray remember that most people from this neighborhood are by the sea. Agitation—as yet—is uncalled for—"

I heard the tap of a stick on the polished floor. Still crouching, I scrambled round the corner of the house, and pulled myself to my feet beside an aged lavender bush outside the kitchen entrance. A stone path led to the door. As I gasped for breath a small lizard scuttled across before me. I was still watching it and thinking confusedly of my uncle's words when a sixth sense made me turn my head. Benedetta's face peered from the scullery window. Her age, her gnarled growth, made her an almost inhuman watcher, as though some prehistoric tree had come to life. Except for Enrico there was little friendliness in this house; no wonder I had been running from it in my dream! Now, what plausible reason was there for my presence out here?

"Please, Benedetta," I called out, "may I have a glass of iced water? The sun's made me so thirsty."

Her face disappeared from the window, and presently she came out carrying a full tumbler.

"You should be on your bed resting, signorina. It's a foolish trick to be out in this great heat. Where is your sense? It's the hour of siesta, even for animals."

"Don't tell my aunt I was so stupid, will you?" I managed to sound almost childishly pleading. "I promise to go and lie down at once."

Benedetta made no reply, but I hoped she was convinced that I was merely silly and not prying. She put her old hand, like a withered bunch of twigs, on my arm, and led me into the house via the kitchen. The shade fell over me like a cool pall. Through the landing window, as I mounted the stairs, I could see my two cypresses, guarding the oblong tomb.

8 Now, rereading my sprawling notes which describe these things, it's simple enough to draw one fairly unpleasant conclusion from them. But then, I was still not too uneasy as I went to lie down on my bed. Even if they were determined not to lose me with my inheritance to someone else, they could hardly *make* me marry Enrico. True, there was that hinted threat of Dr. Carlo. . . . My senses were too dulled, perhaps, to take in the significance of the neighbors' absence by the sea. In any case, once you've been subject to physical blows, and find yourself living in a world without past, fear can develop different levels of meaning. In a way I was—am— more frightened of myself than of those about me.

But now, as I sit here before my mirror late at night, twisting my hair between my fingers and trying to force my mind as though it were a padlock with no key, I have stranger things to record. Far stranger. The first almost sent me running from the house in search of the police. The second was so totally unexpected that— No, I'll write of them in the order that they happened. I must think it all over, try to see it plain. The one comfort for me in this madness of confusion is that I may have found a friend. Or is that illusion too, and have I merely stumbled by accident into another version of a terrifying pattern which I—we—will never understand?

First, back to that evening, before the dinner hour. Carmina called me into her room to show me a white fringed dress of hers which the cleaners had shrunk and which she thought might do for me. She was solicitous as she helped me put it on, but beneath surface kindness ran the continual current on which her thoughts were fixed.

"You know how Enrico likes to see you in white, *cara!*

It shows off your skin." She pinched my cheek as she said it, and involuntarily I drew away.

"So far as *I* know, he's never seen me in it," I retorted.

She sighed. "Sometimes I think you can remember more than you tell us." She eyed me sideways, and I felt myself flush. Roberto, or Robert, was little enough—perhaps a mere daydream—but he was certainly not hers or Cosmo's to command.

"Eh? Am I right?" Her tone sharpened. "You're flushing, Giulia."

"The dress is too tight—I had to struggle into it. It's no good, Carmina. You'll have to give it away."

"Perhaps it could be let out here—" She fingered it. "But no—" Then she pounced: "*Do* you recall anything else, child?"

"Only those cypresses."

For a moment there was a match of eyes between us. Then she tugged angrily at the zipper. As she was putting the dress away I moved over to stand idly staring at myself in her dressing-table glass. I was healthier since those days in the hospital . . . my skin was almost brown. How hard to tell if one's own eyes are vacant or not. . . . At this unwelcome thought I hastily lowered mine. On the dressing table was a clutter of makeup, perfumes, hair brushes. Carmina's jewel case was there too, one flap half open. Tucked into a small velvet compartment were several rings: aquamarine, diamond, black pearl and emerald— My hand went to my throat. Enrico had drawn the pattern too well. Instinctively I closed the case and was rubbing concentratedly at my nose with some of Carmina's sun oil when she came back to me.

"It was peeling a bit—my skin grew soft in the hospital," I apologized.

"Oh, take it, child!" she said brusquely. "It's always a good sign when a woman starts worrying about her looks. It's a good oil, very pure." She glanced downward at the case, but I don't think she noticed that she hadn't shut it. "Now run along—we'll all be late for dinner. Benedetta's so tiresome these days about time, but one doesn't like to fuss her too much as she's so old."

I went with alacrity. Only outside the door did I allow myself to breathe fast, to tremble. They had lied about the ring when all the time *they* had it safe! How had they got it? Did they mean to hide it and claim insurance, if they were short of cash—as I couldn't help but believe was the case? Seeing it there had given me a most curious sensation. I couldn't quite fathom what it was. A ring was an inanimate object, material, it couldn't possibly be evil. But whatever it stirred up in me, no memory came too of the gold and pearl and emeralds heavy on my hand.

So I walked that evening in greater confusion than before, and excused myself earlier to go to bed. In my room I didn't draw the curtains, or put on the light, which would have attracted the bumbling moths and insects of the night. Instead I lay down just as I was on the giant comfortable bed with its scrolled and gilded headboard.

Time went by. The clock downstairs wheezed occasionally and struck: first eleven, then the half hour, then twelve. Everyone else must have gone to bed by now, for the house was profoundly silent. Still I lay there, troubled, discouraged, lacking even the urge to read. The night air, which had been heavy, came in little gusts as though a storm was approaching. Yes—a long way off thunder rumbled. I clicked on my bedside lamp and raised myself on one elbow. It was twenty past twelve, and since I felt disinclined to sleep I got up to look in the cupboard for a wrap. None had been sent up from "the other house," and Carmina had lent me one of hers, too hot for this time of year. I preferred the housecoat that had been left hanging at the back of the cupboard, perhaps forgotten by some guest. It was of frilled seersucker, with a wide skirt and collar. A bit too small and tight for me, but I'd got into the habit of wearing it. After putting it on I sat on my bed and began brushing my hair in long smooth strokes. Someone, I was sure, had brushed my hair like that long ago; it gave me a feeling of nursery peace. "This is the way the lady rides, trit-trot, trit-trot," I murmured to myself. How did it go on? "This is the way the gentleman rides—"

The curtains moved in a more violent gust of wind. Thunder rumbled like an approach of drums. The sky, framed dark violet in the long windows, flickered with sheet lightning. If there was going to be a bad storm the shutters should be closed. I heard a little spurt of rain fall on the stone balcony, and then silence. My hand was still—my left hand, for I couldn't really manage a brush with my right. Not yet. I turned my head toward the window. There was a rattle of something else, not rain, on the balcony. It sounded like pebbles falling. Pebbles—from the sky? Instinctively I quenched the light and sat there in the semidark, my heart pounding, but cursing myself for a too vivid imagination.

Nothing happened. Neither rain nor pebbles. My heart stuttered back to normal. I crept softly to the open windows and stepped out onto the balcony. Beneath me the garden was in darkness. The sky was still darker violet above as the storm gathered. I listened and heard nothing; even the nightingales were dumb. When the next flash came it was so sudden and brilliant that I let out a cry of surprise and clutched at my throat. Just below me, from out of the darkness, came a voice.

"Giulia—thank God, *carissima!* You did come back, she was lying. I've been so worried, so afraid for you—it seemed so odd—"

My knees were really knocking together now. I'd wanted my past to resurrect itself, and here it was, but in an unexpected way indeed. Was I accustomed to welcome the owner of this voice to my room at this hour? I leaned against the window frame and couldn't speak.

"Is it all clear? Shall I come up—Giulia?"

Still I couldn't speak. To shout into the night, "Yes, I'm Giulia, but I've lost my memory and don't know from Adam who you are," was beyond me. An awful quirk of lurking humor made me think that to the Giulia I had been this stranger most probably *was* Adam.

"Giulia?" The voice was puzzled now. "It is you?"

Then I whispered, "Yes, it's me," although my voice could hardly have carried very far. It seemed to be enough for my night visitor. He made a sound of satisfaction, and there was a scrape and rustle of branches as he began hauling himself up by the espaliered rose tree beneath the balcony. All I wanted to do at that moment was leap backward into the room and slam the shutters. I willed myself to stay there, wondering if the face I should soon see would be "Roberto's," or someone else's. The mocking part of me that had thought of Adam was muttering to itself, "Art thou not Romeo, and a Montague?" when an arm came over the balustrade, took a firm hold of the stonework, and gave a heave. Head and shoulders followed. It was a difficult maneuver, and I didn't help, but stood waiting in the shadows.

The man dragged himself clear and stood up as lightning flashed again, temporarily blinding both of us. I gasped, and put up a crooked arm to shield my eyes. He gave an amused tender laugh, and I felt his arms go round me. There seemed no point in evading him, and in fact, while the thunder opened up with a roar like cannon overhead, I found some comfort in burying my face against his shoulder. He was holding me close, stroking my hair, muttering endearments into it. On the

60

whole it seemed best to stay like that and let explanations follow presently.

Just then the rain began falling from the sky in earnest as though someone were emptying buckets over us. The endearments in my ear turned to curses. Still with his arms round me he pushed me before him into the room and followed. It seemed very dark in there and I stumbled. He picked me up easily—he was a big man—and deposited me rather cavalierly on the bed. He seemed to know unerringly just where it was, I noticed.

"Let's have some light," I whispered breathlessly. I was shivering slightly. What if Carmina or Enrico came along to see how I was sleeping through the storm?

"We don't need light."

"We do," I said firmly, though still in a whisper. I wanted a good look at him. Would I recognize Roberto?

He laughed softly. "All right, my love, anything you say. But in that case, the shutters—"

I heard him cross to the windows, and for one second saw his silhouette against a flash before the shutters closed and the curtains were drawn into place. I stretched across the bed to switch on the lamp, and then, leaning on my elbow, looked up at him. This first sight of a past lover whom I didn't even know had a fascination all its own.

It didn't seem to work that way on him.

He made a strangling sound. His mouth dropped open, and he backed away toward the windows. After about five seconds of what's called a pregnant pause he muttered hoarsely, "And who—who in heaven's name are you?"

"Giu—Giulia! I'm Giulia Carminotti." My hands began to shake.

"Like blue hell you're Giulia Carminotti! I—I thought something peculiar was going on when I didn't hear from her. And then—when I was told she wasn't here . . . What have they—and you—done with her? Because— *What are you doing in her room and in her clothes?"*

His accusing glance fell on my housecoat. Automatically I hugged it closer round me. With all the guilt of a child caught in theft I stammered inanely, "It—it doesn't fit me—"

"No?" His glance traveled over me with the same appraising quality that characterized Uncle Vicenzo's. But even Vicenzo's monosyllables never had so biting an edge to them. A guilty flush crept over my face but gradually faded as realization grew that all my groping apprehensions of *wrongness* here in the villa had been justified—in a way that didn't seem possible either. For if I wasn't Giulia Carminotti, who the blue hell indeed was I?

No, I *was* her; here was my home; here my cypresses, my one perfect jigsaw piece of evidence, my proof. I said, with as much dignity as I could manage, since my visitor now looked as though he might well murder me, "You'd better go. You—I—we made a mistake."

"Someone has certainly made a big one," he said meaningly. "And it doesn't happen to be me."

I chose to ignore this and got unsteadily to my feet. Skirting him as carefully as I would a leopard, I made for the shutters.

"Turn off that lamp, will you?" I said over my shoulder. "I'll let you out, and then—"

My behavior must have seemed crazy after such startling pronouncements as my visitor had made. It would have been saner to ask for explanations, to call Carmina, or simply to scream. But I was so shattered when this late-night intruder set himself to demolish my very precarious identity that my one desire was to be rid of him—bar his accusations from my ears and banish this monstrous development into the thundery night. I didn't particularly want to be Giulia; still less did I want to be a question mark in an asylum.

As I reached the shutters his hands clasped my arms. No tender lover's touch this time, more like someone making an arrest.

"Let me go!"

I struggled fiercely, but it was useless. The grip was too tight, my assailant too angry.

"You're going nowhere near these windows till we've had an explanation."

"Unless you let me go, I'll scream, and—"

"Be quiet, you little fool, I only want—"

There was a sizzling flash so close that the shutter cracks turned a livid blue; it was followed by a crash which sounded as though the house were falling down. Simultaneously we were plunged into darkness. I gave an involuntary cry. The grip on my arms tightened, as though my nocturnal visitor thought I might escape him.

"The villa's got a television aerial." He spoke low and angrily, as though I'd set it up on purpose. "I suppose it's been hit." Even then his words struck me as rather ludicrous.

My heart pounded. Breathing was difficult. I wouldn't have minded more of those drugs. "Just let go of me and I—"

Then we both heard them—the footsteps, unmistakably Carmina's. Her high heels tap-tapped along the polished passage toward my door. Her voice was raised as she neared it: "Don't be so stupid, Enrico—why would we need candles downstairs? Fetch me some more up here, that's what I said!"

Over my nocturnal visitor's shoulder I saw a small light—a candle flame—illumine the crack around my door. I felt his hands go rigid and heard him draw in his breath. Then came a peremptory knocking. Carmina's voice, higher and less sultry than usual, inquired, "Giulia? Giulia, my dear, are you all right? Enrico is fetching you some candles." Her hand rattled the latch, and it began to rise—

I've never known anyone move quicker than the man who held me. One moment I was still helpless in his grip and the next I was free, while he was somewhere in the room's deepest shadows and well hidden beyond the canopy on my bed.

9

I stood staring, slightly swaying on my feet, blinking at the candle flame. The door was wide open, and Carmina was a shadowy figure, the white ruffles on her dressing-gown sleeves illumined as she held the candlestick before her and peered toward the bed, searching for me in the gloom. I was thankful for the semidarkness. Standing near the windows, I must have been almost as shadowy to her as she to me. If my face was white, it was a trick of candlelight. And if my voice shook—

It didn't, surprisingly enough; even to my ears it sounded normal. "I—I've just closed the shutters." I never glanced toward the shadows by my bed. Now was the moment when I could have stepped forward to say, perhaps, "Carmina, don't be too surprised, there's a man hiding here." It would have been ludicrous, an impossibility. Not just for the comic or dramatic implications either; I knew suddenly that I could no more give up my visitor to the wonder and fury of the household than I could earlier have considered protecting him. No—not since the accusations he'd been hurling at us all. I moved forward, not too rapidly but fast enough to stop Carmina from coming farther into the room.

"Sometimes you amaze me, Giulia! You're often such a hysterical little thing—at least since the accident—and now you're calm as— Get back into bed, my dear. After such an awakening you'd best have some more of Cosmo's pills." There was almost a note of disapproval in her voice at the discovery of my calm. If I broke into hysterical laughter, as I felt like doing, she would probably find it more appropriate.

"I don't need more pills, really I don't. I've had six today already. Too many make me fuzzy."

65

"If you're sure you'll get to sleep again . . ." She eyed me closely. By this time we were standing at the door together. There was no sound behind me in the room, or if there was, it was masked by the heavy creakings of Enrico's tread. He arrived carrying a many-branched candelabrum from the dining room, with two candles lit; and he looked ridiculously like a flunky in an opera tempting the chief soprano to a clandestine meeting.

"*Mamma mia,* you were right, as always. That foolish Benedetta left the television plugged in. Here, *cara* Giulia, some candles for you, and matches in case you want to relight them."

"Thank you," I said, accepting them, and well aware of those listening ears behind me in the shadows. "Shall we all go back to bed now? I don't suppose we'll be struck again! How's Uncle Vicenzo?"

"Asleep," said Carmina shortly. "He would sleep through anything, that one! Promise me, Giulia, to take just two more pills—or I'll administer them myself! We cannot be too careful with your nerves, however calm you believe yourself to be."

"If I were only shaken up enough I might remember something," I said boldly. "Don't you think so?" I watched her closely, but her dark eyes revealed nothing inconsistent with concern for my welfare. "But I sleep better without pills, and I think the storm's moving over now."

Enrico shook his head at me. "I'll bring you some water for the tablets." Which he did determinedly while Carmina stood by with an approving face. Then he bent to kiss me clumsily on the cheek and murmur, "*Cara cugina,* good night again."

I held the candelabrum high as they moved off along the corridor and called after them softly, "Good night, good night!" Then very slowly and deliberately I shut the door, fastened the latch, and turned back toward the room.

The stranger was already on his feet. We stood taking stock of one another, as much as we could by candle-light. He was tall, thin-faced, with slanting dark eyes and dark hair cut fairly long. Altogether a faintly Renaissance figure standing there in a white, full-sleeved shirt buttoned to his chin. This was chiefly what I noticed about him at that time: the eyes, the Renaissance air, and a look of painful uncertainty, almost of misery.

"Why didn't you give me up?" he said at last.

I shook my head, and placed the candelabrum on my bedside table. I sat down beside it and stared at the floor. Why hadn't I? I must have been mad. My fingers crept to my forehead, which was beginning to ache.

"I didn't know what— Too many pills make me so stupid, and—" My voice trailed away. I should have been afraid of him, of the situation, but I wasn't—only of that terrible mindless mist into which my attempts at remembering always strayed.

I could feel him staring at me across the bed. I roused myself to say, "Why don't you sit? There is a chair."

"You—want to talk? You didn't seem keen on it earlier." But the note of indignant accusation had entirely left his voice; he sounded as bewildered as myself. I heard him cross to the chair, and the creak as he settled into it. When we next spoke, it was at the same time.

"You told me—"

"It seems that—"

"I'm sorry," I said, and he said he was sorry too.

Then he gave a staccato laugh. "It seems we both have something to be sorry for. So you had an accident? And those pills—what about them?"

"Nothing about them. Just that I take such a lot—I mean, I have to. But they make me feel so muddled."

"Since when do you take them?" He sounded rather like a doctor.

Automatically I replied, "Since I was hurt, since I was in the hospital."

"And you've lost your memory?" I looked up and he was staring at me again. "That was why you were in there?"

"Yes, since my accident." I swallowed. "Carmina"—I glanced toward the door and lowered my voice—"*Aunt* Carmina came and found me."

"Identified you, you mean?"

He was watching me very closely. "As Giulia. And—and you really believe you're her."

"I am Giulia," I said fiercely. "I am, I am, I *am!*" I heard my own voice trying to force me back into belief. "What right have you to come here and try to—try to take—" I couldn't look at him any more. I put my hands over my eyes. Even with them shut I could see Dr. Carlo's face. The Carminottis might not be up to much, but I had never valued them so highly till he tried to take them from me.

The stranger's voice sounded oddly far away to me as he said coolly, "And what would be the alternative to being Giulia?"

"The—the hospital again. No, the asylum."

In the lengthy pause I could hear the swish of rain now falling steadily outside, and the sound of my own breathing. Then the chair creaked again as he rose and came to stand beside me.

"Dear God! A mad girl . . ." I felt his hands on my face as he raised it toward the candlelight, examining it as though I were an object. I opened my eyes and blinked and began to cry as I had never cried even in the hospital, huge endless tears that flowed out of my eyes as though there was a waterfall behind them. Suddenly he sat down beside me and put his arms round me as if he had just decided that I was human after all.

"Hush . . . hush."

After a while I stopped crying and pushed him away from me. "I'm all right now." Then I added hesitantly, "But if I'm not Giulia, how could I know about the cypresses?"

"Cypresses?" Now he really looked at me as though my reason was in doubt. Rubbing at my eyes, I began wearily to explain how I'd come to the villa and been reassured to find that the only thing I'd recalled in the hospital had been real. (Still, instinctively, I kept Roberto to myself.)

At the end of this recital he was looking at me in some perplexity. "You must have known this house, anyway. But they haven't had the villa very long, you know. At least you're Italian, obviously. But Giulia was half English. She spoke it like an Englishwoman."

I noticed the past tense.

"So do I. In the hospital they thought I might be English at first. I'm bilingual. I hardly realize which language I'm thinking in."

"A cousin? But I never heard of one your age."

"Aren't you taking it for granted I've accepted I'm not Giulia?" I spoke with more spirit. "Suppose *your* Giulia wasn't the real one? Who are you, anyway?" I began to pluck nervously at my housecoat. My head was starting to ache ferociously.

He smiled faintly, for the first time. I had forgotten how terribly worried he must be until I saw that fleeting smile and how fast the grimness returned to his features as it faded.

"Gian Marotti. And, no, there's no chance of my Giulia being the wrong one. We were friends and neighbors—at their other house—since she was fifteen and I was twenty-three." He looked round him, around the room, as though searching the shadows for someone who might suddenly emerge from them—a girl who should have come to the balcony in answer to that stagy, romantic gesture of thrown pebbles. "And if she's not here, and they've put you in her place, that can mean only one thing . . . can't it? *Can't it?*" he repeated fiercely as I didn't answer.

But I couldn't. I felt as though something gripped me by the windpipe, a hand throttling the air out of me. I gulped breathlessly till he reached for the glass of water Enrico had given me and held it to my lips.

"Here, you'd better have some of this." And afterward he added with some compunction, "But you look all in. Not going to faint, are you?"

"No, but I'm getting a terrible headache." The sweat was gathering on my forehead; pretty soon the shaking would begin.

"Get back into bed. If you've been so ill, all this must be rather a strain. I'm sorry."

Ridiculous remark, I thought, as I obediently crawled back into bed. Rather a strain? "At least you seem to believe now that I'm not in league with them. Why?"

He shrugged. "All three of you alone together, long past midnight. And keeping up a farce of your being Giulia! For whose benefit?"

"Yes," I said faintly, "I see. For mine. For—mine."

He was standing there looking at me very intently from the foot of the bed. He began to say something more, but then fell silent.

"What were you going to say?"

"I don't think you could take much more tonight, could you? About Giulia's disappearance."

"No. Not if I've got to go on living in this house." He made a sharp movement at the word "living," and after that both of us were silent. It was as though we were listening to our thoughts, here alone together in that candlelit room which had seen another girl sleeping in its bed, a girl who had disappeared.

"I ought to tell you," I said at last, "that they're pressing me toward marrying Enrico. There's such a lot I ought to tell you." It all came flooding into my mind. Suddenly I wanted to talk and talk and talk. I sat up in bed. "Please, I want to tell you about—"

"No," he said. "No. Not any more. Not tonight. You'd better not get ill. Take those pills, as Carmina said."

70

"But don't you see, it's important to—"

"I'll be back tomorrow night. There are one or two things I could find out. . . . Tell me the rest then. Whatever they're up to, they aren't moving all that fast."

I leaned forward. "But please! I do feel they're getting worried, because I overheard them saying so—about the marriage, I mean."

He was already by the windows now, and answered impatiently. "They can't force you into one tomorrow, can they? So keep your eyes and ears open and play it cool, *cara mia!* And take those pills. I promise you, same time tomorrow I'll be back." His hand was on the shutters. "Got those matches near you? Then douse the lights, because I'm going to open up—"

As though hypnotized, I obeyed. The room was plunged into darkness as I blew out first one candle, then the other. His voice came out of the gloom saying— a bit incongruously I thought—"Sleep well." Then there was a gray space of open window, a shape silhouetted against it, and he was gone. Cooler air flowed into the overheated bedroom from the gardens outside. I lay back on my pillows listening to faint scraping sounds as Gian Marotti climbed down from the balcony. Afterward I groped on the bedside table for Cosmo's pills, and swallowed two—no, three—with an alacrity that would have amazed and gratified Carmina. And then, surprisingly, I went to sleep.

10

In that household no one's temper was very good the next day. Sleeplessness, thunder in the air, guilty consciences—whatever the cause, the Carminottis were a fractious lot. And I—at least my pallor and increased nervousness could be put down, for Carmina's benefit, to a bad night.

"You should have stayed in bed this morning," she said tartly when she found me wandering around the garden restlessly plucking at a flower stem. "Really, Giulia, you show very little sense. Last night I thought you far more sensible. So cool, so collected."

"I couldn't go on sleeping indefinitely, even on all those pills."

"Young girls often sleep badly till they marry. You would do well to consider—"

But I was in no mood to have Enrico's claims advanced just then. Fear had made me very angry. Fear for the real Giulia—and for myself. And this second loss of identity brought me continually close to tears.

"Don't start on that *again*, Carmina. It's the first time I've heard marriage put forward as an aid to sleep."

We glared at each other. A major row could easily have broken out between us, like lightning flashing from overcharged clouds. But she merely gave me an exasperated look and turned away toward the house, where I heard her bullying Benedetta.

Now I longed to get as far away from the villa as I could go without being followed and brought back. No wonder Carmina had been flustered that day she found me talking to passersby! Even here at the lately acquired villa too many prospective visitors might know the real Giulia by sight.

At least no one ever followed me when I walked

uphill toward the cypresses. Probably because the other side of the steep slope was merely a long sloping meadow which dropped sharply at its farther end to a high stone wall. There were tall iron gates in the wall but they were locked, as I'd discovered on one of my earlier walks.

Stifling hot though it was today, and every movement exhausting, I began to toil slowly up the hill.

The grasses were long, and brushed against me just as in my dream. The large, oblong vault, with its recumbent carved angel, reared up ahead of me against the sky. There were other stones in the grass, gravestones, with carvings almost obliterated by time. Once this place must have been consecrated ground, I thought. Graveyard cypresses. That was right, wasn't it? Graveyard— Could any of these graves be . . . new?

I shuddered. What had happened in this house? When had I been here before—I, who wasn't Giulia? And from what had I run? I turned to look downward at that villa nestling there in the hollow, so peaceful, so invitingly peaceful in the sun. Like an advertisement for an Italian villa—just right. I looked again at the cypresses, so tall above me, reaching up to heaven, and now they looked like enormous exclamation marks of dark gray-green, or pointing fingers, two accusations of guilt. "Leave her to heaven, and to those thorns that in her bosom lodge, to prick and sting her . . ." Why did I always seem to think in poetry, and in English poetry too? I _had_ thought it was because the English teacher, "Miss Howard," had made so deep an impression on my—Giulia's—imagination. . . .

On the hill's crown I stood between those cypresses. The air was slightly cooler here, the gray-green fronds even moved a little. I ran one of them through my fingers, feeling the bumpy hardness of the sprayed-out tiny leaves separating from the spine in fan shapes, as bracken does. The cultivated countryside, the olive groves and river, the small town over to the west, the long steeply sloping meadow falling rapidly away before me were bathed in sunlight. Idly standing there, I noticed with part of my mind that someone had ridden here quite lately. It was still possible to see hoof marks in the grass, and a little farther off there were telltale droppings, dried now by the sun. Otherwise nothing to see.

I stood there for some while wondering dully if things would have been better in the asylum, if Dr. Carlo, with his "modern methods," could have brought my memory back. Could anything have been more terrible, more full of unknown danger, than the situation here? In the asylum I might have lived with humiliation and violence. But what did I live with here—murderers? My melodramatic thoughts were interrupted by the prosaic sound of my "cousin's" voice, far off, calling me to come in for the midday meal.

The day passed without incident till once more the four of us were gathered for evening coffee on the terrace. Enrico was as annoyingly attentive as ever, and with even greater warmth. I felt sure he wasn't a good enough actor to dissemble so, and began to wonder if he'd become genuinely fond of me. The older Carminotti sat reading the papers, ostentatiously absorbed whenever Carmina spoke to him. She was still very irritable, and unleashed displeasure onto me and Enrico, complaining first of this and then of that. Finally she declared she wasn't pleased by my general progress, that unless I could be more sensible—"Look at all this walking in the hot sun!"—and more amenable—"Do you even consider your cousin? See how prepared he is to help you!"—she would have me sent back to the hospital straight away.

"It's so wearing for everyone, Giulia, living with a difficult invalid. You never do anything to please anybody but yourself."

"I've taken every pill I should today," I murmured, clenching my hands together in my lap.

"Which means that you weren't taking them before, I suppose? Tomorrow I shall get Cosmo here to talk with you."

There was no point in arguing. We all sat in silence for some while until Uncle Vicenzo turned the last page of his paper, took his stick, and began heaving himself to his feet, saying, "Well, let us put an end to this delightful evening we have spent together."

The sound came out of the gathering darkness. At first faintly, so that I thought it was my own heart beating. Then louder and louder, until it was obviously just the other side of the hill, beyond the cypresses—the quickening beat of a horse's hooves as it changed from a slow canter into a faster one and then a gallop. For a moment I wondered if, looking up, we should see horse and rider coming over the hill crest. Instead the sound began to die away, and I thought it must have been my imagination till I heard it coming again rapidly, as though someone on horseback was circling the meadow, the meadow with the tall locked iron gates.

"Listen!" I said into the fresh silence that had descended on us. "How odd. Doesn't it sound as though someone's riding in the meadow over there? But they couldn't be, could they? Not at this hour, and with the gates shut and locked."

No one appeared to hear me. They were all standing absolutely still, staring toward the hill. I couldn't see Vicenzo's face, for his back was turned, but Enrico's mouth gaped open—his double chins met on his chest. And Carmina not only stood like stone but seemed to have become one. I've never seen anyone go so gray; as the hoofbeats circled for the third time I thought she was going to pass clean out before my eyes. Then she made a little muffled sound and almost ran from us into the house.

Now the hoofbeats were more distant, then farther

still, dying quite away. Vicenzo grunted and began to tap-tap his progress across the terrace. Over his shoulder he said casually, "How stupid of me—I forgot to tell you and your mother, Enrico, that I've let the grazing." It must have sounded as unconvincing to Enrico as it did to me.

11

As he had promised, Gian came again that night. When the household was really quiet there was a sound of pebbles thrown against my windows. Once more I let him in, but this time we left the shutters undone and I pushed home the wooden peg that secured the latch on my door.

He looked at me silently for a moment. "Better?"

I nodded. Curiously enough, I did feel better. The first shock of not being Giulia had begun to wear off, and it was a relief to find myself in the presence of someone who neither treated me as probably incurable nor saw me as a subject for deceit. I even thought he looked at me approvingly.

"I was worried about you last night—Giulia. No, hell! I can't call you that. What shall I call you?"

"In the hospital they called me Maria."

"How very original!" He grimaced.

"Well, call me Silvia! 'Who is Silvia, what is she—' "

" '—that all our swains commend her?' " he finished for me drily. "What made you pick on Silvia, apart from that overworked English poem? Any connection, do you think?"

"None that I know of, but—" I shook my head, frowning.

"But—?"

"My mind seems to run on Shakespeare, that's all. And other English poets. Perhaps I'm not Italian after all. I put it down to Miss Howard, you see—the English person who taught your Giulia in Switzerland. She wrote about it all in her letters to Enrico. He showed them to me."

"And what about your handwriting? Did you see no discrepancy there?" He was watching me keenly, and I wondered if he really trusted me as much as I'd imagined late last night. Surprisingly, the thought hurt. I raised my right hand, now unbandaged, though still stiff and cramped.

"Ah, the accident." He lowered himself into the only chair, while I perched on the bed. "How well it must have fitted in, for Carmina! Never a woman to waste an opportunity." He brooded for a while till I said suddenly, "Look, I've been honest with you, so far as I can be with no memory. Now you do the same for me. I'm very, very sorry for you, Gian, because I suppose you're—were—Giulia's lover? And I suppose we're both pretty sure she's—dead."

He sat staring at his knees, knitting his black brows together, while I watched him compassionately.

"I had a tremendous—bond with Giulia," he said at last. "Ever since we first met. Perhaps it was because of her English blood, and I—I was educated in England. My father was a diplomat, and I was schooled there while he was in London and Madrid. The Carminottis had nothing against me personally. Although Father retired early because of heart trouble, he's still, even in these days, a wealthy man. In fact he now lives for his hobby of collecting paintings. But they had Giulia and her worldly goods all lined up for Enrico, and competition wasn't welcome." He looked at me a bit defiantly. "As a matter of fact it was more fun than competition a lot of the time. Giulia simply enjoyed living. . . . Yes, we were lovers. I told you we were neighbors up at the other house—it was all so easy. She had trouble fending off Enrico, though."

"She did get engaged to him," I said bluntly.

He grinned. "Poor Enrico! He took it so seriously. He even bought an overwhelming ring. It was after she and I had a soul-shattering row and weren't on speaking terms. Then we saw one another in Switzerland; the whole thing started up again. She said she was coming back here to finish with Enrico, make it plain for good. I

was in Amsterdam then, buying pictures for Father. I wrote and wrote to Giulia and got no answer. I telephoned to Switzerland—they said she'd left. Then I came down here, and got fended off by Carmina—"

"So you came at night to see for yourself." He nodded broodingly. "Gian—she, Carmina, has the ring, now. Enrico drew me the design one day. Then I actually saw the ring on her dressing table, in her jewel case."

"Does she know you saw it?" He stared at me intently. He had gone very pale, as gray as Carmina on the terrace after dinner.

"I don't think so. I was trying on a dress she offered me, in her room."

"So the ring was returned," he said heavily. "And after that—"

"Afterward she disappeared. But why? Just because she'd broken with Enrico, could it be necessary to—to—?"

"To kill her?" His voice hardened on the words. "Somehow they're frantic about the money. Perhaps they've been using it! Or—or— But we don't know what's happened, that's the trouble. She could be still alive, though it seems unlikely since you're— You know, I've an idea that some accident could have happened. It could be—look at yours! Listen, Silvia—Silvie, did anything happen tonight, after supper?"

"It certainly did. We were sitting out on the terrace; suddenly the weirdest thing happened. We all heard someone riding a horse round and round in the meadow above—beyond the hill. The hoofbeats kept circling—but the gates are locked, no one could have been up there."

"And how did the Carminottis react?" He looked intent.

"How did—they seemed shattered! In the end Vicenzo made some feeble remark to Enrico about having let the grazing."

"And Carmina?"

"Oh—she turned putty color and rushed into the house as though she was afraid to stay." I studied Gian curiously. "How did you know?"

He jumped to his feet and walked over to the windows, where he stood, head thrown back, looking at the stars, but not as though he saw them. "Giulia was crazy about riding. She had one of her horses brought up here, and kept it stabled in the village. She used to ride in the cool of the evenings." He turned back to the room, to me. "I played a hunch, went down to the village, hung about till I could look in at the stables unobserved. Her horse was still there. Afterward I found one of the lads and tipped him heavily. He didn't know much. The signorina had returned a short while ago, but he thought she'd gone away again. At least, she'd stopped coming to ride. It was after the bridle was broken that she didn't come back. He'd found it hanging on the wall, and the horse back in the stable, last time she'd been out."

"And tonight, was it you riding in the meadow? But how—?"

He took something from his pocket and held it up—a large old-fashioned key. "I had a copy. That's how we used to meet. I told the lad her horse needed exercise. He's a gentle beast, but he shied coming through the gate. Whatever happened to Giulia in that meadow, he hadn't liked it, not one bit."

A brooding silence fell on us both.

"They don't seem to be very practiced criminals," I said suddenly. "They're so clumsy. Leaving the bridle there for anyone to see. And it must have been impromptu—grabbing at me, I mean."

"The time factor—they must have improvised. Perhaps they're not true criminals—yet."

"But if she's dead, they've hushed it up so far and caused me to—impersonate her. That takes criminal nerve, doesn't it? And criminal intentions."

"Umm, laid open to crime, grasping at it . . . that's what these sudden things could do, I suppose—teach someone who and what they are. Say the Carminottis spent her cash. A wild opportunity—something says, look: here's a thousand-to-one chance, do we take it or not? If it comes off—Villain or hero, perhaps it's much the same thing, turned inside out."

"Gian, Gian, don't be so philosophical, you make my head spin! Listen, who inherited—who would have inherited from Giulia? Do you know? At her age—had she made a will?"

"No, she told me all about it once. Vicenzo was the elder brother, so her father didn't leave her a great deal. Most of the inheritance came through her mother and was in trust for English cousins."

I frowned. These calculations—how they brought on my headaches. I wiped a hand slowly across my forehead. "Then 'criminal intentions' falls to the ground, doesn't it? They needed a comfortably well-off Giulia alive for Enrico—at least a Giulia who wouldn't kick too hard when she found the money gone. If we're right. But they couldn't produce me socially as her. And if they meant"—I swallowed—"to arrange another accident, or—or something, what's the point, with her money left in trust?"

"Ah," he said very gently, "the point, my sweet Silvie, is that on her marriage the funds became hers absolutely, and the cousins lost out."

"And so, if she hadn't made a will, but was married, it would come to Enrico."

"Exactly."

I looked around the room, this ordinary, pleasant room. How long ago had a seed of villainy been planted in these Carminottis? Perhaps "the other house" would give better clues to them as people, since houses that have been lived in by one family for some time do seem to become impregnated with their personalities.

"I can't really see Enrico fitting in with this—I've a feeling that he's really fond of me."

Gian made a dismissive gesture. "Mother's boy. Putty in mother's hands."

"Yes. He certainly wouldn't like to see Carmina, at least, sent to prison. But no, Gian. Carmina's an arrogant bitch, the sort of woman who could see herself above the law, but I don't see her as a killer. So perhaps they wouldn't have killed me—perhaps they would have got me into some—some hospital, after marriage, and kept me there. For Cosmo—and Carmina—"

"Loves fat men. Overfeeds her son, and picks on Cosmo too."

"Don't! It's too disgusting. . . . But really, Gian, I don't believe Enrico's bad."

"Oh, my dear Silvia! We could all do anything, given the right circumstances. It's only knowing that we could which may put us on our guard. I wonder if you always saw everyone in black and white like this?" He looked at me curiously. "White side uppermost! Perhaps we ought to be asking ourselves just why you can't get back your memory. A vested interest in burying something? You must have asked yourself why you attracted circumstances like the Carminottis. Maybe like calls to like."

I could have hit him. The weeks of terror, the fearful striving to see inside myself, like someone futilely throwing the beam of a torch into heavy fog! What did he know of waking every morning to the grip of panic—and now this total renewed lack of background?

"Self-pity too?" he inquired callously. "Well, well, fruitful analyst's ground—ten years at least in all probability."

"Gian Marotti," I said, standing up. "I detest you. If it weren't that I'm sorry for you, and so worried about Giulia . . . You needn't look so sardonic. I *am* worried, I am!"

"You sound more angry than sorry," he remarked.

"Perhaps you're right not to feel too sympathetic. We've all got to die, and Giulia did enjoy her short life first."

"You know what you sound like now? Hard as stone. Not at all the man who came out of that darkness saying he was half crazy with worry. Whose girl has probably been *killed*."

"Silvie—shall we not quarrel? Hasn't it occurred to you that I couldn't go through with this at all if I let myself be anything more than businesslike? I'm determined to get at the truth; that's all there is to it just now. A lot of use I'd be tearing my hair, howling on your floor. I'll keep my feelings to myself, thanks all the same. Anyway, let's get one thing clear now. I wasn't in love with Giulia. I loved her as a friend and a person and valued her. I slept with her—happily. We wouldn't have married in the end, we fought too much. But I miss her horribly, and if her death was anything but accident, no one is going to get away with it."

I felt rather small. "Yes—I do understand. I really am sorry, Gian, believe me. What do we do now—the police?" It cost me a great deal to say that. Gian put out a hand and patted mine. "Yes, the police. I'm truly sorry, Silvie. Don't think I don't see it's going to be hard for you. But I'll talk to my father first, and we'll stand by you in every way; that I promise."

I tried to smile. "So long as you can make them see . . . And Gian, I'm sure I can earn a living all right when I'm better."

For the first time I heard him laugh. "Careful, here comes the uppermost white Silvie." He stood up. "Get some sleep. Tomorrow has its problems too."

There was a nasty feeling in my stomach akin to the feeling in my mind. "Tomorrow. As soon as—?"

"Perhaps not. Perhaps the day after would be best. Yes, I think it would. My father's been away, but he comes back tomorrow. I'd like a long talk with him first about the best approach. If it were Giulia alone—but now there's you as well. We can't have you made ill again. Tomorrow you relax and take things easy."

"Relax, with this hanging over me? I'd almost sooner get it over, Gian—really I would. So please call the police tomorrow."

"Silvie, you let me handle this my way. My father's a wise man, and I value his advice—not only on art. I'm going to have a look round on that hilltop now." He didn't say why, but I could guess. "You go to bed and sleep."

But I simply couldn't bear the thought of being alone with my mind in turmoil, waiting, perhaps, forty-eight hours before the police would drive up to the villa and put the fear of death into the Carminottis—and into me.

"Gian, please. You can't imagine what it will be like for me alone. I'll have to act all the time with them, I'll—"

"You can do that, can't you? It's only for a little while. Oh, come on, Silvie, you're tougher than you're making out."

"I'm no actress." I was stung. "Have *you* ever tried acting in a crazy situation, with an empty mind?"

"How do you know you're no actress? You might well be one with your looks—and your odd memory for words. There's something for you to think of while I'm gone." He was by the windows already. His mind wasn't on me at all.

"Well you're no diplomat, however marvelous your father is," I said angrily to his retreating back.

"Why should I be one? I'm an art historian," he retorted, stepping onto the balcony. I ran after him.

"Gian."

"Lower your voice," Gian said angrily. "Now let me go, there's a good girl—" But there was no "letting" about it; he simply swung a leg over the balustrade and began clambering down.

I trailed miserably back into the room and sat upon the bed and stared in front of me at the blank, blank wall. And after a while, to collect my thoughts on everything that had happened, and to take them off what was to come, I began to write this down.

12

And here I am again staring at a blank wall. A different one, in a totally different place. At least, this wall isn't really blank, but covered in a jazzy pattern of white, yellow, and orange, as though someone had hurled a stained-glass window at it which had shattered into splinters of color outlined in darkened lead. That wall seems to reflect with intolerable accuracy the splintered violence of my mind, the jagged pieces of what may be underneath it.

I'm scrawling this painfully with my left hand. Although my right hand's no longer bandaged, it's still stiff, and cramps when it holds a pen too long. Why do I write at all when to put anything on paper must be dangerous for me? Because now there's no one I can safely speak to about myself, and if I don't communicate somehow, even with paper, I may scream. This can always go in the lining of my bag or be torn up, burned, stuffed down the lavatory piece by piece.

A sound of music rises from the courtyard at the back of the house, amplified by enclosing walls. The insistent blare almost drowns out the gabble of voices and clatter of cutlery from the kitchen. Still, I'm glad this slip of a room looks out over the back and not the house front. There the noise of traffic is intolerable by night. Why do Italians like everything so loud? Color, sound, scooters. Italians: yes, automatically I think myself a foreigner by nationality. I've good reason to know that this time, at least, I've not been in Italy very long.

If I shut the window the heat will be stifling but the noise less. There. It's quieter now. Perhaps, before the heat brings on my headache, I can collect my thoughts—

If only I could be Giulia, a Carminotti niece again! It's not only the Carminottis I'm running from. Why was that beautifully expensive black leather bag ever saved from the accident wreckage? When I think how I used to cuddle it in the hospital, as a child holds a teddy bear for a mother substitute, I could howl with ironic laughter. My comforter, my one and only link with my vanished past. My time bomb.

After Gian left my room that night I sat for some time on the bed, wide awake and frightened. Irrationally afraid, I told myself. Not that the situation wasn't enough to scare most people into fits, but all was coming along, wasn't it? There was Gian to rely on. There was the hospital staff to vouch for my amazement when Carmina claimed me. There was no immediate risk. Perhaps underneath I was terrified I should be left to rot somewhere in a mental home. After all, I'd no knowledge of Gian except those two weird midnight meetings. But one part of me, more reliable than memory, assured me he was honest; that what he promised, he would do. And he'd promised me he and his father would see I was all right. So why was I visited by this suffocating sense of fear, a conviction that everything was going wrong?

I climbed into bed at last and swallowed my two tablets. In my perturbed state they weren't enough to make me sleep like the proverbial baby, and I dozed on and off all night. At six o'clock I woke, heavy-eyed. The bag was on the bedside table, and I pulled it to me as I had in the hospital and lay nursing it against my cheek. Roberto—Robert. I was so pleased when you gave it to me. Why didn't you come and find me, instead of those awful Carminottis? I was still lying there holding it to my face as though it might cure toothache when Benedetta knocked on the door and brought in my tray.

She gave me an odd look when she saw how I was lying. I sat up in confusion, and the bag toppled down onto the floor. Benedetta made no attempt to pick it up, but gave a scornful snort, dumped the tray upon my knees, and waddled away. Of course you scorn me, I thought, watching her. You know I'm not Giulia, don't you? What will the Carminottis give you, I wonder, to keep quiet? Trust someone who's been made use of by other people to scorn someone else now in the same boat. You probably get some macabre enjoyment out of seeing me delicately caged.

When the door was shut I shoved the tray on one side and leaned down to fish for my black leather bag. It was almost out of reach, but I just grasped a corner and tugged it toward me. Now it was near enough for me to grab it and yank it roughly upward.

After I'd drunk my coffee I reopened the bag idly to examine for the hundredth time those pathetic treasures of my forgotten past, sole survivors from the fire. Pathetic indeed to try and trace my history from these—

As I handled them my fingers brushed against the bag's silk lining. Something moved loosely underneath it, something flat, hard, and rectangular, not very large. My heart thumped—then I understood that some piece of cardboard must have worked loose from the base after this second jolt it had received. Anyway, why would there be something important in the bag's lining? It was much too new and well made for anything to have slipped inside, except through a tear, and there was none.

All the same, I got out of bed to find Giulia's nail scissors in a drawer. I sat down, drew the bag toward me, and examined it, turning it so that full daylight shone onto the crimson lining silk. For the first time I noticed a very fine line of hand stitching, not unlike the machine-stitched joinings of the other seams. My heart gave another thump. Clumsily, with my left hand, I dug the scissors' points through the largest stitch and cut. It took a while to undo enough so that I could put in my fingers and draw from its hiding place—

A small flat package wrapped tightly in oiled silk. I

turned it over and over, frightened to open it. What was—what could it be? Why had I taken such immense trouble to hide something so skillfully, even with precautions against damp? The packet was too small to contain bank notes. Bank notes, drugs, or jewels—these were the things that people smuggled through the customs, weren't they? Or—documents. At least, they were the only things I could think of just then.

I sat there staring, half hypnotized, and after a while cautiously peeled off strips of the Scotch tape which neatly sealed the package ends. I unwrapped the oiled silk and a lining paper. Inside these were two pieces of light metal. Thin layers of velvet stuck to their inner sides acted as buffers and protectors to—

I went rigid. What I held in my hands I'd certainly seen before. Memory needn't go back very far, just to a day when, sitting in the hospital gardens desperately trying to recall my past, I'd scanned the English papers with their articles and pictures. I remembered envying— who was it? Lady somebody or other— No, Countess— that was it, the Countess of Waterford—Waterbury, because she'd only lost an heirloom, not her whole past life. Well, since fair exchange is no robbery, I could only hope that she now had my memory, for here was her heirloom, the fabulous Waterbury miniature by that rare artist Nicholas Hilliard, safe and sound after accident, hospital, Carminottis, and all, lying in the moist palm of my left hand.

That was nearly the end of something beautiful which had already lasted centuries. When I started shaking like a road drill, the likeness of that spry twig of Elizabethan nobility, Sir Jonathan Loseley, nearly hit the floor. I moved my hand in time, so that it merely slid onto the coverlet. The painted colors glowed on a slip of ivory five inches long and three across. Sir Jonathan wore a white doublet and mulberry trunk hose. Perhaps he had pleased great Gloriana, for round his neck dangled some order, and from his left ear hung an enormous pink pearl. Hilliard had surrounded him with sprays of dog roses—the Tudor emblem—and the green of his sugar-loaf hat was a darker shade of the dog rose leaf. His looks didn't entirely please me; he was too self-satisfied, too dandified altogether. But I wouldn't have pleased him either, for I must have been white as chalk and wearing a crazy expression as the full implications of this find struck home.

Dear God, I thought inadequately, it can't be true.

And into my mind simultaneously came echoes of Gian's voice saying, "Perhaps we ought to be asking ourselves just why you can't get back your memory. A vested interest in burying something?"

Well, I hadn't buried it. I had simply wrapped it in oiled silk and hidden it in my bag—Robert's bag. Robert, I thought, not Roberto. Robert my—what? Lover? Accomplice? My accomplished fellow thief? For a moment a grim flash of humor illumined my toppling mind. We natural criminal classes—I thought of the Carminottis—we do surely smell each other out. There was I, so scornful of them, so self-righteous, and really I was in a higher criminal bracket myself. No, at least I wasn't connected with probable murder or incipient murder—or was I? Had I been? I must be pretty good at my job if I was already courier for the high international stuff! It made the Carminottis, with their pathetically clumsy cover-up methods, look like small fry. Like children who had got into the adults' league. Then I thought wistfully: I suppose, if I'd been the image of a nice young woman, I might have been drawn into a more pleasant situation. This landing up among frauds, or worse, that's nemesis, surely—or perhaps merely what Jung calls synchronicity.

Sir Jonathan stared up at me, and I stared back. Jung, nemesis, Hilliard: it dawned on me that I was quite a well-educated member of the criminal classes. Whom did I mingle with before I lit out for the Continent with one of the choicest ornaments from whichever circle I graced last? Then I thought of the shabby blue dress I was found in, and the anomaly between it and the very expensive bag. It was all of a piece with everything else: incomprehensible.

How was I ever to explain all this to Gian? Afterward he would believe nothing that I said. Of course, if the English police were looking for me, they might disclose my true identity. But it didn't seem that they knew of my existence, for wouldn't Interpol have seen my photograph after the crash? It was all too much for my addled wits to cope with. I put my head down on my hands and wept.

But I couldn't cry for long—that would certainly bring down on me Cosmo and drugs, fussings and surveillance. I wiped my eyes desperately and got up to secure the lock so that I couldn't be surprised. Hiding the Hilliard was my immediate problem; it was going to be hellishly difficult, with my present clumsiness, to return it to its place. For a moment I actually considered snapping it into pieces and dropping it down the lavatory. Or burying it out in the garden. But looking at that exquisite, masterly work, I knew that I couldn't. This was one crime of which I was incapable.

Eventually I managed to rewrap the miniature, although inexpertly. The packet was thicker than before and refused to slide down and sideways to its original hiding place in the leather base. But using one end of the still sticky Scotch tape, I did manage to attach it beneath the lining of the bag's side, where no one would be likely to notice it who didn't turn the whole thing inside out. I even managed to stitch up the side again, using needle and thread—albeit navy thread—from Giulia's drawer.

By the time I'd finished, Benedetta was knocking angrily on my door, complaining that it was past eleven and she had to do my room. I told her to come back in a quarter of an hour and heard her go grumblingly away. Then I drew the tray toward me and ate my breakfast roll and drank the stone-cold coffee, hard though it was to swallow. This instinctive determination to keep going surprised and delighted me. I'm tough, I thought; really, I'm very tough. And the discovery sustained me as I dressed and went downstairs.

In the hall I met Carmina but, pleading a restless night, escaped her by setting up a long chair out in the gardens and assuring her I meant to sleep. I lay there clasping the bag like an overprecious child, and watched the green and gold leaves swaying overhead—and thought obsessively about the situation as it had developed since Gian's last midnight visit. My first insane reaction had been: how to explain to him. Now I saw it was impossible. I could just hear my stumbling phrases: "Look, since last night I've sort of discovered something—of course, I didn't know it was there. But—odd, isn't it?—I happen to have a really famous stolen miniature in my bag. Would you believe it?"

Discovered since last night? What would he—anyone—believe? That I was trying to get him on my side before the police caught up with me. After that, would he even believe I'd lost my memory at all? Or would he simply think I'd wanted to lie low, first in the hospital and then with the Carminottis, playing as double a game with them as they had with me, to keep my criminal identity a secret?

In spite of sun and heat I shivered, turning my head restlessly to and fro. Well, then: leave my find alone, safely sewn up where it was, and say no more about it? (Oh damn, damn, *damn* the appalling thing—why had I ever looked?) But I soon saw this course was quite impracticable. Once Gian and the police arrived to confront the Carminottis, I stood a great chance of becoming front-page news again. Colder shivers ran down my spine as I wondered what other people were looking for me now. Surely I hadn't made off with the Hilliard just because I loved it too much to do without it, and equally surely I'd never managed it alone.

It was odd that no one had turned up looking for me before; at least this cut out any connection with Dino Il Nero and his friends other than hitchhiking. Could it be that someone was looking for me elsewhere? Maybe I *was* playing a lone hand; or had I simply run out on a ring of crooked dealers? That was a terrifying thought too. And how annoyed—to say the least!—they would be feeling if I had.

Then I realized something else. This miniature must be too well known for the open market. It could only have been "on offer" in advance to one of those fabled people who keep their private collections from the public eye and pay big money to increase them. My disappearance must have caused consternation somewhere, whether I was a lone operator or part of a gang. No! I'd certainly no mind to become a focus of public interest via the Carminotti affair.

So my tormented mind at last reached the point from which it had reluctantly shied away. With no means of support, no memory, and nowhere to go, I had to disappear, leaving behind no single clue for Gian and the police. And the sooner I went, the more time I would have to cover my tracks. I thought of the basic comfort and physical security the villa had afforded, and gave a little moan. How much, oh how very, very much, I longed to be the true Giulia, restored to the bosom of her thoroughly tiresome family. Now the only people liable to suffer as much as I would were the Carminottis themselves, when their getting-out stakes, their fraudulent orphan, slipped out of range.

By suppertime that night my feeble plan was ready. The Carminottis certainly wouldn't call in the police, but Gian just as certainly would. So I must take as few of the things Carmina had provided as possible, since they'd be too easily described. I found a carrier bag and filled it with the most nondescript assortment I could find: cheap underwear (Carmina had been a bit mean over that) and an extra pair of shoes, an anonymous-looking woolly jacket and a long cotton skirt. Small things like tights and makeup—and the rest of my pills— went into that accursed leather bag. For my journey into nowhere I decided to wear a black cotton pants suit. When she gave it to me Carmina had said, rather disparagingly, that the big stores were full of them. It was of better quality and cut than the same sort of thing in London anyway.

In London. Why— I stopped packing. My memory had made another leap at the surface. Only a very minor one, but reassuring. So you're still alive down there, I messaged it, and added—rather bitterly, when I remembered what it must contain—well, have fun.

13 And now there was only one obstacle to my departure: money. Vicenzo hadn't cashed a check for me yet, as I'd had no need of it. Thief I might be on a grand scale, but something in me still quibbled at the idea of picking pockets or Carmina's bag. How reassuring to know that my honesty in smaller matters wasn't dead! Unfortunately cash was essential. Without it I couldn't hope to survive more than a few hours of freedom outside the villa.

I stared into my mirror, examining my face. Hunted and haunted, you there—Silvie? Smile, can't you? Try looking like a carefree tourist, not a ghost recovering from its rest in a winding sheet. Silvie—Silvia is the name, all right. "Who is Silvia, what is she—?" No wonder those words kept knocking at my mind. What is she, indeed?

I picked the pocket of Enrico's jacket successfully just after dinner. It was hanging in the hall, and while he chatted with Vicenzo on the terrace I managed to transfer some thousands of liras to my bag. I was glad it was poor Enrico who had given me this chance. In a way I had a liking for him, and to think that he'd unwittingly provided this essential farewell gift softened me still more—although it might, of course, be Guilia's money, which would be more ironic still.

Fortunately the night was dark and cloudy and stiflingly hot. Carmina complained of a headache soon after dinner, and I also did my bit of moaning in order to discourage Enrico from staying outside too long after she'd gone in. Uncle Vicenzo soon got sick of us and rose to follow her, querulously commanding me to go to bed. Enrico trailed after me forlornly, and the doors were shut.

Everything was now ready for my getaway, and upstairs I lay on my bed fully dressed and waiting. I waited until long past midnight, when all was quiet. Then I took one final look round the room to make sure nothing had been overlooked, covered my hair with a scarf, tucked a pair of dark glasses in my bag, and went out on the balcony. It was easy enough to lower the carrier bag—it fell without sound onto the grass. But I couldn't treat the Hilliard's hiding place so cavalierly, and I had to clamber down the rose tree with that black leather time bomb hanging cumbrously from my right arm.

The gardens were very dark. There was no moon, and it took some while for my eyes to grow accustomed to this lack of light. At last I could just make out the shapes of paths and bushes. How vast the night felt! And I felt alone in it, wearing my new skin that was only "Silvia." Silvia the thief, alone in the intimate, cultivated Italian landscape. Underworld Silvia, on the run. As I stumbled down the drive I was miserably wondering what had started me on the pathway to quick, dishonest riches. I was no average thief, surely, if I had stolen that miniature, hidden it securely, and brought it through the customs. And no average thief could intuitively guess at the right buyer—

Hell! I tripped. Thoughts were no good now. Only action. The road was ahead. Would anyone be traveling it late and offer me a lift? No, I mustn't try yet, I'd be too conspicuous. A single girl hitchhiking alone at night in Italy would be unusual, even for these days. So it must be walking for me—that, and sleeping somewhere off the road, and then walking again until daylight, when it should be safe to thumb a lift—to Rome? My eyes ached, my thoughts whirled as I plodded on through the night trying not to think of dead Giulia or of attractive, desperately angry Gian.

I must have covered at least sixteen kilometers, until I was barely limping along, feeling overpowering fatigue brought on by such exercise after illness. Past a fork in the road a small wood loomed ahead. I turned off under the trees, shivering—even the Italian night would be warmer indoors—and huddled on a dry patch of ground, with the woolly jacket over me, and tried to sleep. But I couldn't. The clouds had gone, and the stars blazed large as torches through the treetops. I shut my eyes. There was too much on my mind, too many terrors. I shifted around, dozed a few minutes, woke, and so on through what remained of that unpleasant night. When the birds started twittering I was on my way again stumbling but determined. It could only have been half past five or so when I joined the main road going south.

"Mother always likes her holidays abroad, don't you, Mother? Not every year we've got the money, see—and kids, they're that trouble in a car. This year they've gone to Auntie. Bognor. Got a caff, she has, serves any thing you please. Give the young lady another cup, Mother. An' a roll."

"I mustn't eat all your food," I muttered. "Please. You've been more than kind."

"*Not* a bit. S'not kindness, is it, Mother, to help a nice kid like Miss—er?"

"Silvia. Just call me Silvia, Mrs. Crabtree."

"That's a pretty name, dear. But you look washed out." Indeed, I was shivering. "Eat up, there's plenty more. Dad and I, we do like to eat well, with no stinting."

"Washed out!" said Dad with a wink. "Burnt the candles at both ends, more likely. That's what all you students do. Mind, I'm a taxpayer, and I don't hold with all that rioting on those grants—all comes out of some- one's pocket, ain't that so? But when you meet 'em you can't help liking 'em, long hair and all."

"Never you mind him, duck. He can't help talking, can you, Dad? Now here's your second cup, plenty more where it came from. And if we're to call you Silvia, you call us Dad and Mother."

I thanked her and smiled waveringly at them both. Dad, so square and reasonable, sitting back on his canvas stool in the camping site, his hair brushed stiffly into shape with too much hair cream, his cloth suit too hot for the Italian sun. And Mother, opulently pretty, two rows of cultured pearls strung tight in the ringed creases of her neck, her silver-blue hair tightly curled, her white and black dress firmly controlling her abundant deep-pink flesh.

They had rescued me with their Ford and trailer early that morning after ten right-hand-drive cars had sped past. (In my frantic efforts to get a lift I'd still had sense enough to stick to "foreigners"—people who were probably tourists, and less likely to respond to police appeals.) Plainly, though they had left "the kids" at home, they had a protective passion for young people that was touching. Now they didn't really want to part with me, but I knew, regretfully, they must soon be shaken off. Oh, if only I could stay with them and forget my inner nightmare—

"I suppose that's the bus stop over there? The bus probably goes straight to Rome."

"Now, let's have no more of that, Silvia." Dad spoke with quiet authority. "Buses! Eyeties pinching you black and blue, I shouldn't wonder. No—I'll run you in later on while Mother cooks lunch and gets things straight. Got anywhere to stay?"

Oh dear. "Not yet. I—I'm just—wandering."

Mother's mouth fell open. "Wandering! Over *here*— oh, not alone, Silvia!" She sounded as though cannibals were waiting on every corner. "I thought maybe you were meeting up with chums."

Desperately I wove a disconnected story of how some friends had set out for Rome a week ahead of me—our dates hadn't tallied—I was hoping to rendezvous with them in St. Peter's between—between three and four.

"Got no address for them, then?" Dad looked at me narrowly.

"They—they were—*we* were—going to look. We all—we wanted sort of—odd jobs. Not—not really official ones."

Dad's jaw looked squarer. "I'll take you in to find these chums of yours."

Oh, this was worse! Hurriedly I said, "Well, honestly, Mr. Crabtree—Dad—it's— Maybe they won't be there today. It could be tomorrow, in fact, because—"

Mother and Dad exchanged a look. For one moment I thought—feared—they seemed suspicious of me. But no—they were simply hurt. They thought I didn't want them to meet my friends. Mother said with dignity, "Dad wasn't wanting to butt in, Silvia; we're not like that at all. But if there's anything we could do—"

"There's nothing truly." I looked miserably at Dad's hurt, square face.

"But, Silvia there *is*." (How nice she was, not thinking of herself at all, or my ingratitude.) "Remember Bernie, Dad? Go on, you remember." She turned back to me. "Bernie's the son of Dad's greatest friend. Plays the guitar something wonderful. Bernie came all through Italy last summer—bumming his way, he said. Told us when he couldn't make a square meal by his music he used to act as waiter—unofficial-like, no labor permits or anything."

"How? Surely it's not easy?" I felt a fresh dawning of hope; I'd been haunted by terror of what would happen when my cash ran out.

"Wait. He gave us the name of some little back-street places he used to work in where they serve cheap food. Gave him an attic room, usually, and meals. No questions asked. If anyone came nosing, he was just a friend's son, on holiday. Speak Italian, don't you? That's right, that's how Bernie got by too." She searched in her enormous plastic bag. "Here, dear. Here's the list. These are the Rome addresses, at the top." She held out

99

a dirty piece of paper covered in a scrawling hand. "I reckon all these places are alike, that desperate for help in summer, they're not too careful about laws. . . . Go on, take it! To tell the truth, duck, Dad's none too keen on these cheap meals. We buy food, mostly, an' cook it in the trailer. So we won't be needing Bernie's list."

Manna from heaven. I was close to tears. A sleepless night, that appalling Hilliard nestling in my bag like a precious, unwanted baby . . . And now this undeserved blessing, the solving of one immediate problem, through Mother's selfless kindness.

I said shakily, "Oh, you're the kindest people I ever met." Mother looked pleased. But Dad was still a bit unbending.

"That's fixed, then. I'll take you in to St. Peter's any time as suits you, Silvia. I ain't going to embarrass you by hanging on, but I'd certainly like a look at these young chums of yours before I go."

He was very silent going in to Rome. I had to force myself to do the talking.

"Look, Dad, you must give me your address. Oh, I've no pencil, damn— Never mind, I'll remember. Then I—I'll try to come and see you when I get back. If I'm not working."

"There's pencils in the locker." He sounded a bit more friendly, appeased. Then came the next hurdle. "And you can write yours for us too. We'd like to know you got back safe an' sound."

I wrote clumsily to his directions, digging in the point. When it came to my turn I scrawled a fictitious Silvia Marshal, hoping it wasn't my real name that had surfaced.

"Dad, I'm afraid I can't give you a real address—"

"Oh, I see."

"No, you don't. You don't see anything at all! You and Mrs. Crabtree thought I was a student—well, I'm not." My tired brain was suddenly inspired by what Gian had carelessly suggested: "I'm an out-of-work actress. P-pretty penniless, in fact. My—my parents don't care for my friends, and— Well, it's difficult to go back home!" I invented desperately. "But I *will* get in touch with you both. If you still want me to."

Dad thought heavily, and sighed. Six motor scooters shot by him, revving; he didn't notice them. "I'm glad it ain't quite like I suspected, Silvia. Thought you was ashamed of us! Now, I reckon you sound like a girl in real trouble, somehow. But there's one thing for sure: these 'friends' of yours sound a right mess to me. If they're not there today, you come on back to the camping site again. Mother an' I, we're staying over till tomorrow, then going south."

"I c-couldn't bother you, it would be too diff——"

"That's all right, an' no arguments about it, so you may as well save time and tongue."

His jaw stuck out. The car slipped in and out of the alarming traffic with aggressive ease. Why, he's formidable, I thought, in confused helplessness. Whatever can I do? No wonder Mother looks so pink and unlined, with Dad so obviously on her side; she's had every battle fought for her all her married life.

14 Rome looked magnificent. And very beautiful. But I felt that sinister influences of past cruelties underlay its splendid surface —and wondered nervously if my own shady past had flourished here. Had I set eyes on Vatican City before? I thought so—no, I felt so: it seemed familiar.

"Not near so cozy as our North Country—ever seen Manchester? Seems these Eyeties has their parking problems too. Never mind, Silvie, we'll just keep on round."

A policeman pointed an accusing baton in our direction as Dad's car shot neatly ahead between two Fiats.

"This looks all right," he said at last, drawing in toward a curb. "Seems other people parks here too. Stir your stumps, Silvie, we've not left you too much time. Big, ain't it?"

"Big" seemed an inadequate word. St. Peter's dome towered against the sky. Dad's right hand was in the crook of my arm, like someone discreetly escorting a prisoner. His other fist clutched my carrier bag. "Heat's something awful. What made you pick on siesta time, dear? Ah, here we are. Was it inside or out you was to meet?"

"Inside," I said firmly, though by this time I'd small hope that he wouldn't follow me. "Dad, I can't thank you enough for all you've done. You've been a saint. Mother too."

"Then they can put us on a couple of pedestals in here." He grinned shyly. But I was right: he was set on accompanying me—which imposed a charade of looking for nonexistent friends. The whole thing made me feel very mean, in contrast to Dad's and Mother's generosity. And when these people weren't forthcoming, how was I to shake him off?

"See hair or hide of them, Silvie?"

I looked about me, taking my time. "Not yet. I'd better perambulate!" I tried again: "Look, you mustn't bother to—"

"Mother won't expect me back just yet." His chin jutted. He looked like padded rock.

Our progress up a side aisle was slow, impeded by tourists. Just ahead of us a sturdy priest was lecturing a group of six or seven young men and women, obviously foreign students—or so I thought. The girls wore pants or trailing skirts, their long hair flowed over their shoulders. Two of them were fair. The boys were mostly bearded or moustached, their clothes a strange mixture of shabby Levi's and sequined jackets. For all their flamboyance they were an attractive-looking lot. Full of vitality. I gazed at them longingly and wished I could lay claim to them as those missing friends.

Dad's voice said, low and disparaging in my ear, "Hope your crowd look nothing like *them*, dear."

I shook my head and pushed past them, murmuring apologies. The priest ostentatiously ceased speaking and gave me a frigid nod. One of the bearded boys grinned sardonically and winked at me. He had very piercing blue eyes. Inwardly I marked him down as possessing personality plus.

"Trying to get off with you," said Dad rather too loudly.

"Oh no—" I hurried on up the aisle, Dad padding behind me. The priest had begun lecturing again in a long-suffering way.

"Did he say Bramanty?" asked Dad. "Sounds Irish. You wouldn't think they had Irish working on a place like this, would you?"

"Not really—"

I'd never thought any building could be so enormous as St. Peter's, or so filled with people. Or that anyone could be so scrupulous about a search as Dad. We dodged in and out of chapels and around pillars. We were the scourge of lecturing priests and docile groups. "Messina," said Dad, "well, at least *he's* not Irish. We don't have much luck up here, do we, Silvie? Think they're in the basement? I mean, old Peter's tomb itself."

I sank willingly onto an empty chair beside three praying nuns. "I—I don't. I'm sure they've seen it. Over and over again." My voice was starting to sound hysterical and I took a firm grip on myself. "Look—you go back, Dad."

"It's already past four, Silvie. They're not here today, obviously. So you come with me."

"Not now. You—you go on back to Mother. She'll be worried. You simply don't know my type of friends, Dad! Time means nothing to them. Why, when they say four they could mean five. Easily. Or six. I'll stick around."

"Or twelve o'clock midnight! I've no use for such people. Want to change your friends, dear." He looked down at me kindly. "You said they could be here tomorrow. Bring you in then for another go?"

I looked dully ahead of me trying to think. The charade repeated tomorrow; then they'd have to leave me, surely, and go on south. But—a camping site! No, I didn't want to stay there, even for Dad's and Mother's kindly company—and their good food. It was too public a place altogether, too much on the direct route to Rome.

Some large Germans, talking volubly, brushed against Dad and almost sent him flying. Where *did* all these tourists come from? Middle-aged men, pale women dressed in black with black lace covering their heads. Candle flames bobbed near us from a pyramid of candles on tall holders. Some women were kneeling.

Suddenly a happy inspiration came to me.

"Listen, Dad, it would truly be too maddening if they turned up later. *Please* go on back to Mother. I—I tell you what I'll do. I'll wait around a bit. If no one comes I could easily bus back to join you—"

"Can wait a bit longer, dear."

"Please don't! You've been kind enough already, truly. And—and as there's no sign of them turning up yet, I—I may as well go to confession now. It's—I feel quite guilty. It's so very long since I've actually—"

"You Irish, then? Like Bramanty?"

"I—no; no, I'm not."

"Didn't guess you was a Catholic, Silvie." Dad seemed to be grinding his teeth thoughtfully. He looked thoroughly embarrassed.

"You going to"—he choked slightly—"join this line?"

"Yes. That's what I thought."

"Half past four's my limit—after that Mother'll get worrying." Worrying Mother, I could see, rejoicingly, simply was unacceptable. "You go right ahead, dear— though why you want to, and you not Irish, I—never mind. If you're through by four-thirty with still no sign of these missing chums of yours, come back with me. Bargain?"

"Oh yes," I said tonelessly, getting to my feet. What had I let myself in for? I shot a sideways glance at the nearest line. It wasn't the longest. But it would certainly seem odd to pick the longest, now.

"You hurry, dear. Someone else may squeeze in first." As Dad spoke, another couple of penitents arrived. "Quick, Silvie."

I brushed my lips against his cheek, murmured, "Goodbye, then, Dad—in case," and stumbled into place, where I stood trying to look devout and confident. My heart thudded. I gazed at the candle flames. Six people ahead of me, four kneeling. Should I kneel yet? No.

A sudden shove at my arm startled me. It was Dad, holding out the carrier bag. "Here, better take it in too. If they'll let you. Case I can't stay."

"I—oh, thanks."

"You're seventh, dear. May just make it if they're snappy." Dad's whisper seemed to bound from pillar to pillar.

I smiled weakly at him. The old woman one ahead of me turned round to glare at us.

"Heathen practice," said Dad impenitently, tripped back across the aisle, and lowered his bulk into my vacated chair. Clutching my black bag and the carrier, I tried hard to arrange my features in a mold of piety. All I thought was, "Dear Lord, make these people have really huge sins to confess. Dear Lord, forgive me for acting out a comedy like this—make Dad go away. If I actually have to confess, what shall I do—what do people say? 'Bless me, Father, for I have sinned'—I know that much, anyway. Lord, I do know the Hilliard shouldn't be in my bag, but could you please stop fate from playing these appalling jokes on me?

An angry little man at the head of the line, who looked as though he ought to confess for at least half an hour, was horribly quick. In, out—more like a self-service counter than a confessional—or was that blasphemous? In, out. Now it was the turn of an elderly woman with gray hair. She took far longer. Wicked or scrupulous. From the corner of my eye I could see Dad staring at me. Why the wary look? I tried to look absentminded, and kneeled, like the others in front of me, fixing my eyes upon the candle flames. Surely it was twenty past four by now? Quarter past, anyway. And still four people ahead of me. The old woman came out at last. We all shuffled up one place.

And now there was only one person between me and the confessional, a young girl, her eyes red from weeping. I don't know which I dreaded more: Dad waiting, or having to make confession when I didn't know the words.

The girl went in. I licked my dry lips. No movement

from that chair across the aisle? None. But the girl was inside a long while—at least her misfortunes were on my side.

At last there was the sound of chair legs scraping back. Dad had risen, and came ponderously over to lean down and whisper and indicate the dial of his watch. Just past four-thirty. Still no sign of the girl. I nodded at him, smiled desperately. He pointed toward the entrance, raised his eyebrows, pantomimed something. What could he mean? Then I got it—would I promise to join them if no one came? I nodded violently. Oh dear, something else to confess.

Now give Dad a few seconds to leave the aisle, and then I could rise and— But it was too late. The curtain was pushed aside, the girl stepped out, more red-eyed than ever. And with Dad still well in sight, I'd no option but to take her place in the confessional.

It was so dark inside. I groped my way, then fell thankfully upon my knees again. My heart was knock-knock-knocking within my chest. I couldn't speak. At least a minute must have passed in silence. Then I heard an impatient movement and a reproving cough.

"Bless me, Father, for I have sinned—"

If I didn't know the other words, would he summon someone to have me ejected as an unruly tourist making an unseemly jest of sacred things?

"Father—I—was in a terrible accident. My head—I can't remember things—I can't remember the words."

My voice wobbled. It must have sounded genuine enough; tears of strain and self-pity were rolling down my cheeks. He was gentleness itself as he led me through the formula phrase by phrase: ". . . and confess to . . . and to you, Father—"

There was another silence. Until in it, to my own astonishment, I heard my voice stammering, "I—I did something terrible. I stole. It was—something very valuable." And then complete terror swamped me. Was the

107

seal of the confessional really secure? Suppose my crazy confession were reported to the police?

". . . before or after your accident, my daughter?"

"Be-before. The worst of it is, I—I can't even remember doing it. All I know is that I must have done it. And the—the thing—I have it still."

Perhaps he didn't really believe anything I was saying, after that first pronouncement about the accident. For his tone seemed almost indulgent.

"The theft was reported to the police?"

"Oh yes—oh yes, indeed it was."

"And you are truly penitent?"

"Oh, I am—I'm truly penitent, Father."

He sounded very young. The gentle voice was talking of God's love and forgiveness and the need of restitution and suffering. "But I cannot absolve you, my daughter, unless you're steadfastly resolved to make restitution for your deed. But this you know—or did know once. Are you prepared to return what you stole, no matter what it costs you?"

Blackness, blackness all around me. In the confessional and outside. Hospital behind me, years of prison ahead . . .

I licked my dry lips to whisper, "Yes, I'll return the thing I took, Father. It may take time. There are so many, many difficulties. But I will do it." Someone else seemed to be speaking, not myself at all. I wasn't even a Catholic, so far as I knew. Oh, I must be far, far madder than I ever thought. This sort of promise, made in this place, must be kept. The voice of this hidden priest was grave as he pronounced my penance. And then, *"Ego te absolvo, in nomine Patris, et Filii, et Spiritus Sancti."*

I crossed myself, rose, and stumbled from the box. A quick glance round to make sure Dad hadn't returned, and then I sank onto that same chair, my heart thudding. I kneeled there a long while, half faint with strain and exhaustion, unable to think clearly. To the faithful

I must have appeared solely concentrated on penance. Perhaps this awful, empty sense of suffering could count as punishment? The idea of rosaries and Hail Marys danced in my mind, but never settled into normal, consecutive thought.

At last I rose. St. Peter's was vast, shadowy. More lights had been lit, and the candle flames on the side aisles leaped and dazzled. Chiaroscuro, they call this mingling of light and shadow. . . . People were crowding in for some service. Carrying my two bags I moved toward the entrance, struggling against the incoming tide. Priests and people: old men, old ladies in black lace, young mothers with young children— There was a great clot of people in the chapel close to where the sturdy priest had lectured earlier. I looked into it idly as I passed, and over the heads of several intervening people a tall fair-bearded man looked at me. It was just a casual glance, one that any tourist might give another. But then he started violently and stared. Recognition?

I backed into the shadow of a pillar. Too late—he'd recognized me, I was sure. But *his* face—the odd lighting turned it to a white mask, mouth writhing open, dark caverns for eyes. Yes, odd tricks of light—light on the fair hair, light outlining—

I turned and blindly, in terror, pushed hard against the incoming crowd. Swinging the carrier bag against their knees, I forced my way through. I wouldn't look back, wouldn't let him see me again. Was it my imagination, or as I successfully battered my way out did I hear a man's voice—an American one by the sound of it—calling after me, rather high and urgent, *"Silvia?* Hi—come back, *Silvia—"*

Like someone hunted, I almost ran from the great church of St. Peter's.

After that everything seemed confused. Vaguely I recall crossing the immense piazza, a dizzy width; leaving Vatican City; following side streets, and peering over my shoulder to make sure no one followed. The sun still blazed down, and speech flowed round me in a stream of sound which was a sheer babel of foreign tongues.

At last my leaping heart quieted itself. I came to a street where tall old houses shaded a small piazza with one of Rome's many fountains at its center. On a stone seat sat two nuns and an old man. The nuns smiled as he opened a large bag of crumbs to feed the hovering birds. Nearby another stone seat was empty, and I sank down with relief. How peaceful it was here! Only a few people about, strolling, or sitting on the grass. Consciously I relaxed, deliberately steered my mind away from thinking of the bearded fair man who had seemed to recognize me. Or had he merely mistaken me for someone else? But the name "Silvia" called after me—that was real enough, surely? And was it Gian who'd named me after I quoted Shakespeare at him, or had blind memory guided me to choose the name myself? I screwed up my forehead, trying to remember—

Across the patch of sun-dried grass a tall blond girl, who had been sitting with some friends, leaped to her feet calling out something that I couldn't hear. They laughed. Two other girls and a boy—they seemed familiar. Why, yes—they were with that pleasant group I'd noticed in St. Peter's. It was good to have my mind taken off my worries, and I watched them eagerly, wishing that I knew them. Now the boy jumped up too and took the girl by the hand. He bowed and stepped back and began to speak, but very formally and with wide gestures. I stared. What were they doing? It was like watching an open-air theater. Theater! Was that it? Were they actors? Perhaps they were rehearsing.

The two girls still seated on the ground began to clap, slowly, in slow time, and then quicker—and the boy and girl began to dance. The nuns and old man were watching too, smiling. It was rather a pretty sight—the gaily colored clothes, the fair-haired girl and dark boy solemnly pacing on pale, burnt grass.

I liked watching them so much that I didn't realize how hungry I was until they stopped. It was hours since Mother had fed me at the camping site. Now was the moment to search out Bernie's restaurant for a job—and food. I took the scrap of paper from my bag, glanced at the addresses, chose one, and approached the elder of the nuns. Could she very kindly direct me? Was it far?

"No, not far at all! But a little complicated. See—" A withered hand grasped my sleeve as she explained: "Take *that* turning from the piazza, signorina. The one which leads to a row of little shops, yes? Then at the end you'll find some traffic lights and a main road. Cross it and keep straight on. Then turn to the right, and to the left again—and you're in the street you look for."

Very carefully I repeated her directions, thanked her, and walked away, passing the group of actors as I went. The strange sympathy which drew me to them made me smile at them as I walked by. The girls looked up indifferently, but the boy smiled back in a friendly way. Absurdly, I longed to stay; and suddenly the carrier bag seemed very heavy, and my solitary terrors almost unendurable. . . . Since I'd reached this piazza the sky and buildings had changed color. They had a mauve tinge, and the shadows were twice as deep, though mistier. The fountain's water ran with a colder light, its rainbows were subdued. In spite of the hot air, I shivered.

The little shops were all in shade. There was a food shop among them which had two or three iron tables outside covered by large shabby umbrellas. It didn't look very inviting, but perhaps I could buy a *cappuccino* here before my stomach ate itself. I was hesitating in the doorway when something made me look round at the passersby. On the other side of the road a large man was striding past toward the piazza. It couldn't be, surely— *No,* I was imagining things! After all, I'd barely seen the face of that man who called out after me in St. Peter's Why should I start thinking that I recognized him now? It was hallucination, caused by hunger. My knees felt quite weak.

"Signorina?"

"Prego, un cappuccino."

But, for precaution's sake, I drank it inside, standing at the counter. And when I'd eaten a rather unpleasant sandwich I emerged very cautiously and set off to look for Bernie's best Roman sanctuary in one of the less glamorous quarters of the Eternal City.

15

"Bianca—Bian-ca!"

I sit, nursing my right hand. How it aches! But it's good for it to write and use these unaccustomed muscles. All the same, I shall develop writer's cramp if the flow of reminiscence continues so—

"Bianca!"

I start, and jump up. A bad memory for things past is no excuse for present forgetfulness. "Silvia" has been discarded here in Bernie's restaurant. "Bianca" is a sour joke—the all-white, puzzled, nonshadow side of myself: the good type that even criminals probably believe themselves to be.

"Pronto, pronto—I'm coming, Cirillo."

I thrust my papers beneath the cheap, lumpy mattress on my bed, tie on my apron, and go clattering downstairs. Making my way through to the kitchens, I pass by the restaurant, which is already filling with its usual clientele: small-time shop owners and their wives; well-paid workers from a nearby factory; and a number of foreign students on holiday, bearded and beaded, accompanied by their sandaled, long-haired, long-skirted girls. But it's not the students who cause me twinges of alarm each time I cross the overheated, smelly room. No, what I dread, probably irrationally, is to find myself face to face with the tall, fair-bearded stranger who recognized me in St. Peter's.

The kitchen's a hellhole—steamy, filled to the brim with angry male cooks hurling insults at each other as they stir, cut, or boil. A waitress's work is exhausting, and I've barely time to breathe. Backward and forward, carrying four platefuls of pasta up one arm, balancing a tray on the other. With both hands full there's small chance of protecting oneself against the Italian masculine belief that women exist to have their bottoms grasped, pinched, or caressed. In forty-eight hours I've learned to keep moving fast, and to control the incorrigible by dropping strands of boiling hot spaghetti down their necks. I ignore the bellows of anger and return to the kitchen for more food.

What a life! As I trail up to bed long past midnight I wonder how long I can survive here. My hair's drenched with sweat, and my eyes are so dark-ringed they look as if I've picked up a paintbrush and drawn blue circles round them. Those terrible headaches have started up again. I fling myself on the bed and stare up at the ceiling. Another day of it tomorrow! If only there were something cheerful to think about before I fall asleep, something less menacing than the actions Gian may be taking since my disappearance, or who's searching for me now—and the Hilliard. Was that man in St. Peter's connected with my accomplices? Does he know them, are they even now alerted that I'm here in Rome? I sit up in bed, my heart lurching. Shouldn't I move on farther south as soon as possible?

But Rome's so big and has so many of these small *trattorias*. It would be most unlikely for— I lie down again, trying to dismiss this attack of horrors. Soon my supply of pills will run out, and I wonder how I'll manage without tranquilizers. That hospital I was in now seems a haven of peace and rest. As for the crazy promises I made the good father in St. Peter's, my mind boggles at the very thought.

Next morning I've come to a decision, right or wrong. To stay on. I scan the paper's headlines—so far, nothing about any Carminottis. I'll try to keep my mind on my work. I enter the restaurant to serve lunch feeling more alive, less like a hunted fugitive.

"The party by the window—quick!" says Cirillo, indicating them with a jerk of his head.

I'm hardly surprised, even somewhat pleased, to see the group of people I found so attractive in St. Peter's.

114

If they're students—of drama?—this is just the sort of inexpensive place where they would come to eat. I flourish the menu before them rather shyly. The dark boy who smiled at me in the piazza smiles again broadly. The tall, fair girl looks through me. She's beautiful, but has a hostile expression. I discover they're English, which makes me cautious. When the young, dark boy speaks to me I pretend not to understand.

"Ashley, your Italian's not so bad as mine. Tell her I've seen her twice already—near here and in St. Peter's."

Ashley, smiling lazily, turns out to be the large, dark one with sardonic looks and blue eyes who grimaced at me when I annoyed the lecturing priest.

"It's high time you learned to do your own tracking, Chris—and talking." He turns to me, and I look back with polite interest as he launches into a flood of adequate though inaccurate Italian. With gestures, faces, and a flow of words he makes a vivid, not to say unusual, translation. Eventually I laugh, and he laughs back. The fair girl frowns and holds out a hand for the menu. They make their choices and I withdraw to the kitchen with some complicated orders. Cirillo gives me the carafes of wine and offers to bring the food himself—which I put down to the fair girl's beauty.

By the time I've waited on them during lunch I've learned a lot about them, even all their names. The third boy's Jack, and the beauty's Helen. The brunette's called Griselda, and I hear Ashley name the other blond girl Janet. She has the type of plain looks that are quite striking in their way—and a far nicer face than the hostile Helen's. I was right when I put them down as actors. It's all theatrical gossip, nonstop. Now and then Ashley tries to draw me into it, or Chris chokes out a few embarrassed words, but I merely smile and shake my head. I like them all, except Helen. But I mustn't get involved with any English people.

We're very busy. For the next forty minutes I'm kept running to and fro between tables and kitchen. Then as

I linger behind scenes for a moment, wiping the sweat from my face, Cirillo thrusts a tray with seven coffee cups into my hands. "For the English, Bianca—quick, I bring the coffee myself."

"There's only six of them." I start removing the extra cup.

"No, no, seven. Hurry!" He jostles me out ahead of him toward the window table. The *trattoria*'s crowded, I've hard work to keep the tray straight and the cups in place, and reach the table without once looking up. When I do, I almost drop everything on the floor. Talking with Ashley and lounging against the window frame, wineglass in hand, is the tall, bearded stranger from St. Peter's.

"—and of course that means we can dispense with sets there altogether," he's saying, "and merely . . ." His voice dies away. He straightens up. I find myself staring into eyes as blue as Ashley's, though without their keenness. Plainly this encounter winds him as much as it does me.

"Si-Silvia—"

There's nothing I can do or say. I just stand there feeling—and certainly looking—both foolish and afraid. Behind me Cirillo has seen nothing, only that I block his way. He swears beneath his breath. Ashley's alert eyes are on my face. So are Helen's. In fact, everyone's staring.

"You know each other, Paul?" asks Chris. He looks puzzled. "But you weren't with us when—"

Paul takes a step nearer the table. In the bright daylight I notice, mechanically, that he's older than the others by some years. The bushy fair beard's almost like a Viking's, though the face it embellishes is scarcely a warrior's.

"Bianca," Cirillo whispers fiercely, "put the cups *down.*"

One of Ashley's eyebrows goes up as he registers this difference in names.

Automatically I place the tray on the table. Then, as the newcomer stutters out "Th-thought it w-was you b-before, only the lights weren't exactly—" I ignore Cirillo's frantic gestures, abandon my duty of dispensing coffee cups, and take off for the kitchen as quickly as possible. Its astonished inmates see me whizzing through like a rocket, en route for the back stairs and my own room, where I burrow my way into bed and lie shaking like a rabbit chased into its run.

But, by five o'clock, I'm thoroughly ashamed of myself. Coward, you, Silvie . . . Can you stay hidden here without a memory forever? It was the shock of being confronted that was so dreadful. There was nothing about that stranger's face at close quarters to give me the sense of distrust that Carmina's had. If one can go by intuition, I'd say it was a pleasant face. And some day, some time, perhaps even very soon, someone else will certainly be on my trail—Gian, the police, perhaps the underworld with which I've obviously been involved. This man Paul doesn't seem an underworld type. Can one tell? But today fate's offered me a second chance to find out something more about myself, and again I've run from it. Which way lies worse danger—in ignorance or knowledge? Heads I win, tails I lose—or is the same answer written on both sides of the coin?

The heat in this back room's stifling. Perhaps I should take a risk—go and get myself some fresh air, if there's any left in Rome at this hour. But first poor Cirillo's owed an apology. I go in search of him to plead sudden sickness. Grudgingly he offers me a second chance, which I accept. Though whether I ought to stay on here now seems uncertain. Suppose I play a gambling game with myself. If this Paul doesn't come back by tomorrow evening, it will mean he's waiting for some sinister friend to join him, and I ought to go. But if he comes, I won't try to run away.

That settled, I spend an anxious twenty-four hours. There's no sign of Paul—or the students—that night or at lunch that day. I'm just thinking that I ought to stick to my decision, and pack my carrier bag, when Cirillo comes to tell me that a signor's outside asking for me. I hardly need his amused expression—quick work, he's thinking—to tell me who it is: Paul. And he doesn't look terrifying at all. He has a distinctly hangdog air.

"Silvie, I don't want to bother you or crowd you in any way, but you don't seem—you don't look altogether — Anyway, the others are all going on, and I'll have to be with them, so it's now or—"

"Please don't be so incoherent!" I say sharply. A shock to see him, yet something in me is relieved. Deeply so. And now I've a real chance to sum him up, face to face, and it's still hard to believe he's any sort of criminal.

"You make me incoherent. You must know you've been acting pretty strangely! I've—I'd surely like to know what it's all about. You're acting as if something's very wrong."

"I—maybe something is."

"Maybe! I should say so—seeing you in a place like this. I won't hang on afterward, but you must see I'd like to understand why—"

"All right—Paul," I say quickly. I'm clutching that wretched bag between my hands. "The trouble is, it's all so—so unbelievable. It will—it would take me literally hours to explain." I shake my head weakly. My indecision seems to make him more decisive.

"Time's the one thing I have just now." He grins uncertainly. Takes my arm. "Come on. Let's go somewhere I can buy you a *cappuccino*—or a drink?"

"Buy us ices, against this heat." I'm making up my mind at last. "And then let's take them to a small piazza that I know of; I think you'll know it too. It's somewhere we can talk in peace."

I lead him there. It's emptier of people than the first time I saw it. Only the old man shakes out a bag of crumbs for the birds. The fountain ripples in the sun; flowing waters are a placid reminder that everything passes.

I lick my ice cone consideringly. "Paul . . . tell me something about myself?"

"What, exactly?"

"Everything. Don't look so surprised! How we met, where it was, how I struck you—who I am and— Do stop staring! Just talk. I'll try to explain—later."

"If that's what you want." His voice is puzzled, worried. Perhaps he thinks me mad. At least he decides to humor me. "Where do I start? We met in London this year . . . But you're kidding, Silvie! You know this by heart. And how Robert made a—"

At this name I draw in a deep breath. I feel as if a thick cloud has obscured the sun: cold. "I'm not kidding. Go on, please. Go *on*."

"We-ell . . . You'd been in that flop at the Cannongate. The night it folded was the night the cast bravely gave themselves a party. It was at the Lamb and Flag."

"So I am—I was acting?" Gian was right.

"I'd say! In fact, I thought you were terrific."

"And you went to see me. But if I was terrific—why did the play fold?"

He looks at me incredulously. "You really want to go through all this as if you didn't know?"

I shake his arm. "Yes. Please. Please, it's desperately important."

"We-ell . . . Your part wasn't quite the whole play. Though I thought you were Duse, and then some."

"A small part?"

"Tiny."

"I see. And now did you get to the floppers' party?"

"Oh, I'm in the theater. Sort of. And a girl I knew, knew you. She took me along—after the performance. Seem to think she said, 'If you must meet Silvia Klavetti, now's the time and place. But I'm warning you—

Robert got there first. And Robert, for all that charm, can act quite ugly when he chooses.' "

Robert . . . So Robert, who can act quite ugly, got there first. Again I feel the sunshine has been obscured by a cloud. I hunch my shoulders to quell a shiver up my spine.

"Klavetti. Doesn't sound real. Stage name—"

"Yes, stage name. Your mother's family. Least, that's how you told it later on. Look, I'll ask the questions now. Why the stale history lesson? You in some sort of—of mess?"

"You could call it that. Yes, you could most certainly call it that."

"You can trust me, you know."

"Can I?" My fingers stroke the bag. Don't I trust people too readily? Fleetingly I remember Carmina claiming me in the hospital. "Can I trust you, Paul?"

"Oh bloody hell, surely you know that by now!" He sounds quite violent. "You really gripe me, Silvie. What is all this, anyway? If you're ready to pretend you don't remember—" He is on his feet, prepared to stride away, full of injured male pride.

I catch involuntarily at his arm. In that second I'm convinced that I can trust him. And know I'll do anything not to be alone again—afraid, among total strangers, as I was in the hospital. "That's just it—you put your finger on it. *I don't remember*. I don't remember anything—nothing about anything at all." And as he stands peering down at me in his bewilderment I start to pour it out, at first in bits and pieces, jerkily, and then everything—like water from that fountain in the center of the little square. Yes, everything except the Hilliard.

It's almost an hour later, and we're sitting hand in hand. To me Paul's hand is simply a hand like any other, but just now a human touch is very comforting. And Paul seems to believe what I've told him. Will he still if I reveal—? I run my fingers surreptitiously along the side of my black bag. He's looking at it as I add hurriedly, "There's one particular thing that confuses me so. It's been puzzling me, niggling away, ever since I've not been Giulia. Those cypresses. The hill. The— tomb in the slope above the villa. I *knew* them. How could I have known them? They were the first things that came back to me in the hospital. And then— there they were. *Had* I been to that place before? What sort of a coincidence is that? Perhaps my mother's fam- ily—before even the Carminottis bought it—"

"You did tell me your mother died when you were small. And you're an orphan—English. And your only living Italian relatives were aged grandparents living somewhere south of Rome—Terracina, that's it."

"But I never spoke about a villa?"

"Not a real one. You spoke about a dream."

"Dream?"

"Yeah. Some sort of nightmare about a place just like— That's really odd. It throws me." He presses his fingers against his forehead as though my dream had got inside.

"Dream," I say slowly. *"When* did I have this dream? Where?"

"Way back in London town. You were half laughing at yourself, but you were scared. The dream did worry you. Perhaps that's why you told me."

"What—?"

"Wait for it—I'm remembering. Here's how you put it. 'It's a vile dream, I don't know why. I've dreamed it three times already, and it's a black one; it's got a sense of threat.' You seemed completely obsessed by it—the trees, the running uphill, just like you've described it now . . . *And* there was another, which had the same effect—something about a van." Perhaps my shudder communicates itself through our clasped hands. "Did that go home?"

"Yes—I—I've dreamed that since . . . Dear heaven,

121

so I accepted Carmina, I accepted everything there in spite of what my instincts said—and all because the place was familiar through a dream! A sort of psychic warning, which I couldn't take. Clairvoyant, too, as well as—" I don't add "a thief."

"Listen, time's getting on. Are you due back at that hellhole yet?"

"Evening off. There's time."

"Your dreams impressed me. No—maybe your fear of them. So I asked, had you second sight? And you said no, but you did dream things occasionally before they happened. That scared you too. Said you dreamed before you met Robert."

"I dreamed—of him?" My voice croaks. My fingers grip the bag.

"Yeah. Dreamed you'd meet him." Paul's voice is markedly colder, but whether toward Robert or to me I cannot tell. He lets go of my hand.

"Paul, help me out a little. You can tell me: Am I someone who—simply slept around? One of a crowd, perhaps—people who didn't mind whose bed they slept in? Sorry—I didn't mean— But you must see, I've got to know what happened between me and Robert. I'm sorry," I add again, since he looks upset, "but you just have to tell me all you know. Of me, Robert, you—us!"

He looks harried, and grows almost as incoherent as he was at first. But in the end I do get it out of him. Everything.

16

So I, Silvia Klavetti, had scaled the foothills of ambition to grab a small part in London theater—not quite West End, but where managements could see me and almost anything could happen. One of the first things that happened to me, apparently, was Robert. No one—says Paul—quite knew what Robert lived on, though he sometimes spoke vaguely of selling this or that for profit. He mentioned stockbroking too, but said he'd left it because it bored him. And he seemed to have a wide acquaintance. Very wide. The sort you acquire through being well connected or born with quantities of charm and push. Yet some of Robert's connections, the more offbeat ones, had little to do with good backgrounds—rather the reverse. Men with flashy cars and suspiciously expensive houses. Men who flew the Atlantic as often as most others take the tube into the City. Men who had an aura of quick thinking and easy wealth.

Is there a hint of jealousy in Paul's voice as he tells me this? More than a hint of jealousy about Robert's attraction for women.

I listen hungrily, hoping I'll put in the right questions at the right time. "Was he—was Robert intelligent? A university type?"

Paul shrugs. "Could have been Redbrick or Oxbridge, *I* don't know." But he seems fairly wound up now on the subject of Robert, obsessed by him. Robert knew about a lot of things, and if he didn't know, then he always knew someone who did. Girls tagged onto him easily—Chelsea types, eating pizzas somewhere off the Fulham Road, or old-time debs ("seen him with them"). Then he'd drop one set and take up another. People talked of seeing Robert in scruffy clothes at country sales, or discreetly dressed poring over *incunabula* at Sotheby's.

"Was he—I suppose he sometimes stayed around—in big country houses?" I murmur breathlessly, clutching the bag.

"And with the latest chick," says Paul scathingly, "whether it was her scene or not."

"So I suppose even someone from a flop at the Cannongate might have got to visit a mansion like the Waterburys'—"

"Heh, what's that?"

"Nothing. Go on."

"There's not much more—you're where I came in. You know, Lamb and Flag party. All that."

"When that girl warned you 'Robert got there first.' "

"Right enough. Silvie, you said you want to know."

"I suppose so." Do I? Or am I too afraid?

"We arrived when a monumental scene was brewing between you and Robert." Paul smiles fiercely, reminiscently. "Seems he was trying to run you and someone else at the same time. It was the last straw, after the show flopping, and you were high on something—pot, wine, whatever—and were getting everything off your chest. It seemed my lucky day all right, if not yours. When you walked out on him you did it with a gesture." He grins an embarrassed grin. "You walked out with me."

"Oh, I see," I say faintly. "How did your current girl like that?"

"She wasn't my current girl. Just a friend. And your gesture fell flat enough with Robert—no compliment to me! When we made our undignified departure he was standing there with his arms round the other woman, laughing. Anita, her name was; she looked fairly special, and I thought I'd won. As if anyone wins, permanently, against a man like that." He sounds more nervous and upset than I suspected.

"I see. My gesture against Robert. I'm sorry, Paul."

"Keep the apologies. That night was as much a horrible flop as your play. I'd no chance against him."

Paul's voice is hard. "He soon had a comeback. New line in moral blackmail, that's all he had to use. First the old one of 'she's gone and I need you.' That cut no ice. Then he came round after you, in a state. Seeing colored lights or visions or something. Obviously high on acid—but his panic, real or false, roused the female masochism in you. Last time I saw you for some while." His fingers stroke mine obsessively.

"But, Paul! One night—and for such a reason. You didn't really care?"

"You got under my skin somehow. At least I made a point of avoiding places where I'd see you—either of you." Paul stares gloomily at his feet.

I'm wondering what else to ask, and if he might possibly believe me if I told— The snag is, without a memory what can I believe about myself? Paul must have felt very involved to want to hang on still. All the same, how much could such involvement take?

". . . bound to meet you in the end. After all, you were an actress. I was on the outskirts of English theater trying to get a foot in—stage-managing. I worked with some other Americans for a bit. At the Roundhouse. You came out there. To a performance."

"Roundhouse?"

"You don't remember it? Some sort of former engine shed, where a lot goes on. We had some drinks together. I asked if you'd got anything going for you in London, and you said no, not yet. But you thought that Robert—"

"I do seem to have had Robert on the brain."

"Compulsion. Or obsession. Girls did get hooked on him. Like the hard stuff."

"Pretty thought. So Robert—had plans for me, did he? Paul," I ask urgently, "what were the plans?"

"Plans?"

"Yes. I thought that's what you meant, that Robert—"

"Oh—that. Something to do with the stage. Not the professional stage, I reckon. Amateur stuff, somewhere in the country. I couldn't see why you were all lit up about it."

Lit up about Robert probably. I'm beginning to take a dim view of myself. But "somewhere in the country" . . .

"Tell me."

"How can I? You were fairly cagey."

"Cagey?"

"Said you never spoke about engagements much beforehand or they fell through. Personal superstition or something."

So I didn't tell Paul anything. Perhaps I didn't even know it. Altogether, I'm not much further on.

"Don't look so depressed, Silvie. You'll get your memory back in time."

"Will I?" I look miserably around the piazza. No one's paying us attention. No one's near enough to overhear—and no one's likely to understand English if they did. Suddenly I find it impossible, unendurable, to keep quiet about my real trouble any longer. "I *must* get my memory back, Paul. I mayn't remember much, but what I do know is that Robert probably involved me in a major theft. Or I involved him in one."

"Silvie!"

"I've got the evidence. On me. And I don't know how I came by it or what to do about it now."

"*Silvie.*"

"Yes."

"Where—for God's sake—is it? And what—?"

"It's here. In this bag. It's a picture."

"Picture?" He looks at me as though the accident has really sent me mad. "In that?"

"Miniature. A famous one. I read about the theft when I was in that hospital. And afterward, at the villa. I found it in the lining—the miniature, I mean. It's the Waterbury Hilliard."

Paul just sits there looking at me. On and on. I look

126

back in defiant misery. We're so still, we might be two of the many stone statues that are dotted everywhere in Rome.

At last he whistles, and says in awestruck tones, "Well, what do you know?" Perhaps it's the best comment that he could have made.

On the way back to the *trattoria* he says suddenly, "Look—I—you've got to get out of here."

"Where do you suggest—a Mediterranean cruise?"

"I'm not joking. Hell, what a mess! I've—well, seeing you so low and obviously—huh—not well off, I, uh—in the light of, I mean—"

"Paul, don't get tied up again. Put it plainly."

"Keeping it short, I wrote to Robert."

"You *what?*"

"Wrote. To Robert. Yeah, after I'd seen you in that hellhole of yours. Seemed plain you'd no use for me, so I buzzed him a line saying where you were. In case he was interested. Masochism, it's catching—and seemed to me you needed someone to look out for you, so—"

"Dear sweet gentle heaven!"

Paul's arm pulls me back from the front wheels of a frantically hooting Saab. We stand on the pavement edge, people milling round us. No one pays attention to an Englishwoman and an American absorbed in personal drama.

"Bloody interference—if you'd left me to look out for myself, but *this*—"

"And you so capable."

"Up to me, wasn't it? Get *out* of here? I'd better take to the catacombs before—" A Fiat almost removes my toes. I leap back and Paul steadies me.

"What's the use of bawling me out? I mean, it's happened. Though in view of what you've just told me, it doesn't seem the best—"

"In view of *that*, not only are Gian Marotti and the Italian police buying up bloodhounds but the trail's probably jammed with gangs of international crooks as well—now directed straight on target."

"Could you stop teetering on the curb, Silvie? It unnerves me. Here, cross the bloody road and be done with it." And as he pilots me across it, gripping my left arm, he murmurs smoothly in my ear. "Maybe you simply pinched that pretty toy all by yourself. Just took a little fancy to it."

We reach the other side and he releases me. I rub my arm resentfully. "You really think I did?"

"How should I know?" The words sting, but at least he's smiling. "Perhaps Robert's the more likely candidate."

"Yes, *Robert*—what shall I do if he comes?"

"Calm down. I'll get you out of here tomorrow somehow. But I must fix it with Ashley first."

"*Ashley?*"

"Yeah. I'm wet-nursing his drama group through Italy. Not that Ashley needs nursing, but—"

"Ashley! You'll never tell him about—"

"Obviously not—"

This time it's a Honda. Paul scoops me adroitly to his side. That's the third time he's fielded me today. I look on him with a more kindly eye.

We've reached my *trattoria*.

"Look, Paul. Don't you think you should cut and run? Because—if I land in prison, you'll land there too. Accessory to the crime, or whatever it's called. For something like major robbery, wouldn't I get fifteen years or more?" My stomach heaves at the thought of it, and at trying to defend myself without a memory.

"Ah, that— One of my best friends is doing time. They pinned a charge on him. Pushing the stuff, they said, though in fact he was merely smoking it."

"But—fifteen years," I repeat dolefully.

"We're going to clear you somehow. Now: plans. Ashley and— We're all leaving Rome tomorrow. As for the hardware, you couldn't bring yourself to snap it up and shove it down the john?" His lighthearted attitude is so reassuring that I almost manage a smile.

"No. I thought. Often. He—it forbids you to touch it."

"Fifteen years is one hell of a long time, I do agree."

"So is four hundred! Wait till you see, Paul. It's so beautiful. So very, very beautiful."

We creep up the jazzily papered back stairs. The usual row is coming from the kitchen as I lock the door behind us. The bare boards creak. There's no chair, and Paul lowers himself onto the bed.

"Quite like old times."

"So it may be. Was the wallpaper like this?"

"I was too absorbed to notice. Now show me the credentials, ma'am. I don't really think you've got the Hilliard, you know. Just blown your nut."

It takes time to undo the stitches, particularly as my hands are shaking. At last I edge the packet from its hiding place and reverently place it in Paul's hands. Until this moment I don't think he'd really believed me. Now he seems unable to speak.

"Well? Scornful, isn't he? A bit of an Elizabethan popinjay perhaps—but what a lovely one."

"The roses . . . ," says Paul at last, lyrically. "Their stems . . . And the velvet! Lord, you'd a nerve to touch this! Don't they keep alarms on it or something?"

"How should I know?"

"Holy, fair and wise is she—but people don't usually come by priceless miniatures without some trouble. Honest or otherwise." His voice mocks me.

"Obviously you think I share Robert's guilt, at least." I swallow. Is Paul going to turn against me? "Don't you believe I've lost my memory?"

"Oh, that, sure. About everything else I'll keep an

open mind." He hands back the miniature and sits gazing at me consideringly, a little grimly.

"Why are you here, then?" My voice sounds angry. Good. Anger is more spine-stiffening than tears.

"We-ell, not many girls look like you *and* provide this high-powered excitement at the same time." He stands up, grins, and lounges to the door. "I'll be back for you early tomorrow," he says briefly. "And mind—don't forget that stream of recollections you say you're writing. Either destroy it or bring it with you. OK?"

"OK."

" 'Bye, then."

He's gone. Sir Jonathan Loseley and I are left staring blankly at each other.

17

"You do understand that I don't believe a word Paul says?"

A warm wind blows Ashley's hair across his eyes. He frowns and shakes his head. Then he sticks an elbow out of the window, leans negligently sideways, and turns the wheel with one finger just in time to avoid a head-on collision.

"You're a very silent girl, aren't you? And so good at countering attack. It leads me to feel you don't trust other people. I wonder why? Something on your conscience?"

I sit hugging the black bag closely and staring down the long, straight road ahead as it flashes toward us, tall trees on either side. The countryside's full of small farms, vines and olive trees. On the horizon lurks a mountain range. We're buzzed by motor scooters. Paul's asleep in the back of the van. The three girls are squashed together like a pile of puppies. With all the stage props and costumes, there's little room for people, but what remains is fully used.

Ashley raises his voice, and starts to sing—

> *Who is Silvia, what is she*
> *That all our swains commend her?*
> *Since she is a mystery*
> *The cops should apprehend her—*
> *And dum-dum and so on—*

I force myself to smile.

" 'Those happy smilelets, that played on her ripe lips, seemed not to know what guest were in her eyes.' "

" 'Oh dear discretion, how his words are suited! The fool hath planted in his memory, an army of good words!' "

131

Ashley's eyebrows rise mockingly. "Dear, dear, so in one thing our Paul has spoken truth. You *are* an actress. Well capped, sweet Silvia."

Again I stare down the long, straight road. A warm sense of pleasure, coupled with fear, rises in me. Since my discovery of the Hilliard I've been too swamped with worry to watch all my thoughts and actions for more signs of normal functioning. And still flotsam and jetsam has surfaced, a speech from my training in that cloud-hidden past. Among other things, Paul's told me that he knows I've done two seasons of repertory in Shakespeare.

What parts—what other words? Think—think gently, like probing a sore tooth with the tip of one's tongue—

> *. . . O spite! O hell! I see you all are bent*
> *To set against me for your merriment.*
> *If you were civil, and knew courtesy,*
> *You—you would not do me thus much injury.*
> *Can you not hate me, as—as I know you do,*
> *But you must join in hearts to mock me too?*
> *If you were men, as—as men you are in show,*
> *You would not use a gentle lady so . . .*

What triumph! Even as I say the words, gathering speed and confidence, I can feel exactly how they should be said. And my memory has cooperatively picked out a speech of deep reproach. As I finish I gaze soulfully at Ashley with what I hope is a piteous expression, lips slightly parted. More triumph, for Ashley stares back, riveted. And someone behind us calls out in anguish as the van swerves, *"Cripes . . .* look what you're doing!"

Ashley snorts contemptuously, settles over the wheel, and leans on it. His black brows are drawn together, his lips purse thoughtfully.

" 'Souls' not 'hearts.' "

"I—I'd forgotten."

"You said it well. When did you play Helena?"

"In—in rep." (Helena?)

"It wasn't John Trebyn's production at Manchester?"

"N-not Manchester."

"I didn't know anyone else had done the Dream just lately."

"It wasn't lately."

Beneath his easy, mocking manner Ashley knows his stuff too thoroughly. He may be only a student still, living on grants and temporarily responsible for this small group of other students touring Italy in a "cultural exchange" experiment, but his innate ability and drive are obvious—so is his keen intelligence. I consider the large, brooding, untidy boy beside me, in his torn orange shirt, dirty Levi's, and bare feet, and feel a surge of resentment against lazy, gentle Paul, who, apart from saying "I must fix it with Ashley," has omitted to mention what story he used to make me an unofficial member of the company.

"You do hedge, don't you, Silvie, love? One more question: You've got a passport all right?"

My hands tighten on the bag. "Naturally. In here. Do you want to see it?" Speak casually—

"Not that interested."

Thank God. I relax.

"We're a bit stretched, as Paul probably told you. One girl dropped out on us. So you can share the understudying for Bianca and Hero. Ever played them?"

No sooner over one hurdle— Hero? My mind tries to track back too hard, fails. "I've played Hero," I say as confidently as I can. "N-not Bianca. But Hero was a good while back. I—I'd like the words."

"You shall have them. Janet, look out scripts of *Much Ado* and the *Shrew* for Silvia."

From the back of the van comes a scrabbling sound as someone leafs through a pile of scripts.

"I—I don't quite see how you're doing Shakespeare with so few of us anyway. Scenes from?"

"We cut a bit. Paul didn't exactly put you in the

picture, did he? What was he doing with his time?" A very faint smile curves Ashley's lips. "There are twelve of us altogether—apart from Paul. Five in the smaller van, which broke down just before we got to Rome. And three gone on by train. Some have to double acting and lights, et cetera."

"Gone ahead where?"

"Just ahead. I'll give you the itinerary some time. It's flexible. We may end up anywhere—even Venice."

"I—I'd like to see Venice."

"There's a slight local reception waiting for us next stop. In case you want to know."

My throat feels stiff. I swallow—and see Ashley grin. "How—what a nice idea."

"Delightful, isn't it? But you'll get by, Silvie, pet. Just open those big eyes at them, and don't answer questions. And don't show them your nonexistent passport, please."

"Paul," I whisper fiercely as we sit together over a small fire while Helen and Janet fry mushrooms and boil spaghetti at the camping site. "Just how did you explain me to Ashley?"

"Said you were having trouble with your family, as well as being pestered by someone else, and had discreetly vanished for a while."

"Oh, Paul, how feeble! Would that have made me run like a rabbit when I saw you in the *trattoria?* Or use another name?"

"OK, tell me a better tale—impromptu."

I can't.

Paul smiles lazily. "Has he accused us of lying?"

"Not outright."

"Then he's accepted you. And Ashley keeps his own counsel, as you'll find. I said you were a bloody good actress, which probably helped."

"He's a pleasant fellow—when he keeps his sarcasm in rein."

"So Helen thinks. And Helen won't take kindly to your presence."

"To hell with Helen. She doesn't own him—and it's not her business."

"Sing small's my advice. You can't afford loud singing, can you?"

For a while we sit companionably side by side saying nothing. My hands leaf idly through the *Much Ado* that Janet has found me. Many of Hero's speeches are so widely separated that—in emergency—there'll be time for me to snatch glances at the words offstage. Fortunately both Helen and Griselda look the sort of healthy girls that nothing, short of broken legs, will keep from acting. As I think this, I feel a stirring of resentment—professional jealousy, a longing for the spotlights. Whatever strong impulse took me to the stage for an uncertain living is still very much alive, raring to go.

"Say, listen, Silvie, about the Hil——"

"*Shush.*"

"No one near. It's courting disaster to lug it with you in that bag."

"Where else?" So far we've signally failed to turn up any good ideas for returning it to the Waterburys.

"That's what I've been thinking about. And here's a—"

"Mushrooms and spaghetti, Silvia? You, Paul?"

Helen's voice is cold as she leans over us in her flowing, tattered sari. I flinch away from the pan's spluttering fat. She smiles and ladles out two helpings into one cracked bowl. "You'll have to share, I'm afraid—we're short of crockery. But I forgot; *you* don't mind sharing, do you?" She moves away before I can think of a suitable reply.

We dig two tinny forks into the pile of food. Paul murmurs conspiratorially, "Listen. When the others go to see the sights, say you'll stick around with me."

"I'll say we're so in love that we need the van. At once."

He laughs, pulls a lock of my hair in a casual way, and says, "That's my girl."

Later that afternoon I'm sunning myself alone on the grass, when Paul appears carrying a screwdriver, squats down beside me, and says with some satisfaction, "Fixed."

"I do rely on you. Too much. Where is it?"

"Under the back seat. I've screwed a bit of plywood over it."

"What if the van needs garaging?"

"No mechanic will look where I've just put it. No reason to."

"Or gets stolen?"

"Chance it. That bag could easily get stolen too. Easier."

"It's always with me." I feel oddly bereft without the miniature.

"You can't hold it at rehearsal. Ashley doesn't stomach eccentricities. Hero with a black bag—no."

"You could be right." I roll over on my back and yawn, shutting my eyes sleepily against the powerful sun. My whole crazy, terrible situation has remained basically unchanged. But Paul's placid reactions are the best medicine I could have.

His lips gently touch my arm.

"Nice . . . I love you as a friend."

"Too hot to argue that."

We lie companionably side by side.

"Listen, when you wrote to Robert—"

No answer. Is Paul asleep? I prod him sharply with one finger. "It's only just struck me. Did you tell him you were with this lot? He may try and trace you if he can't find me."

"I wasn't writing about myself. Said I was in Italy and had met you—in the hellhole."

136

"He couldn't know you were stage-managing this tour?"

"No."

He's determined to sleep. But though I've laid one doubt, another niggles, leaving me no peace. "Paul."

"Ummmm?"

"Friends of yours could know."

He considers. "Two or three. Doubt if Robert would know them." His hand strokes my wrist. "Sleep, Silvie . . ."

"That girl who took you to the pub?"

"Lost her some time back." Paul's fingers stray sleepily up my arm and hold it. "Stop worrying. You've so many worries that if you start on them you'll never stop."

It makes good sense but is hard to carry through. Robert. And Gian—I've thought of him so often, and the Carminottis. If I hadn't found the Hilliard, what would have taken place by now? A confrontation, with Gian beside me. This—with Carmina and Cosmo, Vicenzo and Enrico—wouldn't have been exhilarating! But at least I would have been the injured innocent. The very thought of Gian turning up to find me gone gives me a sense of guilt—even of pain. What must he have thought—a tissue of lies? And what action has he taken? There's been nothing in the papers—yet. I've kept close watch so far, and Ashley will bring one back for me today. If only I could dismiss an inner vision of myself shrinking before Gian's dark, scornful face. He must think I'm the most despicable sort of coward—one who wouldn't even stay to help him find the truth about poor Giulia's death.

The sun feels too hot on my uncovered face. I shift restlessly. Paul's hand tightens on my wrist as he murmurs, "Silvia, *sleep*."

18

"Here's your paper, Silvie. Can't bear to miss a day's news, can you?"

"Just got the habit, that's all."

"We'll make use of it. Italian verbs still puzzle me, so will you help? I'll buy you papers if you'll let me read them aloud and translate to you. OK?"

"OK."

"Funny, you wasting your almost nonexistent pennies on newspapers. Anyway, let's start. *'Dappertutto i giorni di festa—'* "

Ashley does everything with equal concentration. His thick black brows are drawn together above blunt, strong features. It's a dynamic countenance. With his straight black hair and swarthy skin contrasting with those bright blue eyes he's very noticeable. I sit and watch him, thinking how magnificent he'll look in Petruchio's clothes. . . .

"Wake up. Have I read too much?"

"A bargain's a bargain. Read the whole thing from cover to cover."

He takes me at my word. Happily there's no news yet of Gian or the Carminottis—or of the police looking for a missing girl. I lie back on the grass idly watching Ashley's face and trying to still twinges of compunction about poor Giulia.

There's no doubt that an erratic style of living, the traditional one of strolling players—feverish activity and excitement followed by interludes of calm—suits my temperament. I find it oddly healing. In fact, I often revel in it, in spite of missing memory, remnants of illness, and a sword of Damocles suspended overhead. Already I feel as if I've been with the company a long while. I shut my mind to Paul's pessimistic "We've a few weeks' tour, you know—then we'll have to find you something else. Not to mention a passport." And I laugh with Ashley and Janet and try not to notice Helen's barbed remarks and angry looks. I study Hero's and Bianca's words and soon gain confidence at rehearsal. Ashley produces—or Mike, who's joined us complaining of discomfort on the trains and demanding quantities of wine to quench a monstrous thirst.

"Poor boy," mocks Ashley, "did he have a horrid time sitting on a sore arse, then?"

"Sit on yours next time, *amico.*" Mike swigs wine at a dramatic rate and wipes his lips with the back of one great hairy paw. Without lowering his voice he adds, "And why isn't this Silvie understudying for Kate? She's quite as good as Helen—and that tawny hair's terrific."

Helen glowers. Ashley puts his arm consolingly around her. "Because, dear boy, Silvie, though a delightful loan, isn't really on the strength."

"Who cares? It's the result that counts. Impress the peasantry out here, and lo!—a light in yonder window breaks, and it's my favorite member of the Arts Council handing out a fatter grant."

Make matters worse, you clot. "But I'm really 'resting'—and happy anyway, thanks, Mike."

He snorts loudly. "Liar! If ever I saw insatiate ambition on a face, it's yours rehearsing, Silvie. No born actress is ever 'resting' enough not to take the lead when offered."

"Casting's up to Ashley, and well you know it, Mike." Helen sweeps her sari dramatically about her, shoots me a look she's long perfected as Katharine, and withdraws saying over her shoulder, "Come on, we can't sit here all day."

Ashley hunts through his pockets for some liras. Giving me a long, considering look, he says softly, "Mmm, yes. Of course, if Helen's ever ill, you could understudy with Janet. Have a look anyway."

I'm pleased and horrified at the same time. Fear of the limelight—

"One must admit that Helen has a splendid temperament for Kate the curst," adds Mike. " 'A title for a maid of all titles the worst.' Don't look so solemn, Silvie—I'll take you through Kate's words any time you like."

I'm immensely grateful for this strange, erratic way of life: the undemanding company, and the work, which does take my mind off my worst besetting problems. But there are still bad moments when I'm aware there's something sinister, not quite real, about my getting off so lightly. And every overstrung nerve tells me it can't last. The sickening terror of what my memory may contain becomes as hostile a threat to my shaky mental balance as it ever was in the hospital. Soon, I feel—something unspeakable's bound to happen soon.

It's two days later. Ashley, who never misses his Italian hour, is sitting beside me drinking his *cappuccino* in a village *trattoria* and reading remorselessly from daily papers. They're so dull, and his accent's so good, that my attention wanders till it's jerked back when he starts translating. ". . . suspected of the murder of two missing girls . . . The villa's occupants . . . Signora Carminotti . . ."

Everything goes whirling round me; Ashley's face is black against the sun, now on my right, now on my left. I'm rigid with fear, I may begin to scream. My hands clench together beneath the tabletop. Pray, pray Ashley won't look at me. . . . His face rights itself, the sky steadies. I've missed a bit. What did it say—not *arrested?* That Gian has gone to the police, that Carmina and Vicenzo are suspected of murdering *two* girls? So—and I never thought of that. Of course. That's how it must have seemed to Gian.

I rub at my sweating forehead. How long has it taken him—them—to reach the conclusion? How many days—I can't think—since I came down the long road to Rome with Dad and Mother. It feels like ten lifetimes. O heavens, thoughts are shot to pieces, forehead drips sweat. Drip, drip, like in the hospital when memory found gone. . . . I'm unable to make form or sense of Ashley's words. Never—never—never thought Gian might think me dead. Because for one thing the Carminottis would be laid wide open, and how stupid . . . impossible ever to put right.

Ashley's on sport. He reads each word painstakingly. (Time, valuable time, if not for recovery, then to put on persona, mask.) When he looks up I'm clutching at my stomach and giving faint moans of pain.

"Silvie! What's up?"

"Don't—ow—don't know. Been doubled two, three times already—*oh*."

"Touch of tourist's gripes? I've some pills, if you'd like to try them."

"No—I—yes, thanks."

"Right, I'll go fetch them." He lays the paper down beside me. While he slouches off toward the van, I hurriedly begin to read. Three or four paragraphs, not very revealing. Bald statements about missing Giulia and "another girl." Villa's occupants being questioned. Gian's father mentioned as family friend who took suspicions to the police. I sit bleakly wondering what on earth X does now.

"Here. Pills."

"What? Oh—the pills. Thanks." I look them over dubiously. "Are they strong?"

"Quite strong. Soothing. If it's stomach. Of course, if it's something else—" His eyes wander to my hands clutching the paper. I've experience of Ashley's shrewdness and say nervously, "I—they'll be fine. I mean, however strong. It's so"—and if ever I have acted, do so now—"painful."

Impossible to tell if he's convinced. "It looks painful," he says courteously. "Take two now, one later. Good—here's Paul. Hi—take Silvie to the van, make her lie down. She's ill. Oh, don't forget the paper, will you? She may want to read."

.   .

What black responsibilities, not possible to fulfill:
return the Hilliard, and clear the Carminottis of my
death! When I groan aloud, it should convince any
listening ears. Paul, sitting on another bunk, looks up.
He's studying the paper, but Italian doesn't come to
him too easily. I go into details of what's happened.
Does his sympathy wear thin? I'm not surprised. Something's badly wrong, surely, with a woman who gets
herself into so many tangled webs.

"You'll have to go back now."

"But, Paul—"

"Silvie, it's the only thing to do."

"But I can't."

"You can't stay here and let them take the rap."

"They deserve some raps."

"Not that one."

"Not for Giulia?"

"What evidence is there that they killed her? Your
Gian thought it was an accident."

"Yes. Oh yes— Don't look at me like that, Paul! I
wouldn't let them go to life imprisonment or hanging.
Would they hang, in Italy? But they're a long, long way
from that just yet, aren't they? Why shouldn't they stew
a little—how did they mean to treat me anyway? Of
course I'll go back in the end. If the police don't free
them."

"Then why not now? It won't get better, waiting."

"Time . . . I need it."

"Time for what, exactly?"

"Don't know."

Silence.

"Paul—I know it doesn't make sense. It's—call it intuition. Reason says go back, but intuition says don't.
Not yet, at least. Wait. . . . Wait. Time." I push back
my damp hair. Wait! Haven't I been waiting for something to cut these Gordian knots ever since my consciousness surfaced in the hospital?

I look beseechingly into Paul's kind, heavily bearded face and wonder about the person behind it. We're all so complicated. Will he suddenly decide—?

"You'll stay with me on this?"

"Providing."

"Providing I act with copybook decency in the end?" My bitterness is unfair. Why *should* Paul back me indefinitely on a course he finds unjust? "All right, I'll jeopardize myself for those bloody frauds soon."

"I wonder what you're really waiting for? Maybe it's—"

"Robert?"

"Could be."

I shudder. Please God, we've put Robert off the trail—at least till memory comes back. Since I've been rehearsing, acting in parts I may have played before, I've often felt confident that one day my whole past will jigsaw itself into place. Now, at this bad moment with Paul—a shadowy stranger seated on the opposite bunk— and with that piece about the Carminottis spread before me, any confidence is gone. It takes all my strength to repress rising despair.

"I can't think of it yet. I'm going to wait. I'm going to get *well*. I'm going to rehearse. If I can keep my thoughts on something sane, just keep—keep living, things may—could—" Impossible to finish, for I don't know precisely what I mean. But it seems to satisfy Paul, who nods and gets up.

"Right, Silvie. We'll hang on, and—for now at least." He goes out. I reread the paragraphs, calmly this time. Quite soon I'll be able to join Ashley and the others and say those pills are really wonderful, I'm no longer doubled up.

And curiously, quite schizophrenically, with this decision made I'm almost able to behave as if there's no future and no past. Outwardly I behave, and rehearse, with the company as if my only problems were theirs too: work, money, emotions. The heat's glorious, sometimes a bit too much; when we're not actually in some small town we live, eat, and work outdoors. My skin turns golden in the sun; on the stage I should have to block out freckles. In fact, I look so healthy, and throw myself so enthusiastically into rehearsals, that Helen's mistrust of me grows daily. The released and zealous actress in me dies for her to twist an ankle so that I and Janet can alternately play the Shrew.

But camouflaged, sick, and haunted Silvie knows public appearances would be folly. At local receptions where mayors make emotional speeches about England, Italy, and Shakespeare, I turn aside when the photographers get busy, or screw up my face so their shots are quite unprintable. No one but Helen, apart from Paul, notices my reactions. Unfortunately I'm Helen's aching tooth. She's too aware of everything I do.

"For someone so ambitious you're oddly shy," she says bluntly.

"I'm so unphotogenic. I—I'd be very miserable in films."

"Oh no. You'd be very happy in a star part anywhere. Perhaps it's newspaper publicity you mind?" She's always out of range before I can reply. I begin to dread she'll needle me more openly, and in future I try to avoid these social occasions altogether, since every instinct tells me she's only waiting to trip me up.

"Please not, Ashley—I do loathe these meetings. And I've got an awful headache."

"It's all part of the job, Silvie—and you've done this once too often lately. I won't have star tantrums from my understudies."

That clinches it. Perhaps I can plant myself at the far end of the long table, where I can sit out speeches and photographs unobserved? This mayor's a charming little fat man, like a robin. He bobs up and down for toast after toast, and Helen and Janet, on each side of him, are stroked and kissed impartially. When the meal ends, my dreaded moment comes: the advent of the local press. Flash, flash—first Helen's photographed with the mayor, with Ashley, or alone. Then the photographers turn their lenses on the whole company. I bend my neck and fiddle with my napkin. "Speech!" says somebody, and Helen, pushed on (not very hard) by Ashley, murmurs a few gracious words which hardly anyone can hear. I'm just starting to relax when her voice rings out clearly as it does when she's onstage.

". . . not want all the limelight, that's not how we see things in this company, and these plays we've chosen aren't just vehicles for stars." She gives me a wicked grin and says even louder. "Mr. Mayor, how many people realize how much work falls to the understudies? Janet and Silvia both understudy Katharine. Can't the three of us be photographed together? What a memento of a super evening here tonight."

Everyone applauds. Except me. "Cripes, what's got into Lady Bountiful?" mutters Mike. "She must have eaten something." The mayor obviously thinks she has a sweet nature as well as talent.

Someone drapes Janet in position. Paul, looking anxious, stands aside for me to pass. The room seems full of faces pressing toward us in a ring. I'm like an inadequate matador at the center of a bullfight. Pray, pray that these men with flowing hair, bright shirts, and professional handling of their cameras are local talent only—there seem so many of them. As we've moved farther north again more and more people have grown interested. Is the *national* press here tonight?

I efface myself a little behind Helen's right shoulder and flowing hair, but she almost lugs me forward with an arm that feels like an international wrestler's. "Don't be shy, darling. You must be seen." I look down modestly. Click, flutter, flash.

"Could we have another pose, please?"

Of course we can; Helen grabs me and Janet by the neck and draws our heads toward hers so that our hair is intermingled.

"Would the signorina on the left look up and smile?"

Click, click . . . click.

Another brilliant flash and it's all over.

And so, too, is my temporary peace of mind.

19

"It had to happen some time."

"I can't sleep, I'm so scared. If only it hadn't happened yet." I stare down at the national daily paper which we've spread open on the road's grassy verge. Three smiling faces stare up at us. A good likeness of Helen, Janet—and me.

"Yet? What exactly are you waiting for, Silvie? Your memory? You should go back before someone comes to find you—Gian or the police."

Logically that's true; but glimmerings of foreknowledge can't be reasoned with—or proved till they fall out correctly.

"Is it Robert?"

"Robert! That's worse than—" I shake my head. I don't know what it is. Only that it's too soon to return. Paul looks at me in some exasperation. I wonder if such trust as he ever had in me is wearing thin.

"Come on, then, Silvie. Ashley's waiting to rehearse the understudies."

"I'd sooner die than really play Katharine now."

"Oh no, you wouldn't. *Coraggio!*" He pulls me to my feet as Ashley arrives with Chris and Janet.

"Ready? I'll hear these two together. First meetings. Then it's you and me, Silvie. I hope you're all word-perfect."

I quail. Ashley's formidable at rehearsal. I've seen Helen reduced to tears.

Chris and Janet play their scene capably, without much fire. Usually Ashley would have been baiting them, interrupting, groaning, throwing himself between them to show how Petruchio should brag or Katharine snarl. But today he lets them walk through and merely sighs.

"OK. We'll work on it another time. I'll take Silvia through it now. You prompt, Paul."

Subdued, the other pair subside onto the grass while Ashley strips off his jersey to stand revealed in a shirt as eye-catching as any garment Petruchio swaggers in.

He starts almost before I'm in position. " 'Good morrow, Kate; for that's your name, I hear.' "

" 'Well have you heard, but something hard of hearing. They call me Katharine that do talk of me.' "

"No, no, *no*. She's angry, yes—fishwife near the surface. But she's on the defensive too. She's sensed a thunderstorm—can't you hear the difference? Play her too angrily from the start, you'll get monotonous. 'Good morrow, Kate; for that's your name, I hear.' "

He glares. The Tartar's risen.

I repeat my speech.

"Better. 'You lie, in faith; for you are called plain Kate—' " It's a pleasure to watch Petruchio fill out Ashley's skin. When he reaches the line 'Myself am moved to woo thee for my wife,' I find it easy enough to think myself Katharine.

We go through the scene, with Petruchio sometimes changing to Ashley, who swears at me because I'm too slow or too mild or too angry—actually high praise, for I've noticed he's offensive only when his partner's worth correcting. At the end he says brusquely, "Shaping. Take it again from where she's hit him. 'I swear I'll cuff you if you strike again.' "

We rehearse twice more. To my horror I feel myself getting progressively worse. There's a most Petruchio glower in our producer's eyes, but he says moderately, "You were better first go. A bit—muffled later. Not Katharine."

Muffled. Astute Ashley. That was how I felt—as though speaking through a thick fog and dimly aware of known places just beyond it. I'm trembling, and I have an odd conviction that if I look at Ashley long enough he'll turn into someone else.

"I—missed out somewhere, I know. I felt it."

"If you felt it, don't do it! Now the starvation scene:

Chris and Janet. Then you two girls try Kate's long final speech."

My turn to be audience with Paul. I'm thankful to sit. Sounds seem to be coming from a long way off, and my thoughts are jumbled. I stick a blade of grass between my lips and bite on the stem, trying to retain a sense of immediate reality. It doesn't work. Yes, this is how the play should be done, against these yews; in the background the very house where great Elizabeth once watched the players.

My mind jerks between present and past. *Past!* Was it surfacing—is this a combination of ideas sparking off imagination? The "yews" are olives. The only house nearby, a poor Italian farmhouse with a russet roof. Perhaps I dozed in the hot sun, for Chris and Janet have finished, and Ashley comes toward me wearing a preoccupied expression.

"Running out of time. Must take the road soon or we'll not get in a rehearsal with lights before the performance. Scrub Janet. Just you, Silvie: Kate surrendering her women's lib. standpoint. Once through. I'll strangle you if you don't do it properly." He throws himself down on the grass by Paul. A grin belies his words.

I think: Now Ashley doesn't believe I'll ever play the lead; he's sick of me. That smile's too pleasant. It nettles me. I go into the opening phrases of Kate's speech determined to show what I can do. But at the words "A woman moved is like a fountain troubled—" I start to flounder. I was visualizing the scene intensely, as I'd been taught (do I know that?), and a fountain has swum up before my eyes, pale in the dark evening; little moon, a yew hedge behind which people whisper and toward which I run in my full skirts with the harshness of a starched ruff digging into my neck—

Paul's voice prompts me: "'. . . Muddy, ill-seeming—'"

Catch at the words thankfully: "'thick, bereft of beauty—'" Stall again.

" 'And while it is so—' "

" ' . . . while it is so, none so dry or thirsty—thirsty—' "
It's such a melancholy garden by night, and that woman
was whispering to Robert behind the hedge—

"Why don't you bloody learn your bloody words?"
howls Ashley, dragging me back into the present. Beads
of sweat trickle off my forehead into my eyes.

"I—I'm sorry—"

"*Sorry.* Try, you stupid girl, *try.*" He snatches Paul's
copy of the play and intones through his nose quite
ferociously, " 'Thy husband is thy lord, thy life, thy
keeper'—for husband read producer."

And I rise to the bullying; the dark garden sinks from
sight, and after the phrase "One that cares for thee and
for thy maintenance" I flow with increasing speed, like a
very untroubled fountain, to the end.

"Yes, well," says Ashley, untwining his long length off
the grass and tucking in his shirt, "not bad in parts. Bits
of brilliance, acres of sheer idiocy. If you'd rehearsed
enough . . . Heaven send Helen doesn't break an
ankle. *Try* to remember that fountain's not the source
of the fucking Nile." And he stalks off toward the van,
leaving me praying urgently for Helen's health.

I've no cause to worry over that, at least. Helen's
health feeds on rivalry; so does her temper. By the time
three more performances have passed—one *Much Ado,*
two *Shrews*—our nerves are thrumming like violin
strings.

I'm haunted, too, by what happened to me at rehearsal. Suppose it does again! I hardly know whether to
be pleased or sorry at having Bianca's role tonight.
Janet's sorry. It's her misfortune that I should be understudying Bianca, while she would have taken Katharine
instead of Helen. Perhaps her luck will change tomorrow; Griselda's "tourist's gripes" may last two days. . .

Anyway, I think grimly, as the butterflies in my

stomach dance a *cachucha,* one fear casts out another. The sheer horror produced by that published photograph has vanished, displaced by the terror of performance, and a performance while my mind's on the verge of—

". . . you're not"—Ashley's warning Helen—"to go beyond the role when you start battering Bianca. Any real black eyes or cut lips and you won't act again this tour."

"Kate shall batter gently. It's so easy to put poor Silvie off, isn't it?"

How I wish Bianca weren't such a sweet, silly mope. Would Ashley overlook one rousing backhand—?

"Time, ladies and gentlemen, please," says Ashley, and makes toward the dressing rooms while we tail after him in a silence broken only by floods of explosive Italian from backstage, where an electrician's explaining some trouble with the lights.

The makeup seems to melt on my face as I apply it. Hell, this grease stick's the wrong color. A shake doesn't help with lip outliner, and I make some botched shots before Bianca's mouth is set. The dress is virginal white, with false pearls at the centers of big daisies. I start bundling my hair into a snood made of silver thread—

"Take it off," yells Mike, appearing in the doorway and ignoring Helen's seminakedness. "Ashley says wear the blond wig if it fits—better foil for Kate."

"It doesn't fit," I mouth, hoping my teeth won't be heard onstage clashing like castanets, "I've tried it." I'd hoped it would disguise me.

The clock's hands move forward relentlessly. Chris, acting callboy, knocks so hard on the door that the whole room quivers. Helen, strikingly transfigured into Kate, stands up to admire herself, while I admire her calm. My hands are having Saint Vitus's dance all by themselves. Will they ever control Bianca's lute—or will the audience think I'm juggling? I dig my nails into my palms to avert hysterics. Helen picks up a book and settles down to read. The book's upside down. Each time anyone comes in or out an increasing buzz of sound from the auditorium comes too.

Then everything's quiet. The curtain must have risen. Ashley's cut the Induction a good deal, bearing in mind that too much Sly could bore the pants off his Italian audiences. At last someone opens the door again, and we hear the trampling of feet in the corridor as Lucentio and Tranio go past to begin the play within a play. Helen rises, still with that studied self-control, and sweeps past me to the wings. I follow, concentrating on Bianca's speech: " 'Sister, content you in my discontent—' "

First entrance over. Butterflies finish sarabanding as I radiate gentle modesty. Soon I'm making my exit while behind me Katharine starts her ranting. " 'Why, and I trust I may go too—' "

Watch from the wings. One has to admit Helen's very good—an imperious, beautiful scold, who easily holds the center of the stage. Soon she joins me in the wings and stands beside me, watching. Her saving grace is that she really loves her work. She *is* Kate now, and totally absorbed.

The house atmosphere is warm, the auditorium almost full; the only expensive seats left vacant are those right at the sides. So far the play's going well, and Ashley certainly holds them. He's warned us that for a foreign audience we must exaggerate our speech and mime; and when Petruchio exits there's spontaneous applause. It seems next to no time till the whole scene's past and Bianca's called on to defend herself from Kate. Helen's blows are plainly tempered by Ashley's warning. But I turn away my face and raise an arm as though to hide my tears.

My belled sleeve cuts off the footlights' glare. Rows of faces leap out at me from the side stalls. Two people who've just entered, a man and woman, are lowering themselves into their seats. Faces, the faces— My arm still raised, I stiffen.

It's like being frozen in ice . . . or paralyzed.

Robert. *Robert*—

The face remembered in that hospital.

I think time has stopped.

Baptista's " 'Bianca, stand aside. Poor girl! she weeps. Go ply thy needle' " goes disobeyed. There's desperation in his voice as I still stand immovable, and he even takes my wrist to shake me slightly. At last I turn to him with a shattered look which must be extravagant even for Bianca. It surprises him so that he stammers and stutters at Kate, forgets a line, splutters out, " 'Thou— thou hilding of a devilish spirit.' " And sticks. After waiting some seconds for the cue that doesn't come, Helen plunges in furiously with " 'Her silence flouts me, and I'll be revenged,' " and flies after me offstage, where she begins hissing at me like an angry goose.

I'm dazed, can barely hear her. All I see is Robert— Robert, and with him Anita.

"What's the *matter* with you?" hisses Helen. She'll really strike me in a moment, outside her role. "You going to have a fit or something?"

My fingers are tearing at my snood, shaking, trying to drag it off. I mumble something about Janet, yes, I'm feeling ill—

"You fool, Silvie—Janet's not here tonight! You'll go onstage again or Ashley and I'll together wring your neck." Helen's hands hover dramatically, as though reaching for it. But she's really about to push my head down, convinced I'm going to faint.

Janet! She stayed with Griselda; I'd forgotten. I'm trapped, thoughts whirling. Robert, Anita, Janet, yew trees— Must still be Bianca. I straighten up, and Helen, anxiously watching me, straightens my snood.

"All right now?"

"All right." Weak nod. "Pretty odd, I felt. Maybe I—ate something."

"Not you as *well.* There must be some bloody virus going round!"

From the stage Petruchio's voice, and others'. Helen—Kate—still watching me. Robert and Anita waiting for me.

Bianca has no more appearances till Act III.

"Wait in the dressing room. Chris, fetch her a drink." Helen's solicitous for the play, not me.

"No—*please.*" Fighting nausea, I hitch up Bianca's skirts and trail toward the dressing rooms. Safe here? Surely they won't come round, confront me, before everyone? Not halfway through, at least.

Steal van keys from Ashley's pocket? Change? Run for it? Leaving the players—my friends—Paul, in one horrible hell of a mess—

Confession of guilt, confession of knowledge.

Confession I know the Hilliard's there.

Of course I must have known, mustn't I?

If things would clear completely, not swirl toward me in dreadful snatches, odd forms, half hidden by mists.

Anita . . . Anita—Robert's cherished, most loved mistress. That's clear, at least. Paul said— And I see now. Where *is* Paul?

At last Helen comes to join me in the dressing room. "Better? Not going to spoil the play?"

"C-could we send Chris for Janet?"

"He's playing Curtis. *Can't* you—?"

"OK. I'll manage."

"You know, for a moment I thought you might have seen someone—in the audience—"

I look long and shakily into the glass, touch my forehead with powder. "Did you? Strange idea." My laugh's an achievement.

If only I could reach Paul! But he's either in the audience or drinking at the bar. Has he met up with—them?

And here's the call for Bianca's entrance and the third act.

20

I'll never forget—odd words for an amnesiac—this performance. In Bianca's role, anyway, the third act is the greatest ordeal: here's the big chance to shine or falter. Falter? While placid "sweet Bianca" take a music lesson from Hortensio, and her suitors quarrel, unquiet Silvia is swamped. The shattering appearance of Robert has accomplished what all my own endeavors, and the doctors', failed to do. It's as though someone has depth-charged my mind and blown a hole in the dam that kept the deep waters of memory contained. A hole in time as well.

Bianca flirts with Hortensio, fingering his lute, while, as Silvia, I see before me, not the stylized court of Baptista's house and the false orange trees in pots, but the illumined, honey-colored stone façade of Waterbury itself, rising E-shaped, square-towered, glittering with the many glass-set tall windows that prove Elizabethan Clare of Waterbury was almost as wealthy in her day as Bess of Hardwick. Bianca wears simple white and pearls, while Silvia's body best remembers the stiff, gorgeous dress and harsh-pricking ruff of Kate. Yes, we—I did play the *Shrew* at Waterbury—performed for charity, strutted and quarreled on the velvet lawns where four centuries ago the Tudor queen, crimped, painted, and jeweled like some rare reliquary, held court under a silk-draped canopy.

I, Bianca, make dove's eyes at Hortensio, while I, Silvia, stand cooling myself by a fountain in the Long Walk, waiting in the play's interval for Robert to join me—waiting, pretending I'm Elizabeth with her white face and shrewd heavy-lidded eyes—for she'd surely stood by this same fountain in the moonlight, seen Waterbury's towers against the stars, heard the rustle of a night bird as I was hearing it—

A loud night bird to make such rustling! Or perhaps my ears were keener than most people's. Or maybe sound travels easily at night, on a damp air, among pleached alleys and through tunnels of ancient yew hedge.

My slippered foot pressed hard against the fountain's rim. The gardens were eerie at night, but pleasantly, stiff with a sense of past. I felt very much alone, because most of the audience and actors were mingling in the Great Hall for a glass of wine.

"Robert?" softly, "Robert . . . is that you?"

There was no response. The rustling had stopped, but now my senses were all keyed up; I knew people were close to me. Holding my skirts, I tiptoed along beside the yew hedge toward the house. Why I felt secrecy important I can't say—call it instinct which kept me to the shadows. At one place a small tree stood alone, carved into a proud peacock. There I paused. Perhaps I was mistaken? And then I heard the rustle approaching, though on the other side of the hedge. I drew back, watching. Into a small space, where a pathway crossed between the yews, stepped—Anita. Anita, with whom Robert swore he'd finished. Anita, who had spoken no word to him that night, though both were here as guests, who had ostentatiously turned her back on him before my eyes. Was she trying to spy upon us both? How could she have known that we were meeting here?

I stood rigid, but she didn't look my way, only back down the way she'd come, from the long walk parallel to the one where I had waited. She stood and smiled, and waved, blew a kiss to someone out of my sight, and then went on unhurriedly toward the house, moonlight glinting on the green-and-blue pattern of her dress. I saw her long shining dark hair and the gleam of silver bracelets. Then she was out of sight.

I walked back, very slowly to the fountain. Halfway there I saw Robert step out into the space ahead of me and stand waiting as I'd done, one foot tapping thought-fully against the fountain's rim. When I emerged from the deep shadows which ran beside the yew hedge I saw he'd heard me coming, for he stood too still, his listening pose was artificial.

"Am I—early?"

He turned, looked me up and down, and held out his hands, smiling at me. "You sound like 'a Kate conformable as other household Kates.' Not very, love."

I didn't run into his arms, as I would have done before seeing Anita. I just stood there, and he slowly lowered them.

"I thought everyone else was in the house drinking. But there was someone walking behind the hedge—perhaps it was a ghost? Did *you*"—casually—"see anyone?"

He was silent a moment. The fountain was tinkling in silver arcs behind him, and though he wore modern dress I almost expected to see a pearl dangling from his ear, or the outline of a ruff. Then he answered mildly, "Why, no—but maybe a few others came out to get a breath of air. The hall's very hot. Have you had wine, my Kate?"

I joined him at the fountain's edge, thankful my face was in shadow. Anita could have been blowing kisses to someone else; it wasn't probable. I could see no reason for this elaborate charade, this pretense of estrangement, since it wasn't Robert's habit to hide his loves, even from me. I was angry, jealous, confused; at the bottom of it all, wary, and—oddly afraid.

"I don't drink during performances."

"We'll make up for it afterward, then." He moved behind me to put his arms round my waist. I didn't lean back but stared into the fountain as though hypnotized. Robert murmured in my ear, "What appalling garments for lovers! It's like trying to stroke an armadillo." He turned me, to kiss my neck expertly; I could feel his lips traveling down toward my breasts, which were

157

pushed up high by the constraining bodice. I fought off my responses, suspicious that this lovemaking was meant to take my mind off other visitors to these dark gardens.

"The intermission must be almost over."

I could feel him laughing. "Relax, relax, my pretty Kate. You know, you're damned good in the part. Caroline Waterbury's as pleased as Punch, and very grateful. I hope acting with amateurs isn't too much of a strain for once."

"Is acting a strain for you?" I nearly asked, but couldn't. No rows between acts. "I'm glad to help. After all, it's for charity."

"There speaks my correct, my eager little Silvie."

I pushed him away. "Don't be so damned condescending, Robert. It was partly the attraction of the house and—and everything. Taking the chief part four hundred years after it was first played here—"

"You felt the great Elizabeth out there watching you?"

"I did, really . . . *No*, Robert, we've not time."

"You're very fierce tonight. Well in Kate's role. Shall I Petruchio you?"

And then Bianca's words again as the servant summons her offstage. " 'Farewell, sweet masters, both; I must be gone!' " And exit. Stand in the wings while Hortensio's little speech is done. Shake in confusion as one scene at Waterbury is swallowed up in nightmare fashion by another. The Great Hall at Waterbury—

"We simply can't thank you enough. You see, we always have someone down from London to help the local players, but this year, somehow"—a pretty and appealing gesture that aptly describes failure—"nobody! No one at all suitable, only a grand old out-of-work actor who wanted to play Lear! Can you imagine Lear on the lawn? And it had to be this play, now, because after all it's just four hundred years, and everyone said it would be right."

"I enjoyed it immensely. It was like being taken over by the past. Marvelous."

"You're too kind. I can't tell you how much it's meant to everybody. They work so hard for this always. If there's anything we can do for you in exchange—"

"There isn't truly. Robert told you I wouldn't—"

"Yes, but Robert must help you change your mind! Isn't that so, Robert?" She turns to him, smiling like an angel, and for one moment I'm smitten with envy. To look like that! To be such a natural, friendly person, and beautiful, and have two sons and two daughters by the age of twenty-eight . . . Own Waterbury too—at least be mistress of it.

"Ah, Caroline," says Robert, leaning back in the leather watchman's chair that stands by the huge stone fireplace, "you're banging your head against solid teak. For all Silvie looks such a charming girl, she's got a stubborn will. How else did she get so well under the shrewskin? If you want to reward her, let her slaver over Waterbury to her heart's content; there's no corner that won't appeal to her romantic side. And write her down in the household records, so that four hundred years later everyone knows that Silvia Klavetti played Katharine the shrew upon your lawns."

"Reward enough," I murmur. "As Robert says."

Lady Waterbury looks uncertainly from one to the other of us, sighs, and shakes her well-coiffed head. After a minute she adds very determinedly, "*I* know what I'll do. We'll have that engraver friend of Ned's engrave a goblet for you—a scene of Waterbury, with the players, and your name beside Katharine's on a scroll. And its twin done, for the house."

"There's glory for you," says Robert, smiling.

I'm so delighted I can't speak.

"And if you'd care to see all the fragile treasures we don't put on show, just say. I'll give you a personally conducted tour." She rises, smoothing down her skirt.

"I'm going up to see Simon and Jeremy have their baths. Robert will give you a drink, and then we'll all dine together. No one but us, and perhaps the Armadales. He wants your autograph! My dear, you've made a big success." She smiles at me and goes.

"Well done, Silvie angel. At first shot you've breached the formidable aristocratic barricades that keep lesser people out. You've earned yourself this lazy, long weekend too. Now how about a stiff, relaxing drink?"

"What are the 'fragile treasures,' Robert?"

"Oh, infinitely beguiling. You shall see."

Treasures, beguiling treasures—

Paul's hand on my arm. The look of horror on his face is almost funny. "Silvie! Must speak to you—"

"I know, I've already—"

Someone clutches me by the other arm. "Silvia, are you mad? We're waiting—and you should have changed. Bring her dress—*quickly*."

Even Helen helps, gorgeously tricked out for Kate's marriage though she is. Bianca's yellow robe, with its fat Renaissance sleeves, is forced over my head on top of the white dress. The tightness almost chokes me.

"Lucky that white looks like a petticoat—where's her other snood? Someone comb her hair."

I'm pushed, yanked, smoothed into shape. Breathless. Memory and speeches muddled together in a mentally indigestible lump. Ashley's hand in the small of my back pushes me toward the stage.

Thank God for the footlights hiding Robert's and Anita's faces. The thought of their seeing me is bad enough, makes me feel as exposed as someone hung upon a gibbet. A flood of bitterness rises in me at Katharine's words, " 'He'll woo a thousand . . . yet never mean to wed where he hath wooed,' " and " 'Though he be merry, yet withal he's honest.' "

That *is* a stab.

I follow weeping Katharine from the stage.

Paul hasn't waited, and I wonder why. I don't know whether to be glad or sorry—relieved, I think, now that I'm almost overwhᵤlmed by these floods of returning memories. Robert at least can't come and find me in the wings. Helen doesn't bother to scold me; she's given me up as either sick or crazy. We wait together in silence. Bianca re-enters in her sister's wake and for some while has only to react. I find myself, well trained by Ashley, reacting like a sweet puppet outwardly while inwardly obsessed.

"Well, Silvia, are you impressed?"

"I—I've no words—"

No, there are none. None for the glories of Waterbury. I suppose most of us could barely hope to own one object from its store of treasures, and then only if we'd saved for it a lifetime. Lady Waterbury's laughing at me, but kindly—I've been standing, my mouth wide open, before a Samuel Palmer. The ceiling in this high room is by Angelica Kauffmann. A side table was made for the Prince Regent, the silver candlesticks are by Paul Storr, the clock ticking in the corner is a Tompion. It's like that all through the house. And then one comes on some touching object which makes quite recent Waterburys as real as their ancestors. An ivory box of visiting cards, a water color of a favorite dog, signed Nana, and upstairs, in the nursery, a cradle of basketwork with faded bows.

"It must be weird to own all this."

"Ah, but we don't own it. We're just custodians. My husband sometimes says that it owns us. Experts on this or that are always coming to see us . . . very time-consuming."

"I can see that. The house has a sort of sucking power—so strong! And at once you're drawn back to Elizabeth and—"

"Yes, her time's really the strongest draw of all. Of

161

course the main part of the house was built then. It was our greatest period, wasn't it?"

"Elizabeth," I say, dwelling on the word. "Gloriana."

"I'm truly sorry we can't show you one of our special treasures. Gloriana's own gift to the family after her visit."

"That miniature? I remember it on television when the house was done."

"Yes, we had a lot of publicity then, Too much. I was very glad the system had been installed."

"Burglar-proof," puts in Robert, an odd note of amusement in his voice.

"Oh, completely." Nevertheless she wears a slight frown.

"Electronics, rays, the lot?"

She laughs. "Everything! They tell us we're absolutely safe now."

"You don't sound convinced, Caroline."

"We're *too* secure. It goes off if you look at it. In spite of endless scoldings, the children, little brutes, have had the police up here twice already! I'm afraid everyone may get less vigilant if this goes on. And I don't think it's set quite right. Once or twice it's done it on its own—apparently."

"Get the men back who installed it."

"My dear, such a business. It would mean turning everything off for a while as well. Still, while the Hilliard's away being restored by that man you—"

"I should certainly have it put right while the miniature's safe elsewhere," says Robert. And immediately begins to talk of something else.

That night I could see for myself the inconvenience of the elaborate system; it went off while I was in my bath, causing havoc among guests and staff. The police arrived, and the inventory seemed to take all evening. As I went upstairs I heard Lady Waterbury say again, with conviction, "It really *must* be seen to before the

Hilliard comes back." And it was still the main subject of conversation next day at breakfast time.

"Quite sure it wasn't one of the children?" Hubert Waterbury asked his wife.

"Nurse is positive. They were with her and the *au pair.*"

"Someone playing a joke?"

"I don't ask people to the house who have that sort of humor. It would be too wearing."

"Yes. Ring the firm, darling. Before the—"

"—Hilliard's back! I shall. The little man's bringing it down next Wednesday."

"I hope you've remembered that Russian chap's coming specially to see it on Friday. The professor from Leningrad."

"Of course I have."

"It's only that he's flying back next day, and it's his one chance of a lifetime, and—"

"Don't fuss, darling. Robert swears his man's reliable; he's the best. One of the backroom boys, who works for private collectors. I made very careful inquiries. He's all right."

"No joke if he wasn't. Lenin himself might start haunting us, as well as Lady Jane."

"Oh darling! Anyway, I'll have the casket all nice and safe, ready for the gem. They must check the system on Monday or Tuesday. You're looking very thoughtful, Silvia. Isn't she?"

"I was just thinking that all this is going to make my flat seem a little—well, homely, when I get back."

"Ah, never mind, my Kate." Robert casually put an arm round my shoulders. "At least no police and electronics will disturb you there, and you can bathe in peace."

I couldn't help drawing away a little. Inwardly I saw Anita, in her blue and green and silver, walking between the yews. And yet Anita had gone back to London, and here was I, the favored guest, on my last morning here, waiting to be driven home by an attentive Robert.

"I wish—" I said thoughtfully, and then colored. For I'd almost said how much I longed to see Waterbury's magnificent grounds in autumn, and the hall dressed for Christmas with holly and ivy and mistletoe, where the Lord of Misrule used to reign.

I think Lady Waterbury almost read my thoughts. "You must come down to us again. I'll write and invite you for a few days when you're not working and want to get away from stuffy, polluted old London."

"Thank you—I'd love it." She meant it at the time, but in my heart I knew she said it to everyone from a habit of kindness. And there were so many people on her mind. Unless "Ned's friend" did my portrait here for the goblet or I came down with Robert—or paid a guinea fee at the gatehouse—it was unlikely that I'd see the place again.

Sweet Bianca goes offstage after the promise that she should practice how to bride it, stumbling, her head in a whirl. This time Helen's waiting for me in the dressing room—Paul seems to have vanished for good, defeated by the lack of privacy—but before she can complain of my performance I rush past the doorway murmuring *"Doubled—"* and lock myself in the john, where I spend a miserable few minutes trying to sort out some of my mental jumble. All these conversations that I remember word for word—it's like being lent a powerful searchlight and sweeping it round a cave where everything, from homely objects to rare ones, is stored. And I remember other things, and people too: my only surviving relatives, old *nonno* and *nonna,* days in my stage training, myself at school in England; further back still, my Italian mother's death—a lifetime's memories pouring back to fill up emptiness. Then more of Waterbury, and the confusing incidents that happened afterward, now all too explicable.

Someone's pounding urgently on the door. "Silvie, there's a *line* out here!"

And Helen's voice intervenes: "She's ill—it must be Griselda's virus."

"It's curtain up again any minute."

The voices die away; and later I creep out cautiously, back to our dressing room. It's empty. Helen's gone back to the wings. Bianca has no entrance till Scene II. I'm able to drop my head in my hands and sit alone, relaxed. Relaxed!

21

My thoughts turn this way, that way, twisting after truth. Yes—too much truth all at once. And Robert out there, waiting.

We left Waterbury that morning. Robert was so loving, seemed so wholly devoted to me, that I was almost able to dismiss a feeling that he and Anita were up to something. Something—not simply an affair? On the way back to London he said casually, "You're technically 'resting,' aren't you, Silvie?"

"I—yes, I'm between work just now."

"Free to go to Spain?"

"Spain?" I looked cautiously at his profile. "On work?"

"Good Lord, no! You are a career woman now, aren't you? Don't you ever think of anything else?"

"I've got to earn my living," I said stiffly, wondering if Robert knew anything of financial terrors, the driving need to get ahead.

"There are other ways of earning it."

"Like what?"

"Oh, marriage, for instance."

Marriage—but I didn't think *Robert* was offering me that.

"Life's for living, Silvia. I'd like a Spanish trip—London's a dump at this time of year. Come with me, I'll take you down to Andalusia. Heat and color and lemon trees—I can't wait for it. With you," he added, almost as an afterthought.

I sat in silence. A strong breeze through the open window blew my hair across my eyes. Andalusia with Robert. It would be wonderful. It would be wonderful for anyone adult who could take it, who could take unpredictable Robert with a "you play it your way, but

I play it to suit myself" calm. Already I knew that I couldn't. Robert could upset me very deeply because I loved him. Or because I had loved him—did I love him still? I didn't know. But some intuition was sending out warning notes, and I didn't know whether to give it my attention. Life is for living. You can't have life without any risks. . . .

"I'm really keen for you to come." There was greater feeling in his voice now as I hesitated. He took his left hand off the wheel to put it on my knee. Robert, Andalusia—or tramping round the agents'. ("We'll let you know if anything suitable turns up.") There were two hundred pounds in my bank. Everything I had.

"All right. But I'll pay my way."

"Don't be so middle-class, love."

"I've a fancy for independence." It was a long while since I'd felt able to speak in that easy, certain manner with Robert. I felt pleased with myself.

"Well—" He looked sideways at me, grinned. "I've a fancy for you."

"Yes?"

"Yes. Are you going to stick to that throughout Spain? Chocolate and doughnuts in the gutter while I wave at you from expensive *albergos?*"

"The gutter? How do you know what I can or can't afford?"

"I won't call that bluff. Listen Silvie, *I* won't come unless you let me pay for the fun side. You can be as righteous as you like about paying for your journey. Next Wednesday suit you?"

"Perfectly, so far as I know. Unless I'm flying to New York with Paul!"

He just laughed. "I'm going up north for a few days. Let's see. I might travel with you, or I may have to meet you in Madrid. We could hire a car there." Although it sounded spontaneous, I had a feeling it was all worked out already.

"Fair enough." I felt a bit daunted, but it was wrong to show any form of dependence with Robert; it put him off.

We were in the outskirts of London now. He was pulling the car off the road into a lay-by near a pub. He'd become very businesslike suddenly. "Have a drink here. Fix up the details."

"Is there such a hurry?"

"I've said I'm going north."

I followed him inside. He looked around, beckoned to the barman, ordered drinks, threw a packet of cigarettes onto a small round table. "Sit, Silvie. Shan't be long. Going to telephone."

I sat smoking. I smoked two cigarettes and had my glass refilled. Unease had returned in full measure. Why on earth had I said I'd go? Life is for living—but not for rows all the way from Madrid to Andalusia. I was gathering up my bag when Robert returned.

"Apologies. Couldn't get through, there was a block on the line." His eyebrows went up. "Leaving?"

"I—it's getting late."

"You're getting touchy. Sit down, Silvie, love, and let me lecture you. Men don't like women who are always looking for slights. Could I help the line being blocked?"

"You could have waited to telephone."

"No, I couldn't. I want to fix things up with you right now, before you start slipping through my fingers. Don't keep expecting me to say 'I love you, Silvie,' because I'm not the type. But I wouldn't have wanted your company if I weren't entirely keen on the idea."

I felt rather stupid and looked down, biting my lip.

"Umbrage over?" He put his arm round me, drawing me toward him. "It's as I thought—these conferences I'm due at, they could finish early or late. Two in the North, one back here. You book yourself in on the midday plane. I'll join you if I can—and if not, later."

This time I did say, unwisely, "Couldn't we— I'd sooner wait too."

But I knew at once that, for some reason he wouldn't share, he wanted it his way. "Midday will be nicer for you," he said, not even bothering to make it sound reasonable.

"There—there might be difficulties about the seats."

"Nonsense. My secretary will see to mine. She'll make it exchangeable. Business methods!"

"I didn't know you had a secretary?"

"Sometimes." He brushed it off as unimportant. "When you reach Madrid you can go to—" He named what even I recognized as an expensive, famous hotel.

"I—I'd be conspicuous there alone! I'd feel awkward. I—I haven't the clothes."

He looked exasperated. "Who cares these days? Go couture or hippy, nobody cares. Wear a sari, Silvie, if you're going to be grand about my not buying clothes for you!" He grinned. "Your hair's all right, which is what really matters." He stroked my head gently. "Anyway, I've said I'm paying for the fun side—and Madrid will surely be fun. There. Have we fixed it nicely?"

We'd fixed it, anyway. I wanted to back out, but my pride said "you'll look silly." Perhaps I was being silly after all; other women took these tangled difficulties with calm and good humor and independence.

"Fixed."

He stood, and downed the remnants of his drink in one gulp. "Come on." As we walked back to the car he said in wheedling tones, "Could I ask you not to say I'm coming with you?"

I stood still, my mouth open.

"Don't get cross again. It's purely for business reasons. I don't want some people to know I'm away."

My thoughts flew at once to Anita.

"*Business*, I said, Silvie."

It was one of the worst things about my relationship

with Robert: he could be so open, and at other times acted so badly, that it was hard to know when he was really being innocent; it led to paranoia. I got into the car and drew the door to with a bang. He got in the other side and sat silent for a minute. Then he said, "It's true."

I swallowed. I was confused—no more angry with Robert than furious with myself for always getting back into this sort of mess with him. Perhaps I wouldn't buy that ticket—

"It's a fun trip for me, that's all. *If* I come, I'll just say I'm well into the Spanish scene. Why should you think I'd want to boast about it?"

He lit a cigarette and switched on the ignition. "That's fine, then."

We didn't speak again until we reached the house where I was living. I didn't know if he wanted to come in or not, but I wouldn't ask him. He didn't get out, just leaned toward me and kissed me thoroughly in silence. As I began extricating myself he said, "See you in a few days, then, Silvie? And get that seat booked quickly or you mayn't get one."

"*If* I come, I will."

"Please come, darling Silvie." As I looked back at him uncertainly he added, "I'll call you before then, anyhow." And drove away.

I didn't hear from Robert. But as fretting can be a worse source of misery than almost anything else, I went ahead and booked my seat. After all, why shouldn't I have a trip to Spain, anyway? Two hundred pounds in the bank isn't much help these days; I might just as well get it out and enjoy it. Paul rang me several times, but I put him off. The last time he said, "You sound excited. Anything up?" And I said, not particularly. But I was excited all the same—and a bit apprehensive. Robert was

170

so mercurial. I did begin to fret—if he doesn't call me, maybe I should cancel after all—

The telephone rang late on Monday. I'd been filling in time all day—reading, washing some clothes—not eating much, because Social Security for a "resting" actress isn't exactly riches.

"Is that Miss Klavetti, Silvia Klavetti?"

"Yes."

"Hullo. I'm Ada, Robert's secretary."

It was the first I'd heard of an Ada; and a secretary who was on Christian-name terms didn't endear herself to me.

"He's sorry not to ring you himself, but he's been held up all day. He wants to know if you could possibly take a trip out of London tomorrow and meet him for lunch?"

"Where out of London?"

"Not very far. I've looked up trains for you. It's only an hour and a half from Paddington. A little place—Winslow Martyr."

The name seemed familiar.

"Why there, for heaven's sake?"

"He's seeing a—client, nearby. It's his only chance of meeting up with you before Wednesday. Winslow Martyr's said to have a very good pub, the Bear and Crown."

I thought, how like Robert—but I wouldn't really mind a day in the country. . . .

"Miss Klavetti? Are you there?"

"I'll meet him at one if the trains are right."

"Fine, I'll tell him. There's a train reaches Winslow Martyr at 12:30. But he thought you might prefer to drive, in which case I'll arrange with a London garage at his expense for you to pick up a car."

"I'm sure he knows I'd sooner drive."

"Then the garage is Callot's, in Chesterfield Drive—that's not far from you. Would a Mini do?"

"Beautifully. Thanks for letting me know."

"A pleasure. Goodbye, Miss Klavetti."

I was going to ask where she was calling from, but the line went dead.

The boy said, "Miss Klavetti? We got your message and the deposit. The white Mini's for you; had her filled ready. Sign here, please. We'll send you in a bill."

It was probably easier not to confuse an underling with Robert's name and address. Robert could pay me later. I signed.

As I drove out of London negotiating heavy traffic I thought idly that Winslow Martyr, as I'd placed it on the map, wasn't all that far from Waterbury. About eighteen miles. Tomorrow Robert's "reliable little man" would be returning the Hilliard. A pity it wasn't today, or I might have summoned up enough nerve to ask Lady Waterbury if I could see it. But Robert—we—probably wouldn't have the time anyway.

A lovely day. I was now really looking forward to Madrid. I turned on the radio. The Rolling Stones came over loud and clear. Soon I switched off and began to sing.

Three hours later I didn't feel like singing. I was blackly furious. Robert could enjoy being the elusive and sought-after mystery man as much as he pleased, but whatever tycoon games he was enjoying now didn't excuse his not turning up at all or ringing to explain what kept him. At the pub they'd never heard of him, and there was no table booked.

I'd certainly cancel Spain. (If it was possible to get the money back—I had insured.) I ate my lunch, determined not to be put off food by Robert's negligence. Perhaps he was mad. Maybe he had a psychopathic streak. Damn him, damn him, *damn* him. Seething fury, a huge steak, and a large double whisky together gave me indigestion.

The day was still lovely anyhow. As I was out of fumy London, I might as well stay out. See and smell the lush green, forget damnable Robert's damnable behavior. He could bloody well pay for the car—three times over. And my lunch.

I drove erratically. The magnetism of the house must have drawn me, for I found myself later quite near Waterbury. Pity about the Hilliard—but I wouldn't have felt calm enough for social chitchat with Caroline W. From a hilltop I could see the Elizabethan high windows glittering in the valley. And yew hedges, and pleached walks. Hell take you, Robert . . . I clashed the gears, was miserable, knew I couldn't pretend the day was pleasant any more, and turned toward the London road.

22

I reached the house where my flat was at about six, having returned the Mini. As I ran up the steps I thought: bath, sleep, and *not* think. Inside the entrance hall Robert was waiting for me near my door.

He looked quite calm. "Tired, Silvie? Are you very angry with me?"

"Very."

"It wasn't my fault."

"It never is."

"Look, can I come inside a minute?"

"No."

"Please, girl, give me one chance to explain. I've brought you two lovely presents, to make up."

"I don't want your presents or your explanation. But I'm not going to stand out here arguing either."

I stuck my key in the lock. Robert assumed I'd agreed to let him in and followed me inside with an unusually subdued air.

I said curtly, "You can mix me a drink. It's in the sitting room. I'm going to wash off the dust," and retreated into my bathroom. I heard the chink of glass behind me and shut the door.

When I came out again, still tired and angry, but feeling more able to cope, I found Robert sitting crosslegged on a cushion, his parcels beside him, an iced drink in his hand, and a treatise on Zen Buddhism open on his knees. He looked like a zealous youth in attendance on a Master. I repressed a grim smile. A more inadequate description of Robert at any time . . .

"You've made free with what remained of my gin."

"I made you one twice as big, sweet Silvie. You tell me what a hound you think I am, and then I'll tell you why you shouldn't."

"I don't need to tell you, do I?"

"That's shortened it." He dropped my book and reached lazily for my hand. I withdrew it sharply.

"There's a telephone system all over this modernized country of ours."

He made no attempt to recapture my hand, just stared at me with a faint smile. "Agreed. And yes, I left it rather late—didn't know till rather late, in fact. And then I couldn't get through. The line seemed eternally busy. Blocked. Or something.

"Or something. The line's always getting blocked for you."

Robert shrugged, sipping his drink in a maddeningly appreciative manner. "It's the truth. I can't help it if you don't believe me, can I?"

"It's such a—a *despicable* excuse!" I burst out. "I mean, it's quite impossible to fault it, but all the same—"

"All the same, you look enchanting when you're angry. It's almost worth bringing fury to the pink, pink cheeks, et cetera. There wasn't anything I could do about it, Silvie. I was held up, couldn't get a train, couldn't get you mixed in at the same time as this chap I had to see."

"All these mysterious chaps. Explain them for once."

"My dear, it would bore you stiff. I deal with this and that. Call me the eternal middleman, if you like. But all my income depends on being agreeably there when I'm wanted, in possession of certain facts—or things."

"Some sort of commercial racket, I suppose. The business world is so sordid."

"Modern living depends on that sordid world, you know. Economy. Housing, food—the lot. You should be glad you've got a man who knows how to find his way about in it and makes it work for him."

To have Robert lecturing me in that smug way made me angrier still.

"I'm *not* thankful. I'm used to creative artists round me, people like—"

175

"Like Paul, I suppose. He merely works the artistic systems rather more incompetently than I do the business ones. I can see I'm not getting anywhere." He rose, brushing down his clothes. "So I'll take myself off."

"And take your presents with you." I picked up two parcels which were cumbering a chair and almost hurled them at him.

"Ah no, Silvie, it's enough! I know you think I'm impossible, but either you like me or you don't, see? I've said I'm sorry, and I've brought you two of the nicest things I could find at the end of a long day—" There was a fairly pathetic note in his voice. It wasn't often I'd heard Robert pathetic, and the angry hardness within me softened slightly. "Your gentler side would let me off—it's your Italian ancestors I'm up against. A whole long line of matriarchal viragoes hurling platefuls of *pasta* at their spouses—" He looked down at the parcels in his arms, and added mournfully, "Some *pasta*."

"All right," I said rather ungraciously, "I'll forgive you. I'm too tired to do anything else. Though it's the last time you get off so lightly, see?"

"Damn it, not lightly. These two together cost me nearly fifty pounds. Here, don't you want to see them? I thought a bottle of Patou's 'Joy' and—"

The second parcel contained a beautifully fitted-out soft black leather bag.

"Ideal for traveling, I thought."

I examined it, trying to hide some of my pleasure. "It—it's lovely, so well fitted up inside." There was a bit of folded paper in a side pocket. I pulled it out.

"Better keep that. Shove it in your desk. I had them make out the bill in your name, so if there's any cause for complaint you can take it back and row them"

"There won't be any. It's gorgeous—beautifully made."

He was unstoppering the bottle of "Joy" to smell it. "So I'm forgiven?"

"This one last time."

He held me for a moment and sighed. "Lord, I'm tired! Only one more river to cross— Wish I could stay on here tonight, but I only looked in to cull forgiveness." He yawned. He did seem very tired. White under his tan. Perhaps Robert felt the tensions of modern living more than I'd thought. There were those times he'd taken acid—maybe his erratic behavior came from— But LSD didn't tie in with the modern business scene. "Dinner, chairman makes speech, guest of honor replies, blah-blah—" He kissed me. "Thank God, guest of honor isn't me. Enough wine will see me through till four in the morning, I suppose."

"Then I won't look in at *your* flat tonight either."

"You wouldn't enjoy seeing me totter drunkenly in at four. Lemon trees in Andalusia—that's more it. Now— practical matters. Have you got that key I gave you? I'd better leave one with the porter while we're away."

"Sorry," I said guiltily, "but I—I've mislaid it."

"*Where?* In the *flat?*" He seemed very put out.

"Lost rather than mislaid. You see, my awful old bag fell open in the tube the other day and some things dropped out. I thought I'd picked them all up, but I've not seen that key since."

I couldn't think why he was looking relieved, but maybe I was misinterpreting his expression.

"Well, it can't be helped. Sleep sound, Silvie. Got your ticket and all safely planned?" I nodded. "See you either on the midday plane, then—or late tomorrow in Madrid." He kissed me again, picked up the wrapping paper murmuring, "I'll put this out for you on my way," and went. A last, practical touch which left me with a sense of anticlimax.

The combination of gin and reconciliation did have a pepping-up effect, though. My energy returned. I checked the contents of my suitcase, washed my hair, made myself salad and strong black coffee. I dawdled over the meal, playing an LP on my record player and feeling pleasantly relaxed. By this time my hair was almost dry, and as I'd read every book in the flat, there was nothing to do. I rang Paul for a chat, but there was no answer. I might have rung other friends and gone out with them, but I was saving my money for Madrid. I was restless, wanting Robert. Perhaps a walk . . . My bedroom was in a mess when I went through to find a kerchief. I had to root for one in a drawer where the lining paper was all crumpled up. As I smoothed it, my fingers encountered something slippery and metallic. It was the missing key, which I'd thought lost forever in the underground.

Here was a purpose for the walk. No, a bus ride. I put the key in an envelope, scrawled Robert's name on the outside, and let myself out of the flat. Because the weather was fine, there were a lot of people abroad. The buses were full of tourists, and I had to stand all the way to Hyde Park.

Robert's flat was in an expensive block overlooking the park. It had a fine, wide view, and I'd often looked out over the Serpentine, the dusty Row, the curious little restaurant by the bridge where we occasionally dined—a building which always reminded me of plastic eggboxes. Now I'd a fancy to sit alone in Robert's flat enjoying that nostalgic view, and with thoughts of Madrid to come. Besides, though I'd meant only to hand the key in at the desk, the night porter might easily forget to pass it on.

The elevator whined upward to the seventh floor. The passages were dimly lit and empty. There were no sounds, for the block was well built and solid; carpeting was thick, and not even television programs penetrated these walls. I slipped the key out of the envelope to place it in the lock. The door swung inward into the entrance hall. Robert had left a light burning here; he always did, to discourage burglars. It wasn't a large flat, but it had an air of roominess that I approved. Dining room and kitchen led off the hall, and directly opposite me was the entrance to the drawing room, which one had to cross in order to reach Robert's bedroom—this was the flat's one inconvenience.

The drawing-room door was ajar, and I gave it a slight push. A light had been left burning here as well. And another in the bedroom—the glow coming through the bedroom door was reflected in the large ornamental eighteenth-century mirror above the fireplace.

I was just about to cross the threshold when somebody laughed. I froze.

A woman's laugh, low and throaty. She began to murmur in a lazy way—a few words, then a pause; then another few. Afterward came Robert's voice answering hers, deep-toned. It was impossible to hear what he was saying, but—

Nausea rose in me. The one thing I wanted was to retreat from the flat as fast as possible before I was discovered. I didn't want to know who was with him, only to escape; but somehow I couldn't move. It was as though this revelation of a mean little betrayal had paralyzed me completely. I stood with my eyes fixed on the graceful mirror and peered at it as Snow White's stepmother must have peered into the mirror on her wall.

After a few seconds what I had known would happen, happened. The bedroom door was pulled wide open, and the figure of a woman appeared. If she hadn't been occupied in tying a belt she must have looked up and seen me watching, but her eyes were on her fingers which were struggling with a knot. It was Robert's dressing gown she wore; her feet were bare. She said, laughing a little, "You lazy brute! Why should I fetch you wine, as though you were some Eastern potentate?"

"Because I'm more tired than you are."

"You say? You're a somewhat exhausting lover, sweet, did you know? *Damn* this tie—" Still struggling with it, she walked forward into the room. She was going to the side cabinet, where Robert kept his drinks. Her dark hair, her profile, her slim silhouette crossed the corner of the mirror and disappeared from view.

"Are you sure you wouldn't like rum instead?"

"Why should I?"

"Because I would—rum and lemon. I'm in a Caribbean mood. Hot and swinging."

"No comments."

"Besides, rum for a rum go! And it's a very rum go you've involved us in, Robert, my darling."

If I could only have gone! But I didn't dare move. Although she was out of sight, she was closer to me than before. Surely she would hear any stealthy movement—even my breathing.

Perhaps I should have stormed in and had a scene, but some intuition deeper than any mere dislike of scenes or humiliation warned me off. A sense of danger. I could only stand there absolutely still, thankful she hadn't come into the room a few seconds earlier, when she would most certainly have heard me at the door.

The chink of glass, the sound of liquid pouring into a tumbler.

Robert murmured something I couldn't catch, which she answered in a ruminative tone. "You're a bit demonic, Robert, love. Not many men would cold-bloodedly involve a nice, silly girl in this. I'm almost sorry for the little fool—why should she be fated to carry the can for a man like you?"

"Don't you appreciate a man like me? She does, that's all."

Suppose Robert saw fit to come out of the bedroom too? It would be like some awful French farce—a farce with a difference. The sense of danger was a true one.

"That's why I said she was a fool. Who sups with the

devil, et cetera. And I hold a very long spoon, don't forget, my dear."

"Is that a threat?"

"Ah, that would be telling. . . . Here, want these cheese biscuits too?"

"Bring everything. If all goes well, there won't be a can for her to carry, will there? I'm inclined to think my luck will hold. You and I'll both be richer for it—much richer."

"Poor little beast, something tells me the luck couldn't possibly be that good for anyone. I'm coming with a tray, lover, get ready."

The glass reflected her again. This time I saw only Anita's back, her dark hair swinging to her waist, the points of her elbows as she held the tray before her. She kicked the bedroom door wider open, walked through, kicked it almost shut again. There was laughter. Two voices mingled together, muffled now. I took one last look at that well-known and now demonic-seeming room, the gilded glass reflecting it. A Robert-and-Silvia setting that was now the setting for something so sinister and horrible. And got myself out of the flat as quickly and silently as I could go.

23

It's a mercy Bianca has so little to do while Kate's brutalized. No wonder my sick memory's recovery has been so retarded, with this turmoil and terror underneath. So I know now why I ran out on Robert. One thing's clear at least—I'm blameless. Or am I? As Gian said, would someone blameless have attracted a situation like the Carminottis? Something pretty questionable in me must have latched onto Robert and Robert's world, made me refuse to recognize him for what he was: too glib, too moneyed, too evasive about how he came by his income. So, as Shakespeare knew, white Bianca isn't as faultless as she may seem. I walk through the rest of my part, though Ashley's and Helen's furious glances warn me of wrath to come.

"*Smile* at us—or I'll break your neck later," hisses outraged Ashley in my ear. With an effort I drag my attention back to the stage feast. The play's ending and the audience shouting their delight.

One hand in Lucentio's, the other in Petruchio's. Bow. Again. Ashley's grip bruises; I hope Petruchio won't hit me as we go off. In their enthusiasm people are standing, clapping, calling our names.

Ashley and Helen take a final call alone.

I pick up my skirts and fly to the dressing room.

"Silvie, thank God you're first!" Paul, looking strained, is there already. "I tried to keep out of sight, but too late. It would have seemed odd to avoid him, don't you think? He's very affable. Wants you and me to sup with them."

I sink onto a chair and look up at him in dismay.

"Haven't committed us, just said I'd ask you."

"Did he seem—odd in any way?" (How odd he must have *felt*.)

"No. Said you hadn't told him you were coming to Italy. Thanked me for my letter. That's all."

"And what did you say?" (I've pulled off my dress, and start cleaning up my face.)

"Tried not to seem worried. Thought it best to tell him about your accident and loss of memory."

"So—what did he say to that?" My hand pauses in its cleaning work.

"Expressed sympathy."

"Did he, indeeed." I'm about to reveal that my memory's been jarred into activity; but I don't. No time. For here comes Helen, glowering, bearer of angry messages from Ashley.

"One moment, Helen. Paul—" I say, trying to think quickly.

"Well, shall we sup or shan't we?"

"Best not avoid—or seem— Yes." Now Paul's told him of the accident, I can play it as coolly as I please. "Desperately sorry"—I fob off Helen before she can begin—"but I know exactly how Ashley's feeling, and I simply couldn't help it, and I might one day explain. Paul and I have to go out now. Could you save the heavy scoldings until later?"

I pull on my long skirt and brush out my hair. A heavy tan requires no makeup. I dab shadow round my eyes and say "Good night, Helen" very finally.

Paul's arm is supportive as we go through the passage to the stage door. "Wait!" I stop dead. "The Carminottis—Gian? Did you tell him?"

"Nothing beyond the hospital. And meeting you in Rome."

"Good." Now's the chance to add that my memory's returned, but instinct intervenes; let him go on believing in my blankness. It will make things easier for him at supper. After all, *I'm* trained to act.

"Where are we meeting?"

"Stage door. Ah—here's Silvie, Robert."

And I look up into the welcoming face of an accomplished liar, sneak thief—and what else? Things too hard to name.

"Silvie, my poor child! Paul says you've had a dreadful time. I'm so glad we've found you."

I'll bet you are. I almost say, "You were with Anita in the audience, weren't you?" but hold it back—how easily I could be tripped up! I look at him timidly, as if I didn't know him. "Yes. A pretty frightful time."

"Paul shouldn't have run off with you like this after writing to me."

Another chance to blunder. Paul saves us by saying blandly, "Ah, no one knows better than you, Robert, how these things work out sometimes."

Robert squeezes my hands. "He might have let me know."

"Theater people are vague, I'm afraid."

"Paul's only of the theater, not in it."

"Still—it rubs off."

"I must say, for a girl without a memory you're pretty word-perfect onstage."

Is this a dig? "I'm glad you thought so. It's a horrible strain. And good for me, acting in student productions at the moment, rather than risking blackouts on the London stage." (Good thing Ashley's not in earshot.)

Robert's eyes search my face. "You did seem a bit uneasy in the part. A bit—sleepwalking. Shaky sometimes."

"I know. And Ashley isn't pleased."

"Ashley? Oh—ah—the Petruchio. Your producer too?"

Paul interrupts here to say, "Shall we go? Where are we supping, Robert? I'll tell the doorman, in case someone wants to get a message to us about tomorrow."

"Alessandro's. Anita's gone ahead to secure a table." He eyes me penetratingly as we move off. "Remember Anita?"

"I'm afraid not."

Robert gives a twisted smile; he probably felt safe enough about Anita anyway. He doesn't know I saw them in the flat.

Paul puts in, "I remember her. Lovely girl, with dark hair."

"Silvie didn't take to her."

"And yet she came to help you look for me? How very—thoughtful." I hope he doesn't hear the irony in my tone. He avoids the directness of my glance.

"My dear, she's kindhearted. Unlike most beauties. And we're related. She's my cousin, as you won't recall."

My newly found memory doesn't agree with *that*. You pathological liar, I say inwardly, feeling glad of Paul's comforting presence. He swings my left hand in his as we walk. I thank heaven that tonight I've borrowed an old fringed linen shoulder bag of Janet's. I saw Robert give it a searching look. Let him stew. I hope he stews long and hard. As my mind has done.

How badly Anita and Robert must want to know just why I changed my plans—and if I discovered what I shouldn't know. How he must be dying to ask after that fine leather bag! (Now locked in the company's van with all our other gear.) I think: Let them steal it, and it will all be over. . . . Thoughts are brought up with a jerk. Never that! If Anita examines the bag, to find it empty, no amount of lost-memory pleading will save me from some disaster. It won't be Vicenzo, Carmina, Enrico who would be involved in murder then.

"Here we are. They say the food's good." Robert holds open the door for me to pass ahead of him. I press Paul's hand, release it, and walk inside. I hope I'm not just making use of Paul's kindness, as Robert made use of my love. The way the world goes, it's an unkind place, all right. And often fatal to be kind.

Well, here's Anita, drooped glamorously in a shadowy corner, lamplight on shining hair. No need to worry that Anita will prove too kind. I manage to look at her with friendly inquiry as though at a pleasant stranger.

"Hi there, Anita." There's such an edge to Paul's voice that involuntarily I glance at him. Maybe Paul's better equipped for this world than I thought.

"Paul, isn't it?" She smiles a Gioconda smile. "Good to see you. And Silvia."

"And Silvia." Robert gives me a kindling glance—first pouring of treacle over that web for the little fly to walk on. Perhaps Anita doesn't see it as I do, for her smile fixes as though someone's photographed her badly. "We must all be very, very gentle with Silvie. She's had a rotten time." His fingers squeeze mine again as he guides me to my place.

"You needn't be too gentle." I smile up at him. Candid Silvie. Gullible goofball. "In the past they flung people into snake pits to cure them." I look round, wide-eyed. "I'd hate to be flung among snakes, wouldn't you?"

Short silence.

"That was only for madwomen, Silvia."

"Was it? Mightn't some people class amnesia as madness?"

"Of course not."

"So brave of you to go on acting," murmurs Anita. "All those words. Surprisingly—clever." Her eyes challenge me.

"Thanks. But lost memory doesn't affect present learning! Footlights make me feel like a beginner though. I wasn't good tonight, so I'm glad if it wasn't too apparent."

"Not bad at all—a little as though your mind wasn't quite on young Bianca. As though something—you know?—was worrying you. We came in late—I hope that didn't bother you?" She watches me closely.

My hands tense in my lap. Both Robert and Paul are looking at them. "Oh no. What bothers me is about twenty years of submerged memory." Perhaps normal to be tense. But not normal to rush screaming from the restaurant.

Paul saves me by saying lightly, "Much better for Silvie if people don't go on and on about it. Forgive me, Robert, but I'm hungry, if no one else is."

"Ah yes, how right, Paul. Where's the menu—and the wine list? Bet you're both tired to death of *pasta*. Let's have a round of big bloody steaks, or *frutti di mare*, or—Silvie? Anita?"

Robert was always a good host. Look at us: smiling, carefree quartet. Two women, two men, engaged in that happiest of tourist activities, eating, growing voluble on wine. When I fumble in Janet's bag for a handkerchief I notice Robert's eyes fixed on it consideringly. The wine makes me rash, a bit provocative.

"Shabby, isn't it?" I address Anita, one woman to another. "Borrowed from a friend."

"Your bag?" She smiles sweetly. Alert eyes.

"Yes."

Beneath the table Paul touches my knee warningly, seeing me mount the tightrope of my own accord. But he doesn't know that I've thought suddenly of the perfect, simple way out of immediate trouble.

"I've meant to buy one here, but you've no idea how expensive Italian leather goods are. And when you're replacing things—"

"Re-place?" says Robert. In two distinct syllables.

Paul, bless him, catches at his cue, saves me from looking obvious: "Everything Silvie had with her was burned when the car caught fire: her case, passport, the lot. That's why they couldn't trace her identity."

The silence is so profound it almost seems to affect the whole restaurant. Or do I imagine this?

"How—how truly horrible," says Robert at last.

Anita says nothing. Witch face. Gimlet eyes. Shocked look?

"But we have our Silvie, which is everything, isn't it?

Providential that we ran into each other in St. Peter's. Or, poor girl, she'd still be lost."

"Providential," says Anita, as though not sure of something.

"Dear Silvie. What else matters?" Robert's words are just a fraction of a second too late. His fingers touch my wrist. "Still, shouldn't you make sure nothing was stolen from the car? Foreign police often look on tourists as fair game."

"No, no, no, Robert. She was unconscious, yes. But the dead boy was Italian, and the car. There was no reason for the police to see her as a foreigner at first. If there'd been any way to identify, they'd have been thankful. Her passport must have gone with the case. Or the bag. They showed her pictures of the wreck afterward when the doctors tried to jog her mem——"

"*Please*," I say. "Oh please—" Hands clutch at Janet's bag as though it's a lifeline to safety. In my mind's eye pictures they showed me: burned-out car, ominous sacklike form lying on ground beside rescuers. My stomach heaves, as it did in the hospital . . .

If Robert had any doubts of our story, I think that was the moment when they were resolved.

Anita gives an enormous sigh. But she doesn't really look as tragic as someone who's just said farewell to the prospect of a fortune. Trying to ignore my nausea I wonder about the price they asked for the miniature, and who would have paid it. And when—and in what manner—would I have "carried the can" for Robert?

"Don't think of that," says his voice soothingly, making me start. It's a minute before I realize he's referring to the accident. He pats my hand. "Remember acting for the Waterburys?"

I'm almost taken off guard, but manage to pick up my wineglass without shaking, and drink from it before asking, "Acting for the *who?*" An expression of bewilderment comes naturally enough to my trained features.

"Waterburys. Owners of a famous Tudor house."

"No-o-o—should I? I mean, did I?"

"With great success. You played the *Shrew*—only that time you were Katharine."

Paul's looking stunned. Of course, he doesn't know. Luckily the others are watching me. "I—I wish I could remember." I stare at Robert gravely. "What a lovely thing to have done."

"Of course, if even acting in the *Shrew* again hasn't—"

"Hasn't what?"

"Oh, don't be a dumbbell, Paul," snaps Anita, out of her kindly role at last. "Brought back her memory. You'd think *something* would happen, with a grand coincidence like that. I'd say it's pretty hopeless."

"Anita!" says Robert warningly.

"Oh, don't mind *my* feelings." I take the warning note as compassion for myself. "I'm accustomed to seeing it as pretty hopeless by this time." I get up, groping for my woolly jacket. "Lovely meal, Robert. Look, I don't want to be too late, do you mind? I still get tired, and the understudies are rehearsing *Much Ado* tomorrow—Ashley's bound to be hard on me after tonight."

That was an error. Anita pounces. "You *did* do unexpectedly badly?"

My hand fumbles with a button. "I'm not reliable anymore. It—my stage career—" My voice genuinely wavers. This time it's Paul who pats my hand. Everyone's patting me tonight as though I were a really good dog. And I feel like a good dog. With luck, Robert's put off the scent. All that remains is to clear the Carminottis of my murder, tell some convincing story to an outraged Gian, and return the Hilliard.

All!

As we walk between the tables Robert's voice says close in my ear, "And now what, Silvia? Like to think of coming back to England with Anita and me?"

"I—thanks. No, I really believe that—"

Paul rescues me again. "She's got another three weeks

of understudying in these 'ere foreign parts." Heaven send Robert won't ask what's being done about papers for me, and if the British consul—

"I might hang around, then, and wait. See another performance perhaps."

Haven't I put him off after all? Slight uneasiness again.

Anita says petulantly, "You know very well I must be back in England within two days."

"Ah yes, *you* must."

Another inspiration makes Paul say, "Then Silvie thought of giving herself a rest with her *nonna* and *nonno* near Terracina."

"So she remembers the old couple?"

But Paul gets off easily with, "Almost the first thing Silvie ever told me about her Italian relatives was that she loved staying with them on her vacations. Happy childhood memories of Terracina. Well, I've promised to take her there, see her through the awkward moments."

"You're such a good friend." Biting emphasis.

"Why, she needs good friends."

The waiter hands Anita her wrap, opens the door for us, bows us out. My step's light, I'm convinced we've come through rather well. Janet's bag hangs from my arm, and I stroke it as though it were another good friend—which indeed it is. I take deep breaths.

"What a marvelous night, Paul. It looks so good, the sort of night when anything could happen—" I break off abruptly.

A man is crossing the pavement toward the restaurant. He stops in front of me. "Almost anything, signorina? See, *cara mia,* it already has . . ."

Without meaning to, I let out a shriek of horror.

For it's Gian.

24

"I should add 'Ill met by moonlight, proud Titania'—for I must congratulate you, mustn't I, on a sudden Shakespearean career?"

I'm unable to speak.

"It's not sudden. And who the hell are you?" says Paul belligerently.

"It's—Gian, Gian Marotti. You know, I told—"

"Probably what she told me—a pack of lies." Gian's face, by moonlight, isn't pleasant. There's an angry jut to his chin. I look from him to Robert and back again. Hysteria starts to rise. How can I explain either to the other? Why should I, come to think of it? But plainly it must somehow be done before—

"Could we, perhaps, be introduced?" After Gian's angry outburst Robert sounds so civilized.

Gian, staring at me: "Could we—Silvia? I would be interested to know your friends." His sarcasm is obvious.

Paul puts an arm round me. "But do we want to know you? See here, Marotti, you can stop being so damned offensive to Silvia right now. Understand?"

It's like being the center of a prospective dogfight. Gian has made me feel small and mean. I stare down at the pavement, swallowing hard. And in the restaurant it was going so well.

"We're not going to brawl in the streets, like the Capulets and Montagues, are we?" and "Oh, Silvie dear, you do get yourself into *odd* situations," say Robert and Anita at the same time, confusing things further.

Paul breathes hard. Gian looks bewildered and very angry.

"Your memory, I think that it is normal?" he says in stilted English, which makes things easier for Paul, who retorts, "It's not. And what business, anyway, is—"

191

"What business is it to me? It is the same business as to our police, who look for her body, thinking she is dead. Since they had not my advantage of recognizing in a certain paper—"

"Damn Helen," I say suddenly. "Damn all of you. Except Paul."

As Gian mentioned the police, Anita looked quickly up at Robert. For a second he wore an expression of shock—hurriedly disguised by one of polite interest in these strange proceedings.

"I won't stand here being got at by everyone, I—" I shrug off Paul's arm and start to walk away, wanting to run, hide—anything to escape. He runs after me.

"Silvie, come back. We've all got to talk things over quietly somewhere without getting angry. You can't avoid this now."

I only quicken my steps. "I'm not interested in talking over anything with anyone. Not now, not tonight. I'm exhausted. Can't you see? That performance, what a strain—"

My voice, my hands, shake convincingly. If I weren't shattered by Gian's sudden appearance out of the night —what a talent he has for it!—I might have seen the comic side of this situation: myself racing along the pavement followed by three mystified, angry men, with Anita tagging in the rear—something she isn't used to.

It's Robert who grabs me by the arm. "Do stop running, Silvie."

"No good to run from the police," declares Gian on my other side in unfriendly tones of satisfaction. "Though in fact they do not know that you are here, since I do not yet show them that this excellent photograph is one of *you*."

I stop. Everyone stops. Anita cannons into Paul and swears. I switch back into Italian. "You didn't? Oh, Gian—"

"No, I didn't. I don't know why. First I want to know the meaning of this extraordinary flight—"

192

"Must we—you—speak Italian?" asks Robert. I can hear the appalled worry in his voice. Police—body? Why did she run, from where—what has she found that made her leave—did she lie about the bag?

"We can speak double Dutch for all I care. And be no further on." Tears are streaming down my face. In one moment I'll go completely to pieces in the street. Like in the hospital. Even my healed hand throbs reminiscently.

For what must be the first time in her life, Anita hurries to save another woman from an awkward situation. Perhaps all along she's been sure I've found the Hilliard and fears that uncontrolled emotion may make me say something so startlingly incriminating that it can never be hushed up again.

"Listen, *listen!* No one can talk now! Or here. Silvie's too sick." She puts a hand on Gian's arm, forestalling interruption. "Here's what we'll do: go back to Paul and Silvie's *pensione.* Brandy's what she needs—we've some in the car. Then everything will get sorted out with—Gian, isn't it? Yes, and Robert and I—Paul will—" Her voice is so soothing, she's like a sick nurse. Nurse from the hospital. Nurse who may produce two large white pills and say, "Time you took these again."

"Sure," says Paul, relieved, "good idea. Let's find a taxi."

"We don't need one, we've got a hired car. Where did you park, Anita?"

"Quite near the restaurant—somewhere up this side street."

It's a nightmare ride, though Paul holds my hand comfortingly all the way. Robert drives, with Anita beside him. Gian sits in grim silence on Paul's right. I'm aware of his presence like a time bomb's. When we reach the *pensione* I get out first and in the hall turn mutinously on the others. "I'm too tired to discuss anything with anyone. In the morning. Not now. No, Anita—not brandy. I've got a splitting headache."

"I've come a long way—" begins Gian in a voice of iron determination.

"I don't care *how* far you've come. If I go mad, that won't help, will it?"

"You know, she's not strong still. She's surely had herself a tiring day."

"What an excellent nanny Paul would make," says Robert witheringly. "I must say I—"

"It's no use everyone being rude to each other." Anita again, oil-pouring. "*If* Silvia lost her memory—and we know she's been hurt—and she's made too upset, then she *will* be ill." She puts an arm round me solicitously. I force myself not to recoil. "Go to bed, dear. We'll drink Robert's brandy, if you won't. Everything can be discussed tomorrow."

Paul certainly agrees. Robert looks at her consideringly, and doesn't question it. My gaze settles on Gian's face. There may be mute appeal in my look, but it meets stony response. There's a disconcertingly steely gleam in his eye. Like a hawk's. I'm rabbit in wheat field, sinister shadow overhead.

"Wh-where are you staying?" I say hurriedly to Anita, words high and squeaky. No actress should close her throat.

"At the Bertoldo."

"And I'm not staying anywhere," says the hawk, gaze still on mine. "I am yet prepared to sit up in someone's *pensione* all night."

"Ours won't like *that*," says Paul firmly.

"Come back with us and try the Bertoldo." Anita, though preoccupied, doesn't miss a trick when there's a man around. Apart from any other motives, perhaps she wants to pump him.

But Gian is after me, not them. "I've yet to find a *pensione* which won't let me sleep somewhere for a good big tip. Even in the hall—" Obviously he's going to sleep with one eye open, where he can watch any sudden departures. "As for our little Silvie, she's fortunate to have found somewhere that she can afford."

Robert's looking from one to the other of us. I realize that my tenuous connection with someone of Gian's obvious caliber has both surprised *and* worried him. Nice that someone else besides myself feels worried!

A door opens somewhere, letting out a buzz of conversation. I hear Ashley's deep tones and Janet answering. Everyone in the hall glances that way. I take advantage of their momentary distraction to say, "I'm off to bed," and start to mount the stairs.

Gian isn't so easily shaken off. He follows me.

"One moment, Silvia. I insist on one word—tonight. It will be quick."

"One, then," I say exhaustedly. "And you alone. *No,* Robert. Only Gian." I smile weakly at Paul and go upstairs. Thank heaven I can leave that beastly pair, Robert and Anita, safely behind me, in Paul's hands.

Inside my slip of a room Gian leans casually against the door while I sink onto the bed. There's nothing casual about his anger, which can almost be seen as a third and burning presence in the room.

"Silvie. Silvia. So we do have that real name for you at least. Or is this still a pseudonym, or *nom de guerre,* so to speak, taken on since I quoted it back at you?"

"We have a name, yes—and it is my name, and Paul knows it is." I feel sick, not only tired. Returning memories were enough to unbalance me—let alone these shattering encounters. All things come to her who waits, I tell myself crazily. Even something as undesired as a Hilliard.

"Paul knows it."

"Yes—Paul. You've met him. That's Paul."

"Maledetto, I know it. I want to know how *you* met

him—how you knew where to run. The Carminottis are now held, mostly on your account."

"This isn't 'one word.' It's the full-length explanation I don't feel up to giving anyone tonight."

"You've not yet thought it out enough?"

I'm too tired now to be furious. "It's no use being ugly to me, Gian. I knew Paul in the past. I ran into him in Rome, in St. Peter's. I didn't recognize him. *He* recognized *me*. He explained my past—or what he knows of it. He's with Ashley and his company. That's how I got the job."

There's a long pause. I look up. Gian's frowning.

"You were right," I add wearily. "I mean, that inspired guess about my being an actress. I swear I didn't know."

"So—you ran out on me to Rome." I can sense he's wondering about that meeting—was it prearranged? Everything hangs on that.

"How did you get there?"

"Hitched." I tell him about Dad and Mother. I can't see if he's convinced.

"Why did you go?"

"Terror," I answer. He can't know how true that is! I'll never forget my terror when I found the Hilliard hidden in that bag. "I—I simply didn't have the nerve to go through with it. Without—not knowing who I was— am. It was horrible. *You've* no idea how—horrible it was." That, again, he certainly can't know.

His voice sounds slightly less sharp and less disbelieving. "I can see it was a pretty large fence to take blind."

"Oh Gian, yes—it *was*. But I was coming back. Gian? You must believe me. Paul will tell you—I saw about the Carminottis. In the paper. The other day. And—I *knew* I'd have to come back. And I told Paul. He tried to persuade me to go then, but I said 'in time.' Do you believe me?" I look up at him, praying he won't think I'm just acting this pleading look.

"Does that matter?"

He's surprised me. I know that it does, acutely. But I won't say so. I only murmur. "When you've been through what I— Well, Paul does— If anyone believes what—"

Gian shifts from his slightly threatening stance beside the door. "I haven't known you long. Well, I daresay you would have come back. The memory business—how can I tell?" Faint smile. "If I don't trust you, why should I have expected you to trust me? I did think you had courage. That was partly why I got mad when you disappeared."

His tone of half belief is almost harder to take than his sarcasm, but I'm too tired to wonder why.

"The other part of course was Giulia. I thought you heartless."

"I'm not heartless. But you said yourself she was dead! You can bring to justice, but you can't *help* someone dead. And I—I simply couldn't take any more. I knew you'd think it awful of me. But I couldn't bear—" I shy off thoughts of the Hilliard. "I didn't—couldn't," I whisper, "face the Carminottis. Accuse them then, not knowing—"

Silence.

"Yes, Giulia's dead," says Gian abruptly. "They found her. In the grave—that tomb, white in the grass; you remember? Up the hill above the house."

I remember, all right. My dream! Did I tell Gian my dream? I've forgotten. . . . Those cypresses.

My voice is barely audible, uncertain. "It wasn't—*they* hadn't—"

"Oh no. Not murder. Riding accident, most probably. There was an autopsy. Her neck was broken. Shoulder blade and collarbone too. With that stable lad's story— The Carminottis needed her alive. The police are now quite convinced you're the only victim! That you tried to run out, or to threaten them in some

197

way, and they got scared. You have to come back, Silvie, to clear them of murder."

"And convict them of attempted fraud."

"Yes." His voice is deceptively gentle. I sense it hides mething. I look up inquiringly, and the penny drops.

"And to clear myself of being a party to the fraud."

"Will that be difficult—without a memory?"

Surely, surely, my own position isn't invidious—about fraud at least? The doctors could vouch— Think, then, of Gian's last words, and realize how delicately I must tread not to give away that I've got my memory back. Who would ever believe that it happened so strangely? Perhaps dear, kind, reliable Paul would trust me; because at least I did tell him of my eerie experience at that rehearsal, which I half put down to madness at the time.

I cover my face with my hands. This tiredness is overwhelming, dreadful. This is what "dead tired" means. "There're a lot of things I could explain to you, Gian, that Paul's told me. About those cypresses and—and everything. But I can't, simply can't manage a thing more."

"I can see that."

"Leave it till tomorrow?"

"If you won't run out on me again."

"Do I look as if I *could*?"

"No. But when you run, you run! Good night, then, Silvia." Surprisingly, he bends and kisses me. Just as he's leaving he turns back to say, "But this man Robert?"

And I answer, with a sudden flash of energy and renewed desperation, "Oh, that man Robert! *He* can wait until tomorrow. That's one thing I do know."

A laugh. Gian has gone. And I drag off my skirt and roll into bed just as I am, too tired even to wash. Sleep. That's all I want. To sleep like the dead.

25

Far from sleeping the sleep of the dead I keep dozing off and waking up again. It's not just uneasy thoughts that make me restless, for I've violent stomach cramps and, toward two in the morning, sickness. Maybe Griselda did have a virus after all, or maybe the whole thing is psychosomatic. As I lean over the washbasin for the second time I'm reminded of how sick I used to be in the hospital when I tried to probe deeply into memory's murky darkness.

After the second bout I lie drowsing, and start dreaming vividly while half awake. People I've never known rush down corridors toward me. I can see their faces as clearly as if they were present in the room with me. As they approach, each one's mouth opens wide, as though trying to shout out a warning. Each time no words come, and the figure veers aside, only to give place to someone else—

I jerk bolt upright and stare round the room, sweating and shivering by turns. Dear heaven, it's been an awful day! And I can't bear to lie here thinking of it. It's too much, too horribly much. At last I thump my pillows into shape and lie down again. Let me go back, then, past sinister Robert and Anita, past stage struggles, farther, farther back to childhood holidays in Italy, to dear *nonna* and *nonno* holding out welcoming hands — Yes, remember all those lovely summers on the Italian farm with *non*—— Fall asleep once more, this time soothed by tranquil memories.

But sleep itself isn't soothing. Later I wake again, mouth open in a silent scream, just like those warning figures' mouths. My heart beats wildly. Dear God, what a dream! A vile, vile dream, a variation on one I've had before, evidently connected with my accident. . . .

I was in a van, driving and driving through late afternoon, at that hour when light grows more intense just before the sun goes down. It was Italy I drove through, but though the day was golden and the countryside a marvel, I was driving heart in mouth, fast and recklessly. All the time I knew I mustn't turn my head or something terrible would happen. In the driving mirror I could see nothing terrible behind me, only the road winding away into a valley, only an occasional car, already passed, receding into golden distance.

A voice was speaking to me; a man's voice—and I couldn't tell whose—was saying, "Go on, drive, Silvia! Go on, Silvia, drive—you can't stop, you can never stop, you must go on driving, driving, driving."

If I couldn't stop I should die: I knew that certainly—something, someone, would kill me. Was it the owner of the voice? Or was it someone else chasing me, following the van? The wheel swerved in my hands, the van swerved, and I caught sight of the golden road, the whole width of it, and nothing was following me—us—at all; only the voice went on, now whispering, "Drive, drive, drive—"

The sun had gone, and trees were crowding in on each side of the road, which narrowed ahead and wound like a black ribbon, up and up, but instead of winding into light it wound into darkness, as though someone were pulling us on the end of a long black rope. I wanted to stop and reverse the car, but my feet seemed jammed on the controls, and all I could do was hold to the dark ribbon and drive faster, faster, up what seemed to be mountainside. Now the trees were on my right only. To my left there was sheer drop, a sort of ravine where only two or three pines grew at an angle, hiding a small piece of valley from view. There was mist in the valley, curling upward. Mist—or was it fire? A smell of fire . . . blackness behind me . . . and the voice. My feet slipping on the controls, the car veering sideways, its front wheels touching the ravine edge, failing to grip, going, going—

The voice in my ear completed triumphantly, *"Gone. Go on down, you can't help it any more, can you?"* And as the car began turning slowly over in the air I screamed at the top of my lungs, *"Gian!"*

And woke, the scream silent in my throat.

Four o'clock. I get out of bed, hair tangled, sweat pouring down my back and breasts. A drink of water, gulp it down, forget the horrors, forget both dream and yesterday. Crawl back into bed. Sleep properly at last, too worn out to fight the terror of falling back again into nightmare and the smell of fire.

Morning. I'm really unwell, though with no virus. Trauma's my trouble, and a return of weakness. Paul comes to look at me, and reports my situation to the others. One by one they trail upstairs. To sympathize (Janet); to see if I'm acting out a plea for forgiveness (Helen and Ashley); to make sure I'm not foxing for some other reason (Gian); and—obviously—to satisfy themselves that I'm still here (Robert and Anita). These two are accompanied by Paul, who quickly shoos them out again.

"Try to sleep, Silvie," he says, lingering behind.

"I will." I lower my voice. "Do make sure Gian sees I'm not playacting. I *know* he must talk to me again—and bring in the police. But for pity's sake make him see that it must wait till later—later today, at least."

"He sees, all right—you're looking awful, Silvie. Anything you want sent up?"

"Just coffee."

"Could you manage to eat something later? About six, say. We could meet. You, me, Gian."

"Face the firing squad? I'll have to, I suppose."

"Robert—and Anita too? Should convince them—"

I sit hunched, twining my fingers in my hair. When—
what—should I tell Paul about my memory? Must have
Paul, at least, on my side in what's to come. But sudden
resurgence of so much memory's a bit—suspect. Should
have told him after that performance, not covered up.
But I was flapping. Now—can't tell him now. Not till I
can think clearly—push my hair back from my brow—*if* I
ever can . . .

"OK. Robert and Anita too."

"Listen, honey, seems to me that by 'burning' this
black bag you've stopped immediate danger, so—"

"Yes." (Burning—a smell of burning in the dream.)

"Simply treat him as a past friend, hmmm?"

"Ye-es."

"Something more still troubling you?"

"He's worried why I lit out suddenly from the villa. I
guess he thinks I *could* have—found something."

"More reason still to ask them round on a friendly
basis. Nothing to hide, that's how you play it."

"You're right. Paul—"

"Yeah?"

"But you—you think I'm innocent? Without"—swallow—"*knowing?*"

"Dunno, truly. Reason says maybe not. Feeling says
OK."

"Oh Paul"—I smile, tears in eyes—"you're a love. Still
on my side?"

"Even in jail, ma'am. Now, where's that bag? You
mustn't be seen coming out of here with it."

"In the van, locked in with all the props."

"Leave it there. Hidden right away." Exit Paul. I'm
thinking how much his lighthearted attitude helps me,
when he puts his head back round the door to say,
"Food. You mayn't feel like a restaurant. Besides, six is
early for them, *and* they're not private enough. I can
borrow the manager's office at the theater. We'll fetch
drinks from the bar. How's that?"

"Fine. But I must eat something or I'll pass out on you. Something small, like—"

"Honeydew for invalids. I'll bring it. See you at six, then—and don't disappear."

"I won't. I'm going to sleep. All day."

A few minutes before six I walk down to the theater, which isn't far away. I go round to the stage door, and in the parking lot see the vans near one or two other vehicles, among them Robert's hired car and a long, sleek, black one which looks expensive and powerful. I walk over to our van and peer inside. The bag isn't visible anyway—I'd put it among a pile of clothes. Then I notice Ashley's left the keys in the ignition. He's incredibly careless. Anyone could get in and take anything. I lock the van hastily and put the keys in my pocket. Now for the theater.

A drink before facing Gian and Robert at close quarters would be pleasant, but sounds from the direction of the bar prove the company's there in strength, topping up with Dutch courage, and I shrink from facing them all together. I may think it a triumph to stay onstage at all, but they can hardly be expected to agree. The theater manager's room is nearby, and as I enter it Paul, Gian, Robert, and Anita look up, and Gian pulls up a chair for me to join the happy circle. By now I'm ravenous in spite of what's to come, and accept a buttered roll stuffed with ham.

"Nice solid honeydew, Paul. Yes, Gian—gin and Cinzano, please. Long. With lemon and ice."

"Better, I see," says Gian with a faint smile.

Anita is sitting on his other side, close to both him and Robert: a sort of two-sided nestle. I can't tell what Gian thinks about it, but Robert looks slightly put out.

"Yes, better. Here's to us all: to my missing memory and to Gian's—mission; and to Robert and Anita's—succoring. Not to mention Paul." I drink hurriedly, taking a good, long, steadying swig. "I suppose you've been gossiping together, all four of you, and Robert and Anita are stunned to learn that after my spectacular accident I—fell among thieves, so to speak."

A muscle twitches beside Robert's mouth. I look away.

"Darling, we've truly enjoyed ourselves," says Anita. "You have a most wonderful instinct for drama. Almost better offstage than on. But I do wonder why you lit out for Italy like that? I mean, no one our end heard anything about it."

I stare into my glass as though it were a crystal. "I suppose I—I had a sudden yen for escape to a—sort of childhood holiday." Determinedly I fight back those actual memories that *will* rise: panic moments when I wondered whether to cancel my seat on the plane for Madrid, then saw it was best to waste all the money and let the booking stand, in case Robert checked up; my furtive departure on a chartered flight with the airline that all Italian emigrants use—lucky to get a seat at the last moment; the enormous relief as I left the airport behind, the longing for *nonna*— And then the one patch of past which is still shrouded in thick mist.

"You seem to get these sudden urges to—escape," says Gian drily.

"*Touché.*"

"Marotti says you'll have to go back with him tomorrow," Paul warns me. "The police won't be pleased with him for letting twenty-four hours pass already."

"I telephone the *Commissario* tonight, Silvie."

"You must, I suppose. Oh well. Gian, how did you find me at the restaurant?"

"I asked at the stage door, and—"

"Oh yes. Paul left a message. I forgot."

"A message that you were dining at Alessandro's with old friends. These old friends"—Gian looks from Anita

204

to Robert—"who so kindly came from England to search for you."

Anita smirks (friendly cat, stroked by erotic stranger). Robert looks as though he would put an altruistic shoulder to anyone's wheel. Suddenly I'm aware of deep currents of antagonism running between him and Gian. Paul alone looks relaxed. How well he's explained the situation! The "old friends" spiel seems to have been swallowed whole by unsuspecting Gian. Why, all I need do is spend my days sleeping, while Paul stage-manages—

"So, no running off, Silvie?" Gian puts his hand over mine.

"Third time lucky," says Robert lightly. "She might really escape us all for good."

Lightly . . . but with an underlying note that I don't care for. What must he feel toward me since I spoiled his plans? Uneasily I recall Anita's words about his demonic side and wonder if he's given to revenge.

"Ah no, Mr. Alterer!" says Anita, mock seriously. "Why would our Miss Klavetti want to escape her friends?"

Gian's been watching me as she spoke. And I'm baffled by his reaction. A look of incredulity—mixed with what? Shock? Yes, as though someone has put an electric current through him. The hand touching mine stiffens, then clenches itself on my wrist. He looks from me to Robert and back again—and is it my imagination or was that a glance of dawning total mistrust?

"Your name's Alterer?"

"Yes. Any objection?" drawls Robert, insolence near the surface.

"None. It is unusual, that's all."

Gian leans back in his chair, releasing my wrist. Very deliberately he takes out a packet of cigarettes and offers it round the circle. When he offers it to me I look into his eyes and to my horror receive the hard, blackly accusing stare that I first saw when he accused me of plotting with the Carminottis.

"I believe that I've heard my father mention it. Once or twice."

Silence.

"Gian's father is a connoisseur of art," I say too brightly, still held by that hard, bleak stare.

Understandably there's a second silence.

"How interesting! I have a number of acquaintances in that world; like a lot of other people, I frequent the sales rooms."

Gian inclines his head toward Robert but still looks at me. "It is a fascinating world . . . very fascinating. Particularly lately."

"Why so?" asks Paul, looking less relaxed.

"There have been so many art thefts. Curiously enough—this will interest you, Silvie—my father himself has even become involved in one."

"You mean, he stole something?" I say idiotically. My breathing feels constricted.

Gian laughs. A hard, unamused sound. "Not that, yet! But, *as* a connoisseur, he is internationally a name—in his quiet way. He's just been visiting Morocco, and there someone came to him with a most extraordinary story, for advice. Which eventually"—if only Gian would look away—"involved him with Interpol. Strange —isn't it, Silvia?—that the Marotti family should find themselves mixed up with the police on two fronts and at the same time."

That stare. Morocco? Alterer . . . What has he heard of Robert? That hard, inimical stare.

"It never rains but it pours," I say, idiotic again.

"What?"

"An English proverb."

"Ah."

A long, long pause. The only sound: distant chatter from the bar.

206

I'm glad when Anita speaks. Her voice is slightly too high, though otherwise self-assured. (Do I imagine it or is Robert sitting abnormally still?)

"An extraordinary story? In Morocco? It sounds riveting."

"I find it so," says Gian grimly. "And you'll find it doubly so, since it concerns your country, not mine." The stare considers us, one by one. "Art theft has become big business. Perhaps you recall the Chagall that disappeared from Steeplebury? A lovely work—I saw it when I was studying. Then there were the Toulouse-Lautrec etchings that got mislaid on their way to an exhibition. And, most famous of all, the Cellini bronze that vanished from Edinburgh without trace when the Temple family lent it for the festival. Rumored now to be in private, dirty hands."

There's another silence. Paul's looking at me. I hope I'm imagining the look of horror on his face. My conscience is clear, anyway. If Robert's one of a ring, I'm no member of it. But Paul can't know that.

"Ah well," says Robert at last, "thieves will be thieves. And people really should be more careful."

"They should, shouldn't they, Alterer? Because it almost seems that this time someone has overreached himself"—Gian speaks to Robert but is watching me—"with—well, let us call it 'The Waterbury Affair.' A famous miniature which—"

"Say, sorry to interrupt before the story gets going"— Paul leans forward suddenly—"but the glasses need filling. Anita? Silvie—Marotti?" If Paul's bent on giving me a breathing space, he can't distrust me *too* much— how glad I am. But I can see the current of antagonism now runs strongly between Gian and Paul. Gian frowns ferociously, though social training makes his response automatic.

"It is my round, I think." He rises reluctantly, glares at Paul, at Robert. He has a very dark glare.

"I'm drinking whisky," says Robert blandly.

"Perhaps you'll help me fetch the drinks, Alterer."

"Naturally." Robert lounges to his feet to follow Gian.

All I want is to get away. A shiver's beginning, the sort that could lead to spasms of violent trembling. Terror. I cannot, *cannot* sit here docilely and wait till I start shaking like a pneumatic drill—not watched by Anita. In the hospital it used to get so bad that I'd gasp and gasp for air. Drink won't help me—what I need are pills.

Oh God, if only Paul and Anita wouldn't stare at me! If only they'd speak to each other. I look down at my treacherously trembling hands.

"Silvia," says Janet's voice behind me, "so sorry to interrupt, but I've got a message from Ashley. Could he see you in the intermission?"

Why is Robert standing there looking frozen?

"Tell him yes." I turn, thankful for respite. And freeze too.

Janet's holding out my black leather bag.

"Fine. Look, here's this. I thought you might want it, so I brought it in, earlier. But someone might pinch it while I'm onstage. As a matter of fact I rather want mine too. Could we exchange your things?"

"I—yes—do."

Robert takes a step toward us both.

"Coming, Alterer?" asks Gian impatiently. They go out. I cannot look at Paul or Anita as I swap bags.

"That's everything, I think." Janet smiles round at us all, looking embarrassed. She senses something's wrong. I blunder to my feet. "I—I'll come and see Ashley now. Thing is, I—I might go to bed early and not stay—"

I seize the surprised Janet by the arm and almost push her outside. In the passage I glance toward the bar. Robert and Gian are in a line.

"Janet—listen," I whisper urgently, "thank heaven

you came! I'm going back. I feel awful. Tell Ashley to make it tomorrow, see?"

"You *look* awful. Oughtn't you to tell Paul?"

"I'm sure he'll guess." I push her gently toward the bar. Has Robert looked round and seen me? He'll probably overhear the message anyway. It's insane to go, but I can't help it. Nothing would get me back into that room to face Robert and Anita before Gian. Paul must know— Perhaps he'll have the sense to make some excuse, follow me home—

I'll lock my door; not let anyone else in.

Best to go back and brazen it out. How can I if I'm shaking like a leaf? I feel closer still to my old type of hospital hysterics as I scuttle down the passage. Perhaps action will allay those appalling shakes—

I look back. No sign of Robert—coast so far clear. I run down the few steps to ground level and out across the parking lot. Back to my own room. Back. Lock door—wait for Paul . . . Taxi? But where? Bus—no, horrible idea. My forehead's throbbing. I'll walk— No— take the van of course. Ashley's keys in my pocket.

Fumble at the lock, into front seat—warm from the sun. Switch on, let in clutch. The van's clumsy. Maneuvering it deliberately out of its parked place slightly steadies my nerves. Concentration. My right hand aches.

In first gear move to the car-park entrance. I'll have to cross the road, turn left. The traffic's not too bad at this hour; pretty awful all the same. I wait, longing for a gap. Glance in the driving mirror and see Robert emerge from the stage door and come running toward me—

I step on the accelerator and shoot across the road. Someone shouts. Horns. A slither of brakes. Nothing that's not normal Italian practice though. I'm safely across the road now, in a slow stream. Glance sideways, and back. Robert's standing at the entrance, staring after me. He turns and runs for his own car . . .

26

To drive and think at the same time takes all my skill. Another glance into the driving mirror. About two hundred yards behind me Robert's car is just swinging out of the car park. Unfortunately there's a clear patch for him to cross the road. Devil's luck. I grit my teeth—lights ahead. Changed against me. Where—oh *where?* With Robert following me, the *pensione*'s out.

Nowhere. No place to go or hide. Just get out of town. Is that sane? No—panic sets in. With the lights still against me I stare hypnotized at the mirror and see Robert's car has edged up closer. Someone begins hooting. Lights have changed—I've not noticed. The van leaps like a kangaroo. I'm trying to remember what I can of this unfamiliar place. Usual piazza in the center, a church, as in so many Italian towns. Can one park in the piazza? Probably. Then, perhaps, hide in a *trattoria* somewhere, lose myself. Lose myself till I can creep home late, take refuge with Janet or Paul. Though come to think of it, both may be searching for me by that time. With police. I suppress a mad giggle, see a boy on a motorbike stare at me, and straighten my face.

Drive, stop, drive, stop. Straight road, lights, stop again at the corner. Robert's car still behind me, skillfully driven even closer. If I can shake him off . . .

Yes—*then* I have it: back to the theater. Park on the other side, wait in the dressing room. Dead easy if he's first shaken off. But his car's simpler to handle than mine is, and he's tough and determined. Steady, I must remember where that theater is. Here's the piazza—not a place empty. We've gone round toward the *pensione* now. Let him think I'm heading home— Damn this family Fiat in front of me, *bambini* in the back shaking miniature fists. Miniature . . . Robert's car only three cars behind.

So now it's obvious I'm heading away from the *pensione*. Must shake him off soon or the theater turning will have come and gone. If I can go round in a large square I'm all right, otherwise heaven knows where we'll end up. A tinny clang as my bumper just scrapes another car. Memories of last night's dream come to life. Driving the van, darkness, the fall. Burning. Careful—I must be careful. Maybe it was the warning of another accident.

Hands sticky on the wheel. Robert's car has fallen back, displaced by an Italian thruster's enormous red tourer. He's still too close for me to confuse him before turning toward the theater at the next left turn. What if this road goes straight on and on out into the country? I'll turn right instead, try to get rid of him.

And that *was* the theater turning, I'm sure. I feel small and afraid. A mistake to run; how could I know Robert would be so quick after me? Thoughts muddle—Paul knows—Paul, Gian—what action will they take? Sooner police than Robert, Robert tailing me in ungovernable rage, convinced I've double-crossed him. Demonic Robert—running from Gian as well as after me?

Lights ahead still signal Go. Here, maybe, is my chance; they change as I rip across the road. The red tourer reaches a standstill, effectually stopping Robert from passing them to follow me. Now, where's the next right-hand turn? Not far.

I turn suddenly, to a blare of horns and shouting. The van heaves across the road like a charging elephant. Entering the side street, I can glimpse Robert's car, still immobile. Now, if I'm really clever, he's shaken off. My heart thuds with my relief. Mustn't black out whatever happens—I might kill someone, probably myself.

No triumph. Luck's against me. The road ahead's full of people. Pedestrians, motorcyclists, two huge black cars—bride and groom getting a send-off from suburban wedding. One could hardly move in a smaller car; the van crawls forward. Hand on horn, blare. Indignant faces. I might have sworn publicly at the Pope. No one attempts to move. I drive slowly straight at two cyclists, who reluctantly swerve aside. Must I mow down this bunch of bridegroom's friends?

Halt, sweat; and honk again. Faces turn, people shout. I've lost my start. Behind me Robert's car enters this avenue, with no red tourer between it and me.

I put my head out of the window and let fly a volley of theatrical Italian, with some effect. People stand slightly apart, I edge between them. Another turning to the left. I take it—can see Robert's car behind me, moving quicker than I did. Sea of celebration hasn't quite closed up again.

My brain feels stupefied, my body like part of the clumsy van. I drive on and on, aware that I've come straight into a maze, a new housing estate. Round about I go, mouse in a trap, with Robert roaring after me—and here we are, coming out into the first avenue again, that damn wedding ahead. I honk well in advance this time. An angry chorus of yells. I accelerate wildly, screech almost to a halt at crossroads; zip across in time to avoid a bus. People scream and point. It won't be long before I've the police after me just for my driving's sake, even in Italy. Oh, bless bride's mother—she's arms akimbo in road's center giving Robert the rough edge of her tongue.

No more fancy efforts up side streets for me, though I must get back to the left if I can. Best to abandon the car in a cul-de-sac and run for it? Hitch, catch bus, anything. Several cars stream behind me, and Robert has escaped from bride's mother to join them. Dear sweet gentle heaven, what shall I do? Ask a policeman? I don't think.

The road forks. I take the one that veers slightly left. Good—that's got rid of most of the traffic; I can accelerate. Robert's hired car isn't very fast, that's one comfort. I know well what an excellent driver he is—if he had something good here, I'd stand no chance. The van's sturdy and reasonably fast, whereas Robert's hireling seems to have poor acceleration, thank the Lord.

Does *this* road never turn? Evidently not. It stretches ahead of me on and on, like a ruled line. . . . The Romans made it, no doubt. Only a scattering of houses on either hand now, and the country ahead looks flat for some way, till it rises to wooded hills. The light's very golden—light of early evening; the sun won't be with us long. Black bars of cloud on the horizon. Stare in the driving mirror. Robert's tooling along in the rear behind two or three other cars.

A glance at the speedometer. Seventy—not bad for an old van. Gas OK too. Has Gian reported our disappearance? Will the horizon fill with an overflow of cops on motorcycles? What an insane idea, to try for the theater. I should never have let myself be forced out of town either—

The road narrows very slightly. There have been one or two side turnings, but they looked bad—led straight across flat country, with worse surfaces than this road has. Two other drivers have turned off though. That's one left between me and Robert. He seems to have lagged; maybe I can shake him off now on the open road. Fear. Of drill-like shaking. But I'll shake worse after this, surely. And everything will have to come out now. Robert's bound to try and pin something on me, that's obvious. How can one think what to do when one doesn't know the full plot? Drive, drive, drive. Sun behind bar of cloud, cold wind blows in through windows.

I wind one up. The road ahead curves slightly to the right, starts to rise. The dream: golden light, voice driving me on, narrowing road ahead, rising, curving. It's the start of the hills. One lonely house on the left with gravel drive. The third car turns off into it. Now we're alone, I and Robert, racing onward like mechanical puppets in a children's racing game.

The road twists in a number of long, easy bends, with

a sign ahead that reads "Steep Hill." It's getting dark, surely? No—trees close in on either side. I watch the line in the road's center. I'm almost mesmerized by it. The road winds, I accelerate, slow, accelerate, negotiate the bends, each sharper, higher than the last. Between tree trunks I see a wide view to my left. My eyes search the way ahead desperately, the land, the driving mirror. Robert's nearly one bend behind. If only, just round the next, there would be a fork in the road—

If it happens I must have a decision ready. Driving on the right, natural to go on round perhaps? So go to the left . . . No, stick to the natural course and hope Robert does the second as more cunning. That's decided. No sign of a fork at present anyway. Darker, thicker trees. Sun's glare shut out, except for golden pools, dazzling, deceptive pools, here and there on the tarmac. A car coming down almost takes me by surprise straight in the middle of the road. I swerve violently. If only it would hit Robert! But he comes inexorably on.

Now the road straightens again. We must be quite high. A scattering of trees to my left, the ground slopes away. Wood to my right. The sky seems closer. It's cold in the van. I can accelerate up here, all right; and I do and watch, satisfied, as Robert's car gradually drops back, laboring. If only its engine would catch fire. (And if only mine doesn't.) I begin to feel sure I can get away, with his car's performance falling off. What then? I don't know. Just get away from Robert. Hide somewhere. Lie in the woods, and shake, and cry.

But now faint, odd exhilaration creeps over me. Robert, you bastard, I'll show you! If anyone takes the rap for something you've done, why, it won't be me! If I can outdrive you, I can outwit you too.

Steady. Another car coming fast. A big black one. Past me. I've swerved in time, but Robert loses more ground as he brakes slightly to avoid it. The van goes hurtling along as if it's developed flight pinions. Another bend—

Beyond it, what I've prayed for: a fork in the road. No, a sort of crossroads. A track goes plunging down to the left, while the main road goes straight on to a second convenient bend within a hundred yards or so. Opposite the track is another road, a secondary one by the look of it, to the right. Well, he has three choices. I go to the right without hesitation.

And within fifty yards regret my choice. For the black surface is gone, changed to rough earth and stone. I'm ploughing upward in second, foot hard down, gripping the wheel as though I can propel the van upward by force. Upward it is. Very steeply too. The trees make an archway behind me, boughs almost meeting overhead, dark road. Pray heaven he drove straight on. If he's stopped to listen he'll surely hear the van. But I can still win, because I must be miles ahead, and that rotten car he has should be finished by this final climb. Should I have stopped, let him get out of earshot? But then, if he'd followed me up, gained on me—

I'm at the top of something, of the roadway at least. It's no longer a road; it leads straight into a ploughed field on one side and, at an angle, into a quarry. Dead end. No way out if he's behind me. I aim straight for the quarry, drive in at full tilt toward an overhang. Cut off the engine. Quiet. Strain my ears. Nothing. A bird sings, that's all. Silence. On such a clear evening I ought to hear his car if he's driven on past the turning, for the main road curved to the right too.

And then I do hear him. He's been playing hide and seek with me. His car's now only about a hundred yards below the quarry. He's been listening too. And he knows the way I've gone. The car's coming slowly and powerfully in first—it must be shaking itself to pieces on this rough ground

I jump from the van. There's a wretched-looking way up the quarry side, which I wouldn't ordinarily attempt: it looks like mountain-goat stuff. But desperation drives me, and I lurch toward it as if drunk and start the crawl upward. Briars snap back in my face, my feet slip and slide, my right hand clutches at holds that seem too flimsy to support any weight. Sweat pours into my eyes. A bramble drags across my left instep, digging large thorns straight into it. I'm brought to a halt about halfway up as Robert drives with precision into the center of the quarry below me.

He leaps out as fast as I did, for perhaps he was expecting to find me cowering in the van's front seat and is thunderstruck to find it empty. He looks up. Shouts. Runs across the ground below me—and I see the gun, small, black, and dangerous, in his right hand.

27

"Come on down."

I stare, horrified, at the gun.

"D-don't w-wave that thing at me, I c-can't move."

Robert laughs. "Anticlimax! Expect me to come and get you?"

All feeling seems to have left me. I'm drained dry, exhausted. If he means to shoot, I hardly care. It wouldn't make sense anyway. He'd be immediately picked up. I'm trying clumsily to disentangle myself from the briar.

"Don't pretend."

"I'm not—ouch—" I'm free at last and begin my slow, ignominious descent. That odd calm still holds. When I reach the ground I sag and lean my back against the steep quarry side.

"Can't you put that thing away? I'm not likely to knock *you* out."

"Cool little beast," he says lightly as he pockets the gun. "And cunning little beast too. To think I was on the verge of believing you about the bag."

There's nothing to say. If I hadn't been so proud of my wits— If I hadn't lied, or, having lied, if I'd then had sense enough to hide the bag in Paul's room, and not leave it where it was, in the van— The lies were damning. To run away, the final touch.

"Where is it?"

"In the van."

He puts out a hand and draws me relentlessly with him.

"Show me."

I'm limping, and Robert clutches my arm: warder with prisoner. The van door's still open. My eyes go to the ignition, and Robert leans across to remove the keys.

217

My bag lies on the front seat. He picks it up and prods me in the ribs.

"Get in the driver's seat."

I obey. Mindless doll.

"And no monkey business. Sit on your hands—and stay like that." He clambers past me into the van's interior. I hear a clang as he lays down the gun.

"Now, let's see."

A ripping noise as he tears open the bag's lining. I daren't look round. Silence.

"Where is it?" he says at last. His voice is very soft, but there's that in it which makes me wince.

"It's n-not there."

"I can see that, can't I? Where were you off to in the van? Going to find someone?"

"N-no. N-nowhere. I was—going home, then you came, I started—"

"You started running. Not surprisingly. Back in your room somewhere, is it?"

I don't answer. I don't know what to answer. If I say yes, and we go back, we may find the others there. A relief, even if it's Gian. But "we"—would Robert ever let it be "we"—wouldn't I have an accident first? So, not at home, that's dangerous.

"Is it?"

"No."

"Where—exactly—have you—*hidden* it? *Silvia?*"

"I—I won't tell you."

Another silence. That odd calm of mine seeps away. Then I feel Robert's hands on the back of my neck, his fingers groping on both sides. Pressure.

"Silvia?"

I shrink away. Say nothing.

The hands are round my throat, pressing harder.

"Perhaps this will—"

"I can't speak if you throttle me!"

"No, my dear, you can't." I'm released. "Let me say that I admire the way you keep your cool. Or the way you've kept it so far. Turn round. Now—do you know what this is?"

"Yes," I whisper, feeling sick.

"Good. Have you ever seen a human face that's been carved up by a razor?"

"N-no."

"Do you think I'd use it on you—if necessary? *Do you?*"

"Yes."

"I'm glad that's clear. To keep a bit of painted ivory. Is that worth going through life with a face which makes other people sick to see? It's not, is it? I'll count ten, and if you don't answer— One, two, three—"

He hasn't reached "five" before I say hoarsely, "It's here. In the van."

"Sensible girl. Where exactly?"

"Under that seat. There's a piece of plywood screwed over it."

"Is there a screwdriver with the tools? Come on, come on, find one for me. We haven't all night. From what friend Marotti let fall—"

Clumsily I crawl from the front seat and kneel to pull out the toolkit that Ashley keeps beneath it. My fingers are wet and slide ineffectually on the tools. Robert eventually pushes me aside to search himself. I glance at the gun, but he's quicker, and it's there in his left hand.

"Give up these funny tricks, Silvie, love. Here. Now, let's see. I want to make quite sure you haven't lied again." His hands are deft. The gun's laid by again— well out of my reach—while he extracts the miniature from its hiding place. Quickly he removes Paul's carefully placed screws. I think: He's a born thief; that's the sort of adroitness a crack operator would have.

He looks up, grinning. "So. Back in Papa's hands at last. I don't mind saying you've given me some most uneasy moments, Silvie. When did you discover it? Before you ran out on the Spanish trip, I take it?"

Careful. My memory's still supposed to be a blank. Is

there a point in clinging to the fiction now, since I'll need every bit of memory to help me clear myself—if I survive this evening, which seems doubtful? All the same, once admitted—if, in my terror, I could only think—

"Lost your tongue as well as your memory? But I think somehow your memory's all right—whatever you've palmed off on other people as a story. I assumed you'd found me out and hidden to think it over."

"I—I found the miniature after—when I was with the Carminottis at their villa. The night after Gian came and found me."

He frowns heavily. Robert's vanity is disturbed. I can see he's not flattered by the idea that my first disappearance was solely to avoid Spain with him.

"So that's what made you run the second time, and annoy Marotti, was it? Sheer panic." Angry laugh. "Heavens, Silvie, I'm sorry for you, my poor, sweet fool. What an almighty shock! How did you think you'd come by it? Stolen it?"

"I—yes. I couldn't know." Careful! If I survive, no one, even Robert, must be allowed to think that I knew then I wasn't Giulia. So I explain: "Bits of memory came back—I remembered you giving me the bag. And—little, puzzling things." I stare at the wrapped packet. Swallow nervously. "Paul talked about you later, of course. I'd read about the theft in the hospital. I guessed you stole it."

"It was fantastically simple. People are so stupid." (Criminals are always said to boast.) "It was being restored by a—friend of mine. Reputation above suspicion, I assure you! He took it back a day earlier than it was expected. The alarm system was off—the workmen still working on it. We knew that, of course. I gambled on the Waterburys thinking that their muniment room was pretty secure just for one night."

"But—how did you get in?"

"Keys," says Robert briefly. There's no need for him to tell me how he got them. Pleasant house guest, so good at copying—

"The Hilliard was in its velvet box inside a glass case, as usual. Thirty-six hours later Caroline took some visitors round the house and found— You remember Caroline?"

"No," I lie positively.

"Oh well, we've no time for all the ins and outs now. I'm just going to wipe the outside of this—so! In case anything goes wrong." He's unwrapped the miniature and is looking at it approvingly. "A very pretty likeness. How I wish you could see the joke."

"Joke! You were a monster to involve me in—"

Robert's not listening. "My entry of Waterbury in the small hours ranks as a major triumph. Of course I'd had some opportunities of—er, surveying the land. You had some too."

I stare, speechless, while he continues, "Now, let's see: I'm going to rewrap this, we'll put it in your bag, and with any luck you'll both— Did you tell friend Paul about how you found it?" His voice has suddenly sharpened. I look into his eyes and see them as blank, hard points of steel. Not human.

"I—no—"

I can feel him thinking that over. There's deep rage behind Robert's eyes. Rage against me. Against Paul. Against whoever may be on his—our—track. And I've involved Paul. I will Robert to believe me. But he won't. Because Paul has helped me, and helped me lie about the bag.

"I'll have to see about that," he says very softly. "If I can. It's a pity things don't seem to be altogether running my way, but one can't tell— Now, hurry, Silvie. You put the miniature back in your nice bag." He holds it out.

"Robert, I—"

"Do as you're told." The voice cracks with menace. Is ugly. The face—the face seems to look through me as though I weren't there at all, as though I've never existed—as I never have, truly, for Robert.

I obey the face, the voice; though my shaking fingers find obedience difficult.

"That's it. Leave it open. Then it should burn, all right."

"You're—you're going to—" The words won't come.

He doesn't answer, only takes the van keys from his pocket and hands them to me. "Wipe them. Put them in the lock."

"I—I can't—" I can barely find or see the lock, let alone put the key in.

"I can wait. But not very long. Oh, Silvia, pull yourself together! We all have to die some day."

His brutality stiffens my spine. Cold cruelty. Something in me that was beaten into the ground by his callousness begins to rise up again, to fight—at first passively, by not giving up hope, then with a desperate seeking for any minute opportunity that may come its way.

Robert climbs into the seat beside me. "I hardly think we need bother to scrub up the van. The screwdriver." He reaches for it and hands it to me. "Wipe it."

"You're going to kill me."

"Safer now. This isn't what I'd meant to— Things have altered."

I'm whimpering like a child. "Not that, n-not, not b-burn, please, Robert, please—" On and on, hopelessly.

"I can almost swear you'll be unconscious."

I'm sobbing, starting to jerk like a marionette.

Robert's fury comes uppermost. He hits me, hard. "Stop whining. That's better. Now: you're going to drive this van back to the road. Stop before you quite reach it."

The gun's pressed to my side. I would be clumsy any-

222

way from terror, but I force myself to even slower, clumsier movement. Oh God, God, God—I'm praying soundlessly for something to happen, anything. Someone to come along. A chance to scream. And be shot. Or would Robert do anything so inefficient? If the chance comes I'll scream, because he wouldn't risk a shot.

Unless the gun's silenced.

Obviously.

The van's stiff in reverse. With deliberate error I make the engine roar, and Robert says venomously, "Don't rev up like that, you little fool."

Backing completed, I change gear. The van jerks forward and down the road up which I drove only twenty minutes earlier.

"Stop."

"I—*Robert.*"

"Shut your mouth, you damn tiresome girl."

I watch him listening for oncoming cars with the fierce expression of a predator fearing a trap. But there's no sound. The light's going rapidly. A thick band of cloud, westward, engulfs the sun.

Robert takes a large handkerchief from his pocket, meticulously wraps it round his left hand, and presses down the handle of his door. His movements are slow, deliberate, and terrifying. I'm almost mesmerized by them—these methodical preparations for my own death. Engulfed. Like the sun. But no sunrise.

"Hoping for rescue, darling?" The voice is urbane again. He used to sound like that on the telephone. "I'm afraid your time's run out. Because luck's always on my side."

His left hand, wrapped in the handkerchief, holds the door closed. His right presses the gun against my side. He gives the road careful scrutiny; listens again.

"They'll know you've murdered me! Ch-chasing after me like—"

"Oh no. I'll say you blew your nut. You drove off so

dangerously, I had to try and save you. Sad failure. She went clean over the edge, couldn't stop her. Quiet!"

Still nothing. One sleepy bird calling to its mate. How safe that tender sound— Life ticks away. Tiny span of remaining time marked on the van clock.

"Right, over we go. Cross the road and turn left, as though you were returning. No lights."

We cross. Not smoothly, since I'm barely in command of my movements. I turn left and the van slowly descends along the road up which Robert hunted me. The drop is on my right. Round the first bend, into the straight bit, while Robert glances back over his shoulder and then peers forward to see if luck still holds. It does, dreadfully. The coast's clear.

"Next bend, I think," says that urbane, conversational voice in my ear. "Your brakes surprisingly just fail to hold."

"No, no, no—"

"Stop it. It won't help you."

I'm half blinded with tears. Useless to try and fight Robert off when the moment comes. I'll have no time, nor a chance to open my door; and if I had, how could I jump clear, with that fearful drop beside the road and the van leaning toward it? There's no proper bank but an untidy verge of mud and unkempt grass sloping upward about a foot high. After that it falls again— Falls.

The road's flying backward beneath us. Accelerate, he won't be able to jump clear.

"Stop that! *Take your foot off.*"

Robert's gun hand comes down crashingly across my legs. The steel hits my right kneecap and my foot jerks up and off the pedal. His right foot feels for the brake pedal and presses. The van, which has been gathering momentum, shudders and slows. My own voice is screaming and Robert's yelling, "Damn you, damn you, damn you—" I'm trying to fight back, but the van's just

224

where he wants it now, pointing at the verge. His foot comes off the brake, shoves mine out of the way, taps the accelerator once—

And then, as the van heaves up over the verge, myself screaming and hanging onto the wheel as though it could save me, Robert draws himself back like a steel spring and flings himself sideways against his own door. For that second, hanging on, trying to brake too late, lost between life and death, I hope he's left his own escape too late.

But the door's wide open—he's tumbled clear. The sky's moved sideways in front of me. Back wheels rasp on the verge, fail to hold—

I scream. Van plunges downward.

Emptiness. A grinding, crashing noise, a series of violent jolts—

Shut your eyes, Silvie, here's your death.

There's no further movement, no sound except my gasping breath and the faint tick of the van's clock. I'm alive, though nearly scared to death.

Robert's somewhere up there on the road waiting to see a burning wreck, with a dead body in it. Or to make good his luck.

This bit of knowledge, filtering through my state of shock, rouses me. How and why has the van failed to achieve his object? Gingerly I pull myself up. Thank God I was clutching the wheel as though trying to fight it, otherwise I'd have gone straight through the windshield. My side of the van's almost lying at right angles against something. I can just see out, and my heart nearly stops at what I see. Three pines, growing together from a bump in the almost vertical slope, have arrested our descent. The van's prevented from plunging farther—but only just. Its front end lies insecurely wedged in a sort of triangle of narrow trunks. The back wheels must be in the air.

Something cold and hard rests against my left ankle.

The gun—slipped from Robert's grasp as he jumped clear. I bend toward it. Even this slight movement makes the van rock ominously. Hastily I abandon my attempt to get the gun and cautiously turn my head, trying to see backward up the slope. Impossible. I can only see sideways, through the left-hand window. That door's still ajar. That door's my one way out; right-hand door and window are jammed against the trees. Pray heaven the left's not jammed too. I can see a crack of daylight, but the force with which it must have closed— If I have to shake it, the movement will send both van and me slithering onward down the terrible slope.

Shift sideways in the seat, inching centimeters at a time. Any movement from the van and I pause, holding my breath. At last my left arm can push the door. Carefully, carefully. It *is* jammed? Sweat pearls on my forehead . . .

There. Without shaking it, it's opened. Now: push myself very gently, pressing with my right leg, which feels almost crippled after Robert's blow.

Creak. Van sways like a bird on a bough.

Sit still, eyes shut, waiting for the lurch, slither, plunge.

Nothing. Cautiously, try again.

Three more attempts; three more horrible shakings of the van before the door's pushed wide, and stays that way. And—now—I—

Inch by inch, centimeter by centimeter. If only I could take the gun, but I daren't make any extra movement. I'm sure the van's gradually shaking free; the back end, with some gear and props there, must be fairly weighty.

Gun: to kill Robert. Not worth the gun if that kills me too.

Left arm outside the van pulling me gently up toward the tilted door. Left foot gropes for the gound. Gently, gently, pull, pull, pull—

226

Steep reddish slope close before my eyes now. I'm sitting on the van's floor, both feet outside and on the ground.

Safe. If the van goes, I'll simply tumble backward into the trees.

I look up, and see Robert climbing down to me.

I'm past screaming. Robert's luck against my luck. And Robert has strength on his side, and a better position.

Knock me on the head, throw my limp body into the van, wait for the jolt to tear it free. Yes—that's what he'll do.

Can't fight him, so play for time. Time? What hope has time for me? Who's going to see us down here, playing out a deadly game, unless someone takes an evening stroll along that lonely, remote road up there and looks over the verge to admire the darkening view!

Edge round to the van's front? That's the only place— where it won't topple on me as I try to escape my furious assassin, now only a few yards above me on the slope, clambering steadily with a dogged determination that—

Fighting the mesmeric horror of wanting to watch him, I drag myself from the van with one movement which sends me forward onto my knees, nose to the slope. The van rocks behind me, I can hear its side scrape against the trees. A quick glance. Yes, the back wheels are in the air. All that stops it from falling backward is one branch of the young trees, pressed at an angle along its side, like a small extra brake. If only I'd managed to pick up the gun!

Start crawling round the van's front. What I see makes my chest heave with cold horror. Beyond a few small bumps and edges of outcropping rock the slope's almost sheer, tufted with grass—a drop of at least fifty feet onto hard earth. This sick giddiness . . . I put out my aching right hand, clutch the front bumper, and work myself gradually where I want to be. Don't look down. One of the pine boles is about two and a half feet from me now, rearing up from the slope; the side of the van's blunt nose rests hard against it.

There's nothing to hold to here except the bumper. I half sit, half lie, right hand on the chromium plate, knees scraping into earth. Hopeless: trapped like a fox that has run into a blocked lair.

Scrabble, scrabble. Robert's closer. By twisting my head round I can just see the top of the slope where the road lies. Nothing else.

Sit, hardly breathing.

At first I don't realize what I'm seeing. Must be dizziness, these faint flashes of light before my eyes. No. Outside me. Real. Flash, flash. Flash, flash. Two pencils of light approaching from the right. Some car's headlights blazing as it comes full tilt up the farther slopes, bend after bend, the reflection of its lights bent up through the trees—now extinguished, now stabbing clear. The sound of a powerful engine—a car climbing the steep hill as Robert's car and the van climbed some while ago.

I don't know if Robert's aware of it, or whether, hell-bent on my destruction, he's failed to notice the lights and vibration that betray the oncoming car. In any case, how can it help me? We're hidden from above, and the car will go by on the right of the road.

If only we were in England, where the driver would be driving on the left, he might catch a glimpse— Don't hope. Hope's worse than not hoping.

But what's Robert doing? Nothing? I've expected him to edge round the van's front, as I've done. Perhaps, coming down backward, he's not seen that I'm outside. Perhaps he's merely intent on learning if I'm dead, really dead—or unconscious, shocked— Then he'll push me over.

Suddenly instinct tells me what he's doing. Of course

228

he's seen I'm out of it—and the gun lying on the floor. Every bit of my imagination shows me how he's reaching carefully into the van's interior. If I don't—don't burn entirely when the van catches fire, no one would be surprised by a bump on my head—dropping from that height.

The pencils of light are jabbing straight up into the sky now. The oncoming car gathers itself below the bend to zoom up and round it.

And Robert, of course, has certainly heard. He's still, waiting for it to pass.

No. Not still. He's fumbling in the van. I know, because the front end rocks and moves slightly toward me. New terror. With unnecessary, instinctive force I push against it, still clutching the bumper. The sound of the oncoming car grows louder. I'm listening, and automatically push, push hard, harder.

There's a creaking, slithery noise as the young branch, pressed against the van's back end, starts to bend away from its weight. A shifting, rocking movement. Robert must have been almost fully inside at that moment as he leaned forward gingerly toward the gun. The open door must have caught him, and drags him with it, for I hear his feet desperately scrabbling on the earth as the van starts sliding, dragging me with it too. The whole of the back end swings inexorably round toward the drop, the movement accelerates, Robert's screaming like a trapped hare, it's Robert screaming, not I— But I almost go too, paralyzed into holding the retreating bumper. Just in time I let go, and my forward and sideways skid flings me against the tree roots.

The van's plunging, falling, turning slowly over as it goes, Robert still screaming—

A tremendous and terrible crashing sound below. A series of bangs. A flash of light.

I drag myself on my stomach to peer over the bump of earth where the pines are rooted. Looking between them I see smoke and flame mounting upward in serpentine coils of gray and orange. I can see—something sticking half out of the uppermost door. A dead-looking foot, swaying aimlessly to and fro as though a wind's blowing it.

A sudden violent explosion. Flames roar high into the air, though still many feet below me where I huddle retching and gasping between two tree trunks and watching Robert's funeral pyre: my deliverer.

On the road above, pencils of light have steadied into full, stationary glare as brakes squeal, doors slam, and a confusion of voices joins with that only other sound on the still, evening air: the hiss and crackle of flames.

28

It was a police car that found us. For which I must thank Gian. Losing both Robert and me, he immediately made some wrong deductions and rang the *Commissario* who was dealing with the Carminotti case. Soon after I had driven out of town they were searching for us.

Memory I have back; even so, it's hard to see what happened then as anything but one long, horrible confusion. Police arrival and rescue; shocked state and another hospital; moments when I sat, dazedly, a nursing sister by my side, answering questions about that dive over the edge. Two large, solid *carabinieri* sat at the bottom of my bed, one questioning me, the other taking down my replies on a typewriter.

Perhaps the skies are about to fall on me. Heavily sedated, I'm almost too torpid to care. Not too torpid, though, to notice that these particular inquiries seem oddly restricted ones, considering they concern attempted murder which misfired. No one asks me why Robert wanted to murder me. No one seems to disbelieve me when I say he did. Perhaps—considering my first stay in the hospital and that other accident—they simply think I'm mad? But gradually I realize that these are just local men setting up mechanical groundwork for an inquest which will be adjourned. They've probably been warned to keep to the bare, basic facts. The big encounters are to come.

For two or three days I'm too listless to care about what's going on behind the scenes. I eat, sleep, and do exactly as I'm told, like a child. And then one day I wake feeling better, and about twelve o'clock Paul comes to see me. He arrives looking faintly embarrassed and bearing a large bottle of wine. I'm in a cubicle alone, and he looks round surreptitiously for glasses.

"There's only my toothbrush glass. It smells of tooth-paste. Better ring for the nurse."

"No, honey." Firmly he washes out the mug. "She's dragon stuff. You and I are going to drink most of this between us. So here you are—first whack."

"What are we celebrating, Paul? My survival? Because there must be—I mean, I'm surprised they let you in without police dogs. And I must be their hot property. And I don't know how the law works here. Is it innocent till guilty, as in England? Or the other way round, like France?" I take a long swig of the cool, pale wine and hold out the glass. The horrors that have been dwelling at the back of my mind, including the one of Robert's death, retreat a little further.

"Your very good health, ma'am." He lowers his voice. "Police dogs are sharing another bottle with the sister in her office."

"Paul, you're an organizing genius."

"Can't claim all the credit." His voice hardens slightly. "Marotti's here. Waiting his turn at the bed-side."

Quick sense of alarm. I snatch back the glass and drink some. Dutch it is. I remember when I last thought that, and shudder. Paul's watching me rather sadly.

"Is he expecting to crack an entire bottle with me too?" An attempt at lightness.

"Left his with the dogs. You're being bunched, I believe. Fill up." He does. "My turn?"

"Go ahead. Paul—"

"Uhh?"

"You know what's worrying me? I—I don't mean all—all the horror about R-Robert."

"I can think of some other things. Including a future choice between me and Marotti."

"Be serious. It's"— I look round nervously, hardly able to believe that we're truly left alone together—"the van."

"It was insured. Ashley won't hold it against you."

"Don't be obtuse, love! What was hidden there—you know."

"Ah, that," says Paul, putting down the glass and regarding me thoughtfully, "is sad."

"*Sad!* There won't be any extenuating circumstances. . . . Fifteen years. And—oh, Paul, it was a crime. So beautiful."

"Now, Silvie, don't get excited. You'll relapse."

"But I do care, so— Paul! Are you holding out on me?"

"Naturally. I was only allowed in if I promised not to talk of anything—controversial."

"Come closer—whisper?"

A man's shadow appears on the thin curtain that closes my cubicle's entrance. Paul stares at it. So do I.

"Dog's under the bed."

"Ah, Paul . . ."

"An' you could save one glass of the stuff for Marotti, Silvie. Much as I hate his guts." Then, bending over me, he mutters urgently, "Don't scream, but I think you're maybe more off the hook than you think," and straightens up as the curtain's pulled back and Gian stands there, scowling darkly at him. The scowl is framed by a mass of flowers.

"Hello," I say a little unsteadily. "Are those for me?"

"For Paul of course. First visitor out, please."

"Goodbye, Paul, love, thanks for the wine and—and everything." Beseechingly, "Will I be seeing you?" But behind Gian appears Sister's formidable face.

"One at a time in here, I said. Now, who's leaving?"

Paul flees, grimacing at me in a way that might mean anything.

My throat feels constricted. Briefly before my inner eye appears a small, sharply etched picture: the theater manager's office—Gian looking from me to Robert and back again with dawning mistrust; and then the hard, bleak stare—

"Lovely flowers, Gian." Almost inaudibly.

"Half from Ashley and Co. and half from me."

"Oh—thanks very much. To you all."

"I've a message too: that no one's cross with you any more. Lots of love and sympathy, and Ashley says you can play the *Shrew* with him in Lancaster this autumn if you've nothing better." So the keynote is lightness—an ignoring of darkness and confusion, of attempted murder, and sudden death . . .

"Thank him from me, Gian. But you could say I may be in prison." What use pretending? *I* won't guard my words anymore. I won't try to hide anything. I'll try to accept that my life, my career, may only start again when I'm thirty-five. This inner admission rewards me with a sense, if not of peace, of freedom. I can even look at Gian and not fear a bleak, suspicious look.

But he doesn't seem bleak at all. He sits down comfortably on my bed and deposits the flowers in my lap.

"I won't say that. Did Paul mention a glass of wine?"

"Here"—I hold it out. "Vintage toothpaste."

"To a happy issue out of—of all your afflictions, Signorina Klavetti."

"Gian—Gian, do you know anything? I mean"—I twist a rose stem between my fingers; it reminds me of the Hilliard, and I let it drop—"Paul seems to, but he won't t-tell me."

"Very properly. I, like Paul, am allowed in on probation. Limits: exchange of affection or goodwill."

"Oh . . . I see. When, or rather—"

"Except I'm allowed to say that you're judged fit to travel tomorrow." Still he doesn't mention Robert.

"Wh-where? W-with the police?"

"With comrade Paul, most probably. Though by police car. To the villa of the Carminottis."

I catch my breath. "With you too?"

"No. I go today. I have to. Are you feeling better, Silvie?"

I look up and see that I'll get no more out of him. But he's smiling. He looks younger and less strained, and we gaze at one another for a long moment. In it I decide that now, and for the possible future, there can be nothing but honesty. So I say, "Did the sister tell you I've got back my memory?"

"Yes. Another accident—another shock. It can happen."

"Yes. But, Gian—" I take a deep breath. The value of our relationship seems to hang on his reaction now. "That's only what they think. I got it back before."

"You—"

"Yes. Onstage. And I haven't even told Paul yet, first because it was a bad moment, with—with Robert waiting, and I was afraid Paul might get muddled—and then afterward I was so afraid no one would trust me—" Hurriedly, words tumbling over each other, I start to describe what happened. But in the middle Sister's face comes round the curtain, and she breathes one dragon word: "Out."

"Please, I'm perfectly fit now to—"

"Your lunch is coming. And I won't have visitors cluttering up my ward."

"And I'm leaving tomorrow!" I say, outraged.

"It's no use arguing, *cara mia.*" Gian smiles sweetly at us both.

"C-could you tell Paul what I said? And explain—don't let him f-feel hurt—"

"Out."

"And Gian, ask him to tell you about my *dreams*—the cypresses, I mean—"

"Your dreams. I'll remember. *Ciao,* Silvie. See you at the villa." He bends to kiss me. There's no way of knowing how what I've said affected him. I seize his arm—

"Do I have to call the doctor?"

And Gian, with a glance of complicity and an amused wink at me, hurries out.

We go north by police car. Two *carabinieri* in front, Paul and I together on the back seat. At three o'clock we approach the villa. All the way up in the car Paul has been very silent, and I've not felt like speech either, but gaze out of the window, my hands gripped tightly together, sweat moist between my fingers. Return to the villa . . . It's hard to breathe. I have a terrible fear that my memory may disappear again, swallowed up by some oubliette in the structure of my mind, where hospital and accident terrors, and terror of being at the mercy of other people, jostle each other like strange fish swimming in a dark pond.

But all too clearly now I remember myself in the hospital telling my doctor, "There was this garden, with cypresses"; the doctor himself coming into my room, smiling broadly and saying, "Signorina *Giulia?*" Carmina speaking to her son: "I don't think you should go on and on asking her if she remembers things," and to me: "Dr. Carlo says he would have put you on deep sedation for at least three weeks"; and—last and worst of all—Gian's accusing voice: *"What are you doing in her room and in her clothes?"*

Oh how, with all this at the back of me, have I ever managed to laugh and work with Ashley and the others, or dared to take a part onstage? The thought appalls me now. I feel there must be several people living inside my skin—people I barely know.

"Paul," I whisper drily as the sweat trickles down my palms, "I don't think—"

"Say, is this the place?"

I look up.

And there's the villa before us; and beyond it, to the left, the hill with my cypresses' feathery tops outlined against the sky.

"Paul . . ."

"Scared, Silvie? But it's surely less unnerving than a police station." He takes my hand, and the nightmares retreat a little. Strange how all inquiries have come together at this house I dreamed of: a sort of crossroads at which they meet. I'm still staring at my cypresses and the hill; the oblong vault just as it was— No—it's been moved. The stones are differently arranged. I catch a glimpse of piled earth, a spade . . . and shudder. Giulia—

"Paul, do you—do you suppose Carmina will—will be here? And—and the others?"

He shakes his head, meaning, I suppose, that he can't tell. We get out of the car, and still clutching Paul's hand, I follow a policeman into the house.

No difference in the hall. Yes—there is. No flowers. Carmina always kept some here. And the tiles don't shine as when Benedetta polished them each day. Has she been arrested too? I shudder again. Oh, how horribly sick I feel, fearing some dramatic confrontation. But when I'm ushered into the dining room—Paul's left sitting on a hall chair—the Carminottis are conspicuously absent. The room has been turned into a temporary adjunct of the police station. One man sits at a side table. Before him is a typewriter. Uncle Vicenzo's big, flat desk occupies the center of the room, and on it are piles of documents. Two men in plainclothes stand talking by the window. As I walk in, they turn, and Gian, who's sitting on the window ledge, looks up. He appears preoccupied.

The shorter of the two men smiles at me and goes out. The taller comes forward. I judge him to be in his early thirties, dark-skinned, red-cheeked, side-whiskered, and slightly long-haired. Not my idea of a policeman.

Gian rises. "*Commissario,* this is Signorina Silvia Klavetti."

I smile nervously and nod.

"Will you sit down, signorina?"

I settle myself before the desk while he glances through some papers. He starts by satisfying himself about my identity, etc. The policeman at the side table types away. Then there's a pause while the *Commissario* and I scan each other.

"Signorina"—he puts the tips of his fingers together

and smiles discreetly—"you are an actress, one who has a talent for involving herself in explosive, not to say dramatic, situations. You find drama comes easily to you?"

"I—no. On the stage, maybe."

Again he examines his papers. "We have a good deal about you here already. Statements from the hospital staff where you were taken after the first accident. Statements from police who examined you at that time, when you could remember nothing." His voice is so soothing, so smooth, that when he suddenly shoots at me, "You did really lose your memory?" I almost jump off my chair.

"Oh—of course I d-did! S-surely they must have told you the c-condition I was—was in? I was almost m-mad for weeks, I was—" Close to tears, I stutter into silence.

A long pause. The *Commissario* eyes me, then continues smoothly: "At least we have Signor Marotti's statement that on the night he—er, made contact with you, you were plainly unaware that you weren't the Carminottis' niece, and that the family were behaving, even in private, as though you were indeed the missing Giulia. *Did* you ever doubt that you were?"

"N-not really. Only—I felt uneasy sometimes. But there were the cypresses—" Feeling like a circus freak, I explain, stumblingly, about my dream, and add hastily that Paul knew about it—and other dreams as well. He nods noncommittally. Perhaps he sees these peculiarities as part of my instinct for drama. Or my madness—

"Yes . . ." the *Commissario* turns over another paper. "Signora Carminotti made one attempt to involve you—so foolish, we need barely consider— But I must ask myself: what motive would she have in trying to throw blame on you?"

"She—she hated me, I think. Because I was holding out against marrying her son."

He nods again, thoughtfully. "You spoiled her plans.

You and Signor Marotti. They were clumsily improvised . . . it seems hardly credible that she and her
husband ever thought they could succeed. Of course,
he's getting old . . ."

"She's—she's terribly arrogant," I venture nervously.
"She couldn't imagine anyone not doing what she
wanted; I saw that. D-did Enrico and his father try to
incriminate me too?"

"You're not here to ask me questions, signorina."

"I'm sorry."

He looks at me piercingly for a moment and then
relents. "No—and Enrico Carminotti in particular in-
sists that you were never in their confidence. Indeed,
how could they have told you? Later they would have
had no option but to—remove you somehow, before
friends and neighbors saw the substitution." He rests his
chin on his hands; there's a pencil between them and he
fingers it, looking straight at me. "Possible intent to
murder is no easy charge to make stick."

"They—they might have got me certified. Because of
the accident. And Enrico would only have wanted me
put away, I'm sure," I blurt out. "I—I mean, *he*
wouldn't have wanted that, really. He—I think he'd
begun to feel genuinely for me, and—"

"He would *only* have wanted you put away? Signorina, your charity does you credit. Enrico Carminotti
may be weak, but there's a point at which weakness
becomes culpability, no? Anyway—" He frowns, twid-
dling the pencil. "We shall talk of this later. The
cousins from England—the young Giulia's cousins—are
on their way out here. We'll take your statements during the next day or so. I hope that staying in the villa
won't remind you of too many unpleasant experiences."

This is all so civilized, so polite. So unexpected! I'm
an almost innocent lamb, cared for by everyone . . .
but of course, during the Orthodox Church's Easter
rejoicings the lamb's throat is suddenly cut. When will

this kind, thoughtful *Commissario* produce his knife? His dark eyes are regarding me blandly.

"There's now the question of why, having made contact with Signor Marotti and agreed to expose the Carminottis, you—left?"

The knife.

"Would you care to comment on my last remark, signorina?"

There are so many different things that could be said. I say none of them but lick my lips and remain silent.

"Yes," muses the *Commissario* sweetly, after my silence has lasted some while, "it's a question we're all profoundly interested in, signorina. I can imagine that your reply gives you some trouble. However, the question's of much interest also to two other *actors* in your drama." His white teeth flash at his own joke. "They arrive"—he looks at his wristwatch—"in about one hour's time. In the meantime, being English, you'll doubtless welcome a cup of tea."

He rises. I rise. Everyone rises. The *Commissario* is very charming, with his red cheeks and woolly side-whiskers, and his smile. Nevertheless I'm scared to death of him. Gian's not even looking my way. Meekly I turn and follow the policeman from the room.

"Everything OK, Silvie?"

I look at Paul mutely, silenced by the policeman's presence. As we follow him to the back of the house, where more policemen have taken over the kitchen, I whisper sharply "What have you told them?" But as Paul whispers back anxiously, "About *what?*" I feel no better off. When the promised cups of tea are brought—disgustingly weak—I sip mine unenthusiastically. I long to talk properly with Paul, but can only smile at him feebly and discuss Ashley and the company. Impossible to discuss the miniature like this. . . .

It's five o'clock before I'm summoned again. This time they let Paul accompany me, and usher us into the

240

L-shaped drawing room. How well I remember it like this! Shadowy, because the shutters are closed against the heat. There's a scent of lilies and roses and a drone of bees. In the greenish light the *Commissario* looks enormous, like a whale under water. There's no stenographer present, and the policeman who shows us in goes out again. But as we walk forward into the room, with its aqueous green shadows, I realize suddenly that the *Commissario* isn't alone: in the short arm of the L-shape three men are sitting, grouped on the spindly sofa and chairs where I've so often sat with Carmina, Vicenzo, and Enrico. Gian—and two strangers. One's small and brisk-looking. He might easily be a lawyer or accountant—he has the air of someone who deals efficiently with facts. The other is an older edition of Gian, with white hair. And to him Gian says, rising, "Here's Signorina Klavetti. My father, Silvia, is interested in paintings, as I've told you. His particular interest is—miniatures."

"How—how do you do?" I falter. My throat seems to have closed up, and Paul clears his uneasily behind me. His Italian is still not as adequate as Ashley's, and he's probably afraid that something important may be said which he can't catch. Now the skies seem really about to fall. But the older Marotti doesn't look at me accusingly, simply with an appearance of interest. He bows over my hand.

Neither Paul nor I are introduced to the other man, and I wonder if this is intentional or an accident. I look round to see what the *Commissario* is doing, and see him standing by a table, frowning down on a small black box which is displayed there. He glances up and catches me watching him.

"Signorina, these two gentlemen have brought me an extraordinary story—or rather, they've brought me one half of an extraordinary story. It's my hope—and opinion—that you'll supply us with the other half. Will you have the goodness to open this box and examine its contents?"

Is this some sort of trap? Everyone may be watching me curiously as I move forward, but I'm intent only upon the small black box. I feel like Pandora. What fresh troubles may fly out when I release the catch? It's stiff. For a moment I fumble with it. Then it gives. I raise the lid, peer inside; gasp.

Against a background of red velvet lies a small rectangle of delicate ivory. Arrogant and aristocratic, the features of Sir Jonathan Loseley lie before my startled gaze. Here are the Tudor emblems and the deliberate, casual pose. The colors: wild-rose pink, green, and mulberry. Everything the same as I last saw it, held between Robert's fingers in the van.

29

I let the box fall. Luckily it was a mere inch or so from the table's surface.

"It—it wasn't burned with the van!"

"You recognize it?"

My voice is barely audible. "Th-the W-Waterbury miniature." I look round me bitterly. "You meant to trap me. And you've succeeded." Beauty has triumphed after all; outlived Robert, survived to put me in the dock.

"You're sure that's the missing Hilliard miniature, signorina?" Gian's father stands beside me. We gaze together at the painting.

"Oh yes . . ."

"Then what about this?" He holds out a hand, palm uppermost. On it lies a second miniature, an exact replica of the first: Sir Jonathan Loseley, resplendent in his same exquisite colors, stares haughtily from another ivory rectangle. Perhaps my brain's worse affected by my last accident than by my first!

I can only stutter out, "It—it's incredible."

"Can you tell which is genuine?"

"Genuine? I—no, I shouldn't think—" I've almost forgotten my own awkward situation as I pore over the box, then over the second portrait, which Signor Marotti has deposited on my palm. The fine strokes of paint dance before my eyes. Is there a fraction of clumsiness here . . . a feather not quite so—

"I can't tell at all."

"That one you're holding is a first-class forgery."

"I don't understand! Was—was one to be substituted? Yet they didn't . . . And R-Robert"—swallow—"p-planted it on me. Or was I—was mine the real one? Which was it?"

"Neither," says Gian at my shoulder. "For you, Silvie,

243

carried a second copy! You were quite right, it *was* burned—when Alterer died in the van."

"But it doesn't make sense."

"It makes very good sense: an unscrupulous Englishman, your dead friend, thought up an ingenious way to make his fortune." There's a bad-smell-beneath-the-nose look about Gian's face when he mentions Robert.

"Three, though . . . But a *burglary* was reported! So he didn't mean to substitute a fake?"

"At first. That idea had to be shelved—late in the day. The Waterburys themselves innocently spoiled it for him by revealing that some Russian enthusiast was coming to see the Hilliard the very week it was returned."

"Oh yes, I remember—" I catch myself up.

Gian doesn't seem to notice. "A great piece of misfortune for Alterer and his friend the restorer! They must have known that every European expert had already seen this famous work. The fraud mightn't have been discovered for fifty, sixty—a hundred years. And then the one man who hadn't seen it . . . Inevitably a fake produced by the restorer who cleaned it would have pointed straight to himself and his friends."

"But a *Russian* . . ." I stare at the "fair copy" in my hands. "Could he have known?"

"Very likely. He'd seen others. Experts develop an instinct. And instinct leads to tests. No—the threat was too great. After that it had to be straightforward burglary."

One thought comes to my mind and I blurt it out.

"You—you couldn't have guessed this—or got it from Paul. So how . . .?" I find myself looking up into the *Commissario's* face.

"There are still gaps in the story, signorina. You'll fill them for us, no? Because you're quick. And perhaps luckier than you realize! For Robert Alterer had a friend, who came with him to find you—"

"Anita? Of course! I'd almost forgotten her."

"And when Anita has hysterics," murmurs Paul behind me in a satisfied voice, "does she have them! And when she hates—"

"She hates me . . . yes, I suppose she feels I caused Robert's death. You'd think she'd incriminate me! Well, she must have said I was carrying the Hilliard. Or—as it was a copy—you'd never have known. Unless Paul—"

"How that dame's jealousy overrode her hatred! It sure was good to hear her, Silvie. She nearly burned up the room. She was too crazy to see she was doing you service. You're a born dumbbell, you'll like to hear, and a real female fall guy."

"Poor Silvie," says Gian, grinning a lopsided grin. "She wasn't complimentary about your looks or character."

"You—you suspected me, Gian. I mean, at the theater. You were looking daggers before I ran."

"Ah, my father had indiscreetly told me— In short, I'd heard too much of Alterer already. And then I found you in his company."

"But—but that night, outside the restaurant . . ." I wrinkle my nose. "Didn't anyone mention Robert's surname?"

"Not till that woman called him 'Mr. Alterer' at the theater."

But at this point the *Commissario* takes over. Quiet-voiced though commanding. Evidently he feels we're getting out of hand. The fake's removed from me; the box is shut.

"And now, signorina, before we satisfy your questions you will satisfy mine."

I'm led to a chair, and he sits opposite me, motioning the others to seat themselves too. Paul takes the chair on my left, Gian and the others occupy the sofa.

And so, stumblingly, I tell my side of the story. Everything from that moment when I found the Hilliard: my flight, the meeting with Paul— Here I pause; am I involving him too deeply? But he touches my hand reassuringly and murmurs, "Ok, Silvie, I told them." So I hold nothing back and go on to relate how my memory returned after Robert's and Anita's appearance at the theater.

"—when I overheard them in his flat she spoke of my 'carrying the can' for Robert. And he said, only if things went badly. They meant to point a finger my way if anyone began to look at Robert closely?"

"Indeed—and we've learned from the woman what pains Alterer took to involve you. The car hired for that Tuesday. The trip down to this English village with the strange name so that someone might remember you in the neighborhood of Waterbury on the very day the miniature disappeared. The receipt for the bag—which you say the Englishman told you to keep in your desk. A bag which she went to buy for you herself, wearing a chestnut-colored wig and dark glasses."

"But—but I came back to London the same *day*. The miniature wasn't stolen till that *night;* Anita must have driven him down after I saw them at the flat!"

"That is true. But why were you in the neighborhood at all? A sudden urge for a day out? Or a meeting with some local accomplice? Your plane didn't leave till midday on Wednesday."

"Yes, there would have been plenty of time for someone to slip me the miniature. What fun he must have had working it out," I say bitterly. "He never meant to come to Spain at all, but if necessary *I* could be picked up there. Waiting, in an expensive hotel, for someone who didn't come!"

"It would have seemed they were afraid to come. You would have said it was the Englishman, which he would have denied, having already arranged to be in Scotland with the woman Anita."

For a while I sit in silence contemplating the extent

and detail of Robert's perfidy. Then I blurt out, "But, *Commissario,* if I'd *had* to be picked up, there was still a risk of that Russian professor saying it was a fake."

"No—by then *he* would have been back in Leningrad."

"Then suppose—suppose someone only thought of questioning Robert later, after I'd come back from Spain?"

"You would still have had the fake," points out the *Commissario.* "It would have seemed you failed to sell on an abortive trip abroad. Presumably, when any trouble died down, they would have taken steps to recover it from you. *Some* risks they did take—you cannot commit crimes without them!" He smiles at me meaningly. And I shudder, thinking of the Carminottis. And how, without criminal intentions, I've certainly taken some risks myself.

"Of course I see now that they—R-Robert was just improvising after he learned about the Russian! I must say he did pretty well. I was with him at Waterbury—it was on our way home that he—asked me—about"— I shoot a nervous look at Gian; after all, Paul knew all this before—"coming to Spain."

"The bastard," says Paul feelingly. "Three miniatures, though: that's surely a lot for one man to handle. It's greedy."

"Exactly, signor. Excessive greed. First he would steal the original and sell to—someone as yet unknown, an 'undercover collector.' And the fake would be substituted. But the copy was brilliant; so why not another like it?"

"To Signor Alterer and his friends the world is full of rich fools, some less knowledgeable than others!" puts in the elder Marotti. "If the cheat was discovered, he could always claim he'd been deceived himself, that the countess kept a copy on display."

How cunning of Robert! The holders of hot property

aren't likely to approach the police—as I know. Recalling my sensations in the villa when I found the Hilliard, I drop my head on my hands. Yes—how brutally, with what imaginative efficiency and bravado, Robert acted throughout! How he must have enjoyed himself, dovetailing his jigsaw into place. Well, Robert's dead, but . . . "I'm glad," I murmur, "of the horrible shock they had when they lost me."

"It does my heart good to think of it," says Gian, and the quiet satisfaction in his voice makes me look at him and smile.

"Please, *Commissario,* may I ask one more question now, since I've told you all I know?"

"Signorina?"

"Well, Gian—Signor Marotti—had heard about"—it's still hard to say the name—"Robert, through his father learning something in Morocco—"

"And you want to know how—and what?" The *Commissario* puts the tips of his fingers together and looks at me with what I hope is mock severity. *"If* I satisfy your curiosity, signorina, it's because your innocence is—almost established. You have been through a terrible time. But you must understand I have still some inquiries to make about you."

There's a nasty sensation in the pit of my stomach. He continues to look at me till I murmur feebly, "Oh yes. I understand."

"And it's also understood that nothing said inside this room goes outside it?" The *Commissario* looks round at us all impressively, then gently inclines his head toward the one person who hasn't spoken yet. "Perhaps my colleague from Interpol would kindly—" They exchange smiles. "My colleague from Interpol" immediately rises like an after-dinner speaker and turns to me.

"Signorina, you've heard my good friend"—he bows slightly toward the *Commissario*—"speak of the man Alterer's excessive greed. Naturally it's unwise to sell

248

the same painting twice at the same time—particularly unwise to try and trick a gentleman with more money than sense, one who finds it suits him to live snugly in Morocco. We won't name him, since he's still outside the law—just. At least he showed enough sense, when an intermediary offered him a certain miniature, to call for advice. He'd met the elder Signor Marotti"—here he bows to Gian's father—"on two occasions, when they were staying at the same hotel. So he went to him with a request: could he identify a genuine Hilliard? What a moment to put such a question! Signor Marotti assured him that he could—and that the beautiful thing he was shown was a mere copy. Of course this didn't prove that the seller, though fraudulent, was the man who walked off with the original. But in the end, both inquiries came to the same person."

A third bow. "My colleague from Interpol" is very polite. Now he exchanges another smile with the *Commissario* and returns to his seat. He's said his piece so neatly that I almost feel I should applaud him. Or at least say something. I mutter awkwardly, "R-Robert seems to have been every bit as big a fool as he thought me." A moment's triumph, quickly eclipsed by thoughts of that appalling death.

"Vanity is the hallmark of criminals, signorina. Don't you know that truism? Let us take a quick look at the London end of this complicated crime. London—which Robert Alterer has just left on receiving a letter which tells him of your reappearance in Rome. It's another truism to say that a major crime is sometimes solved through the trail of a minor one leading across it. You knew Robert Alterer took drugs?"

"Drugs? It was mostly pot: cannabis." There's a defensive note in my voice. Gian's father has given me a denigrating look.

"Mostly cannabis—occasionally LSD. Acid. Sometimes a drive against these things slackens. But unfortunately for Alterer this was a moment when a number of intensive checks were being carried out in London—at what you call pubs and at nightclubs. Certain people in certain sets were often seen at the same parties. Your friend's name was known. And so his flat was searched when he'd already left for Italy, and a trained dog sniffed out the stuff, hidden behind a panel—a small packet, plainly for private use. And then"—the *Commissario* holds a dramatic pause while we all contemplate the thought of paneling—"something else is found in the same hiding place: the Waterbury Hilliard."

A long silence. The heat's intense and seems to have increased during this last dramatic hour. The whole of this long nightmare, while I've fought and struggled in the double snare, has been accompanied by constant heat. I would like to live at the North Pole for ten years.

After a while I let out a sigh.

"Well, signorina?"

"I—there seems so little left to say. I was unlucky. And I'm glad, in spite of his horrible end, that Robert had a share of bad luck too."

"Accident, theft, attempted fraud, attempted murder . . . young woman, you were certainly unlucky in your associates," remarks the elder Marotti rather stiffly, and gives his son a considering look which bothers me. Am I to be condemned as unsuitable company? Well, perhaps I am. After all, as I've so often wondered before, how did I come to attract such a bunch of crooks around me? Even when I hitched, it had to be psychopathic Dino whom I picked on. . . . And yet what about Dad and Mother? Ashley, Janet, and the company? Giustina? And—above all—Paul, who now comes to my defense. (Perhaps Gian doesn't care? Perhaps Robert has been too much for him—and me—altogether.)

"We could say she's surely lucky *and* courageous to have escaped them all for good."

"For good?" Gian speaks at last, briskly. "There are two trials ahead, at least. You'll be a principal witness in both, Silvie—English and Italian. One for each bit of ancestry. Good thing you're bilingual. Paul and I must see to it that you get the best possible lawyer's advice."

Again that scrutiny from his father. I find myself hoping, rather apprehensively, that Gian thrives on parental opposition.

"I'm not sure I could ever trust a lawyer again," I remark, thinking of the Carminottis, and then of Robert, as I add, "any more than I could trust a man who exudes charm. It's a horrible attribute."

"That's all right. Neither Paul nor I exude it, as you must know."

"Say, you speak for yourself, Marotti." Paul lounges to his feet yawning, which breaks the tension. The atmosphere becomes informal, and the group starts to disperse, the *Commissario* talking earnestly with his colleague from Interpol. Signor Marotti senior lingers, eyeing me with the look of one who doesn't mind what he sees but fears what's behind it. I'm a little embarrassed and quickly turn to his son, saying the first thing that comes into my head:

"Gian, your father told you what happened in Morocco. But you weren't really concerned with—"

"*Then* I was more concerned with poor Giulia's disappearance—and yours! Not to mention that bolt from the blue, the photograph of the Three Graces. . . . It was a genuine shock to find you with friend Robert, and a worse to learn his name."

He's dropped his voice. His father turns away and contemplates the garden from the window.

"Your expression scared me sick." I lower my voice. "I was—once—really in love with Robert, you know. That was why the whole thing happened."

"Poor Silvie. I blame myself for making things worse that day. *And* for handing Alterer clues that he was already in deep water. Our friend the *Commissario* was furious; the man might have got away. Frankly, I wasn't thinking of my careless tongue, only of trying to press home the truth with you. But at least my call to the police brought them after you like a pack of hounds. I can pride myself on that, can't I?"

I know my smile must look like a sad effort. "Yes. Considering that all the time you must really have been haunted by those lines about 'Who is Silvia, *what* is she . . .?' "

It's three days later, and the *Commissario,* for whom I now cherish a cowering sort of fondness, has done with the three of us—for the present. Our statements have been taken, our questioning's temporarily over, and we've been told that an inquest on Robert will open in ten days' time. There's no longer a policeman with a typewriter sitting at my elbow, and I've handed in those pages of notes that I kept so painfully both here at the villa and later at my Roman *trattoria;* since Robert's appearance on the scene Paul has taken care of them. My conversations with Gian or Paul are no longer interrupted by one or other being called away.

"My colleague from Interpol," still unnamed, has put the true Hilliard in a black velvet bag, and the copy in a plebeian brown envelope, and flown with both to England. On the same plane went Anita, not handcuffed but suitably escorted. Anita, not me . . . I shudder when I think how easily she could have put me there as well.

"They'll have to toss coins, here and in England, honey," says Paul, putting my case in Gian's car, "to see whose trial comes first. You're sure going to be one very busy witness—and soon."

"I feel bad about Enrico. Very bad."

"We know. Heard all those kind messages you were trying to pass on via our friend the *Commissario.* Gian, let's stop off someplace en route for *nonna,* and buy this scab Enrico a bunch of flowers."

252

"It's not a laughing matter, Paul." I tie on my kerchief—Gian's car is an open one, and fast—as Paul gets into the back and Gian into the driver's seat. As we move off, the *Commissario* appears bulkily in the doorway, and I exchange smiles and waves with him.

"No passes at the police, Silvie," says Gian severely. "Please! It unsettles them."

"But I love him. He has a sadistic way of saying 'There's still much to be discussed, Signorina,' which I find most attractive."

"It must be quite a change after Alterer. What are you staring at so solemnly?"

"My cypresses. The whole darn peculiar view that got me muddled from the start. It's curious—I did run from the villa in the end, but not quite that way. Though there *was* horror in the house—and up the hill." I stop, wishing I hadn't said that.

"Up the hill . . . In the vault. Don't look so unhappy, Silvie. It's all past. It's dead."

"And—and Giulia too. Oh, I'm sorry, Gian. I'm sorry about everything."

"No use being sorry." He smiles at me briefly. "In the end the Hilliard will outlast us all."

"Unless it meets with another—criminal."

"Forget it, Silvie," says Paul from the back seat. "Keep your mind on your own troubles—you'll have plenty, with both Gian and me around."

"*Cara mia?*"

"Yes, Gian?"

"Where am I going to sleep? Will they have enough beds for us all?"

"Oh yes. *Nonna* has two spare rooms at the farmhouse. I'll have one—and you and Paul share the other."

"I'm not sharing a bed with any of your devoted Italian admirers, Silvie."

"I'll toss you for Silvie, then—and I always cheat."

Squabbling amiably, we drive along dusty summer roads and through the villages.

"Stop a moment! I want to send a card to 'Dad and Mother.' Though I simply can't think what to say."

" 'Don't believe all you read in foreign papers.' "

"Oh, Gian, I hope they can't read them!"

"Well, how about this, then: 'I may be getting married soon. His name's—' "

"Paul," says Paul.

I get out hurriedly and go into the post office. At the counter I turn the postcard round and round between my fingers. My mind's a blank— No, I mustn't think that way ever again. Glancing out of the window, I see that Gian and Paul seem to be engaged in serious argument.

"I do hope to see you when I'm back in England"— No, too stiff. Oh dear. And the argument looks as though it's getting hotter. "Things have been rather strenuous since I saw you last" ("You can say that again," Paul would say), "but they're all right now. In fact I'm having"—no, "going to have a wonderful time. Hope to see you soon, love from Silvie." There.

I post it and go outside to the car.

"I've tossed him for you," says Gian as I get in. "Three times. And the name is Gian."